The Meticulous
Messenger

The Meticulous Messenger

Wendy Burdess

ROBERT HALE · LONDON

ISBN 978-0-7090-8542-3

Robert Hale Limited
Clerkenwell House
Clerkenwell Green
London EC1R 0HT

www.halebooks.com

2 4 6 8 10 9 7 5 3 1

Typeset in 11/13pt Plantin
by Derek Doyle & Associates, Shaw Heath
Printed and bound in Great Britain
by Biddles Limited, King's Lynn

CHAPTER 1

Paris, France
April, 1789

IT was not that Wilhelmina was particularly fond of her name. In fact, had she had any say at all in the matter, she would undoubtedly have suggested to her parents that they should choose something a little more fetching with which to christen their only child. That point aside however, she had, over her relatively short lifetime of some nineteen years and two months, grown quite accustomed to Wilhelmina and was therefore not about to relinquish it without some form of protest.

'But what we require is a name that is much more romantic,' expounded her cousin, Lavinia, as she marched briskly along the filthy French cobbled street, her blue silk skirts held a little higher than propriety generally allowed to avoid soiling the hem in the murky puddles. 'A name that is more appealing; more *Française*. Something like . . . like . . . Delphine. Yes, Delphine shall suit you very well indeed, dear Cousin,' she declared triumphantly, tossing Wilhelmina a satisfied smile over her shoulder.

Wilhelmina, who, in her efforts to keep up with her longer-legged relative, had been forced into something of an energetic trot, was not at all impressed with this suggestion. 'Really, Lavinia,' she puffed, 'I can see absolutely no need for me to change my name. Why the very notion is ridiculous.'

'It is not ridiculous in the least,' countered Lavinia, as she swerved to avoid a cart of rags being haphazardly manoeuvred by a man with a grubby eye-patch. 'Your own name will not serve at all if we are to create a favourable impression here in Paris. It is much too . . . too . . . *pas de Française.*'

As was so often the case during conversations with her cousin, Wilhelmina felt strongly inclined to roll her eyes. Fortunately for all parties concerned, however, she had, at that opportune moment, focused them on a half-starved dog speedily crossing her path in pursuit of a mangy, black cat. She avoided the animal with a nimble piece of footwork before replying, 'Well, given that I have been born and bred in Chipping Sodbury, Lavinia, it is perhaps not surprising that my name is *pas de Française.*'

No sooner had the words left her mouth, than Lavinia came to an abrupt halt and swung around to face her relative, an expression of horror clouding her beautiful face.

'Shhh!' she hissed, looking frantically about her. Then lowering her voice in the manner of one discussing a matter of the utmost confidentiality, 'I do so wish you would refrain from such declarations, Cousin. Why think of the consequences if someone were to hear you.'

Wilhelmina, who had managed to come to a standstill just in time to avoid knocking Lavinia over into a stinking pile of rotting debris, stifled a giggle. Having been brought up close to her cousin, she was by now well accustomed to the girl's elaborate efforts to disguise her background as the daughter of a wealthy merchant and portray herself as a refined young lady belonging to a class infinitely higher up the social ladder than her own.

Wilhelmina on the other hand, whose own father had established the business with her uncle, was immensely proud of the success of Crump & Crump Sugar Importers and extremely appreciative of the comfortable existence which it awarded them all. Knowing her cousin's strong opinions on the matter, however, she could not resist teasing her just a little. Feigning a look of wide-eyed innocence, she therefore declared mischievously, 'I confess I have no idea to what consequences you are referring, Lavinia.'

Lavinia inhaled deeply and cast her deep blue eyes skyward causing the curled feather in her tower of blonde hair to quiver with exasperation. 'It is perfectly obvious, Cousin,' she pointed out in hushed, impatient tones, 'that in order to procure husbands of the aristocratic variety, we must do our very best to present a more

... refined image. Why it would not do at all if such gentlemen were to discover that we were the offspring of mere ... *merchants,*' she concluded, adopting a low and disdainful tone for the final word of her observation.

Gazing at the girl's perfect, anxious features, Wilhelmina attempted to control her twitching lips before pointing out what she perceived to be two quite obvious facts. 'Firstly, Lavinia,' she observed, 'unlike you, I have not the slightest interest in marrying a gentleman of the aristocratic variety and secondly, even if I were so inclined, it is highly unlikely that I would encounter such a suitor walking along this very street.'

Lavinia wrinkled her button nose as she surveyed the display of poverty and deprivation surrounding them. 'Well, I blame the fact that we are lost, and now likely to miss the most magnificent royal procession we are ever to encounter, on those wretched, selfish Fitzgibbons. It is completely inconsiderate of them not to loan us their carriage today. Quite what that boring little pair could be engaging in that is of more import than an event presided over by the King and Queen of France, is beyond me.'

Having sensed their unsuspecting hosts' chagrin at being unable to oblige their guests today, Wilhelmina sprang immediately to their defence. 'I hardly think that one can class the Fitzgibbons as wretched or selfish, Lavinia,' she observed shrewdly. 'It is, after all, exceptionally good of them to accommodate us so.'

The scornful look which Lavinia threw her cousin left her in little doubt that she was most definitely not of the same opinion. 'Well,' she sniffed disapprovingly, before wheeling around again and resuming her vigorous march, 'given that they were so keen for us to visit them, I do think the very least they could do is be a little more obliging.'

This time Wilhelmina thought it wisest to bite her tongue. Despite numerous heated discussions with her cousin and her aunt on the subject before they had left Chipping Sodbury, she remained unconvinced that the banal sentence in Mrs Fitzgibbon's letter: 'The weather is at last much improved,' constituted an invitation. Lavinia however, having apparently set her mind on a trip to the Continent, had been adamant, insisting that the woman had obviously meant they were to visit the city to experience the pleasant April conditions for themselves. She had succeeded, as was usually the case, in winning over her indulgent mother who had agreed that actually, having given the matter a great deal of consideration, the statement did indeed sound quite 'inviting'. No sooner had these words been uttered than Wilhelmina had found herself bundled into a carriage with a large number of trunks, portmanteaux, valises and band-boxes and whisked off to Southampton with her cousin and an elderly wizened chaperon – the inappropriately named Mrs Charmsworthy – who was an old friend of her aunt's and was passing through Paris on her way to Spa to take the waters.

The speed of their departure had, of course, meant that they had arrived at the modest Parisian townhouse of her aunt's cousin, Mrs Ermintrude Fitzgibbon and her husband Mr Percival Fitzgibbon – a childless, greying couple of some middle age – without a single word of warning. Not surprisingly, the unassuming pair had been unable to conceal their astonishment on finding two unexpected young guests and an extremely large pile of luggage deposited on their doorstep some five days earlier. Despite the disruption to their tranquil household, however, the Fitzgibbons had done their utmost to accommodate the two girls and had dealt particularly well, Wilhelmina considered, with Lavinia's long and unceasing list of demands.

She picked up her skirts once again and made to follow her cousin, aware of the strange looks the pair of them were attracting in their finery. She was not, she had to confess, unaccustomed to being observed, particularly by gentlemen and particularly when accompanied by Lavinia. Although it was often said that the two of them looked so alike as to be sisters, she had always considered that it was Lavinia, her elder by some two months, who was also the prettier: her honey-coloured hair a shade brighter than Wilhelmina's; her large oval eyes a shade bluer; and her tall, slim figure a shade comelier. Not that any of this signified in the least to Wilhelmina, however, for, despite Lavinia's capriciousness, her affected manner and her extraordinarily naïve view of the world, she was exceptionally fond of her cousin – indeed, she could not have been fonder of her had the two of them been sisters.

Following her along the filthy street today, however, Wilhelmina had the impression that the looks being thrown in their direction were not of admiration, but of something markedly more sinister.

Since their arrival in the capital a few short days earlier, she had been conscious of an almost palpable undercurrent of unrest bubbling away in the city, though today was the first time she had experienced the feeling of being in any personal danger. Their unsuccessful efforts to locate the scene of the royal procession – which was to take place between the Church of Notre Dame and the Church of Saint Louis – had taken them to a hostile and neglected area of the capital.

Now, approaching a huddled knot of some ten or so ragged-looking peasants, deep in heated conversation, her sense of unease intensified still further and she began to wish that she had paid much more heed to Mr Fitzgibbon's sensible recommendation not to wander the streets unchaperoned and much less heed to her cousin's melodramatic proclamation that, should she miss the procession, she would most likely die from a fatal attack of disappointment.

Lavinia, now a little ahead of her and oblivious to the antagonism swirling around them, did not appease matters in the least when she suddenly screwed up her nose and exclaimed loudly, 'Good lord! Can these people really think of nothing better to do with their time than stand around gossiping all day.'

Wilhelmina, whose grasp of French was infinitely better than that of her cousin, had succeeded in comprehending the gist of the fiery conversation which immediately ceased as the group became aware of the girls' presence and all heads turned in silence to observe them. Sensing the hatred emanating from their glares, a stab of panic pulsed through her: her heart began to race; her legs to shake; and, not daring so much as to glance in the direction of her intimidating audience, she lowered her head and focused her eyes firmly on the filthy pavement.

Having passed by the crowd without further incident, Wilhelmina sighed with relief. Lavinia on the other hand, still a little way in front of her, with her nose now stuck well and truly in the air, evidently remained in ignorance of the danger they had so narrowly skirted. Having no desire to find herself in a similar situation in the future, however, Wilhelmina considered this an appropriate time to enlighten her cousin on the current perilous state of French affairs. Quickening her pace somewhat, she succeeded in catching her up and fell into a brisk step alongside her.

9

Deliberately lowering her voice, she said, 'I do think it perhaps wise to be a little more sympathetic to the people's plight here in France, Lavinia. They are experiencing a desperate shortage of food following the most appalling weather conditions over recent months. I have even heard that the situation is so bad that many of them are facing starvation.'

Obviously unable to comprehend such an alien concept, Lavinia tossed her blonde head and declared, 'Well, that's as may be, Cousin, however I do think that rather than standing around gossiping all day, they could make much better use of their time and clean up this disgusting street. What the poor queen would think if she were ever to set eyes upon such squalor is quite beyond me. Why she would most likely never wish to leave her beautiful palace ever again and I, for one, should not blame her.'

Having ceased long ago to be amazed at her cousin's lack of understanding of the world outside her own pampered bubble, Wilhelmina felt that this time it was worthwhile persisting in her explanation.

'But I rather think it is that very point that is upsetting the people, Lavinia,' she pointed out patiently. 'They believe the aristocracy to have little or no interest in their suffering. They see the upper classes as living in the very height of luxury whilst the common folk do not have enough to eat.'

Lavinia threw her cousin a disbelieving sidelong glance. 'You mean they resent the queen for living in the height of luxury?' she enquired incredulously. 'But that is utterly ridiculous. How could they possibly expect her *not* to live in luxury when she is the queen?'

'Perhaps,' continued Wilhelmina tolerantly, 'they feel she should be doing more to assist their cause.'

'Assist their cause?' repeated Lavinia cynically. 'But how on earth can they think for one moment that a person of such import would be interested in such a tedious cause? I am sure the woman has far more pressing matters to attend to than filling peasants' empty bellies.'

Realizing that her cousin had not the slightest inclination to concern herself with such unappealing matters, Wilhelmina decided to drop the subject for the time being, though having experienced first-hand the menacing mood of just a small sample of the

French people she could only hope for her sake that Queen Marie Antoinette did not dismiss her subjects' problems quite as blithely as Lavinia did.

CHAPTER 2

IT was some ninety minutes and several more erroneous turns later that the two girls, in an intermingled state of fatigue and bad humour, eventually arrived at their ecclesiastical destination: the Church of Notre Dame. Not only had they failed to spot a single cab during their protracted expedition, but they had also been issued with a set of what they now realized to be false directions from two quite separate but equally scruffy-looking individuals along the way, both of whom had undoubtedly found it a source of great amusement to direct two of the unpopular royal family's apparent supporters in the opposite direction to that in which they desired to go.

Despite her aching feet, dry throat, rumbling stomach and frayed nerves, however, Wilhelmina could not help but gaze in awe at the magnificent architecture of the Gothic cathedral as they approached its western façade and set eyes upon the spectacular rose window. Lavinia, conversely, was looking less impressed as they drew closer, for it was obvious to even the most short-sighted of visitors that there was no procession at all taking place – least of all one involving the entire French royal family.

'Damn those wretched Fitzgibbons,' proclaimed a now seething Lavinia, as she came to a standstill outside the imposing church door. 'This is all their fault – them and their wretched carriage.'

Wilhelmina's mind was busy forming quite a different theory as, by the normal display of everyday hustle and bustle taking place, she concluded that no grand display had taken place there at all that day nor indeed was planned to.

'Are you sure you have the correct day, Lavinia?' she enquired tentatively, uncomfortably aware that they were attracting a great deal of curious attention from the passers-by. 'It certainly does not look as though there has been any great procession here today.'

Lavinia rolled her eyes in annoyance. 'Of course I have the correct day,' she snapped. 'I overheard a woman in the baker's shop speak of it yesterday.'

'One of the French women in the baker's shop?' asked Wilhelmina cautiously.

'Of course, one of the French women,' retorted Lavinia. 'There were only French women in the baker's shop.'

'So you heard it in French then?'

Lavinia tutted. 'What is your point, Cousin?'

'Simply that I do not recall French being one of your strongest subjects when we were in the schoolroom together,' observed Wilhelmina.

Lavinia placed her hands on her slender hips and confronted her relative. 'Are you suggesting that I have misunderstood the date?' she demanded.

'I am merely saying,' pointed out Wilhelmina, now unable to suppress the edge of impatience colouring her own tone, 'that it would not be the first time you had confused your French numbers.'

A look of fury spread over Lavinia's countenance. 'It is bad enough,' she growled, 'that not only have I been forced to suffer more time than I care to recall wandering around this stinking city and miss the grandest spectacle I am most likely ever to set eyes upon, without having to endure offence from a member of my own family. Now if you have quite finished insulting my intelligence, Cousin, I suggest we attempt to find our way back to our lodgings for I have no desire at all to spend another moment being gawped at by these odious little peasants.' And with that she threw the group of a dozen or so odious little peasants – who were observing the argument with some amusement – a look of ripe disdain, before poking her nose in the air, picking up her skirts and swinging around on her heels in the most theatrical of fashions. No sooner had she done so, however, than all the observers watched in amazement as she wobbled precariously on the spot for several seconds before landing with an abrupt – and unladylike – thud on the filthy cobbles of the pavement.

There immediately followed a loud guffaw of laughter from the

13

grubby group of spectators, which both girls opted to ignore.

Wilhelmina, having not the first idea what could have caused her cousin to be suddenly sprawled about the ground, bent down to her and enquired concernedly, 'What on earth happened, Lavinia? Have you hurt yourself?'

Lavinia said nothing, but instead affected an aloof expression in defiance of the continued sniggering from the rabble behind. Rummaging under her skirts for a moment, she produced one of her blue silk slippers – minus its heel, which had lodged itself in a perfectly-sized gap between the cobbles. Observing the superior countenance which Lavinia was using every ounce of her resolve to maintain as she held up the damaged shoe for her cousin to examine, Wilhelmina felt a gurgle of laughter rising in her own throat. Not wishing to cause her relative any further embarrassment, however, she managed to choke it back, before reaching out her arm to assist the older girl to her feet.

After slipping the damaged shoe – minus its heel – onto her foot, a still silent Lavinia accepted the proffered arm and brought herself to a standing position in as dignified a fashion as she could manage, ignoring the mocking round of applause from the increasingly large group behind.

Defiantly jutting out her chin, and with her arm linked through Wilhelmina's, she then announced stoically, 'Come, Cousin. Let us be on our way,' and with that the two of them took their leave of Notre Dame with Lavinia hobbling away in as decorous a fashion as she could muster.

Just when one would have hoped that fate had completed its delivery of cruel blows for the day, the girls had been walking in silence for no more than ten minutes, when the heavens opened and the ominous group of dark clouds, which had been steadily forming throughout the morning, began doling out a torrent of large, heavy drops of rain. Not wishing to point out the obvious, which was that they were still quite some way from their lodging and that the rain was rapidly becoming heavier, Wilhelmina said nothing, choosing instead to squeeze her cousin's linked arm reassuringly and to carry on walking. A sudden loud sniff from Lavinia caused her to come to an abrupt stop.

'Come now, Cousin,' Wilhelmina coaxed soothingly, as she

turned towards Lavinia and observed the tears – intermingled with raindrops – rolling down her cheeks. 'We shall be home soon and I have no doubt Mrs Fitzgibbon will arrange for us both to have a warm bath and a cup of hot chocolate.'

The indifferent look which Lavinia flashed her indicated it would take a good deal more than a lump of soap, a tub of warm water and her favourite beverage to put her back in countenance.

'Oh, I wish we had never come here, Cousin,' she wailed loudly, the once proud feather in her hair now matted and bent and looking decidedly sorry for itself. 'I desired only to visit Paris because Verity Drinkwater told me she had the most marvellous time here last year. But it was quite obviously lies. It would be impossible for anyone to have a marvellous time here for it is quite simply the most hateful place on earth and that Drinkwater strumpet has now made it perfectly obvious that she will say anything – anything at all, Cousin – in her pathetic attempts to make me jealous.'

Knowing without a shadow of a doubt that, where Verity Drinkwater was concerned, her cousin gave just as good as she received, Wilhelmina bit back a smile. Lavinia's rivalry with their equally young and beautiful neighbour had been a source of amusement to her ever since Verity had first moved to Chipping Sodbury when the girls were but six years old but, for once, it was not Verity Drinkwater who was the sole target of her cousin's torrent of blame.

'And of course that mouse of a Fitzgibbon woman is also not without responsibility for luring us here,' she continued between sniffs. 'Quite why she insisted we visit when she cannot even do us the courtesy of loaning us her carriage is positively beyond me. It is my sincerest wish that we return to England as soon as possible, Cousin.'

Wilhelmina, who had expressed not the slightest inclination to make the trip to the Continent in the first place, decided this was not the wisest time to point out that fact. Instead she said, in as soothing a tone as she could muster, given the fact that she was standing in the most torrential of downpours, 'Come now, my dear. I am sure you shall feel much better once we are back at the house.'

Lavinia wiped away a drop of water dangling impudently from the end of her tiny nose. 'Indeed I shall not, Cousin,' she countered. 'I shall instruct Mr Fitzgibbon to make arrangements for our passage home as soon as possible for I have not the slightest wish to spend a moment longer in this odious place.'

At that announcement, a crack of thunder sounded directly above them, sending forth an even heavier downpour.

'Ugh!' squealed Lavinia, stamping her broken shoe on the ground. 'I wish I were dead for even that has to be better than being in this wretched city. Now let us hurry – the sooner we arrive at our lodging, the sooner we may instruct Mr Fitzgibbon to arrange our departure. I wish never to set foot in Paris ever again, as long as I live.'

Deciding that there was not the least point attempting to console the girl when she was in such dark humour, and that any further efforts to do so would merely result in the two of them becoming even more soaked – were that, in fact, possible – Wilhelmina said nothing. Instead she made to follow Lavinia who had already adopted as brisk a trot as circumstances would allow, in her impatience to reach the house and begin making the necessary arrangements for their return to England. The rain was pelting down with such vigour now that it was stinging her face and eyes. Rivulets of water were flowing freely down her throat and neck and under the thin silk of her gown, causing it to cling uncomfortably to her skin. Her painstaking arrangement of hair, meanwhile, had collapsed and was insisting on plastering itself with enthusiasm to her face. With both girls intent on nothing more at that miserable moment, other than reaching their warm, dry lodging, they were about to make their way across a wide cobbled road where the rapidly flowing water had adopted a worryingly river-like appearance, when they became aware of one of the elusive cabs they had been hankering after all day, rattling along behind them.

Before they could indicate for it to stop, it drew up alongside and a male voice stridently commanded of them, '*Montez! Vite!*'

Startled, both girls stopped in their tracks and turned towards the carriage. There, at the open window into which the rain was now pelting they saw a handsome young man who appeared puzzled by the drenched sight before him.

'You are English?' he enquired, obviously attributing their stunned silence to a lack of understanding.

The girls nodded their heads.

'Come then. Get in quickly,' he chivvied in a thick French accent, as the dripping wet jarvey, not looking the least bit impressed by this impromptu protraction to his miserable, soaking journey, leapt down from his seat and yanked open the carriage door.

Exchanging a look, which said they should be mad to refuse such an offer, given the appalling conditions, the two girls marched quickly over to the carriage where the disgruntled jarvey, muttering something in incomprehensible French under the broad brim of his hat – was now drawing down the steps. Wasting not a moment, they accepted the man's grudgingly held out, dripping-wet arm, climbed inside and took their places opposite their gallant rescuer. The jarvey meanwhile, still mumbling his stream of imprecations, slammed the door shut behind them, in a manner which left no doubt at all, had there been any, of his displeasure at the diversion.

However sensible the idea had appeared but a few short, wet seconds before, as the carriage pulled away, there was no disguising the fact that being in the close proximity of the conveyance with a complete stranger had the effect of rendering both girls a little awkward. The realization that they were not only extremely bedraggled and dripping water all over the cracked brown leather seats, but also that their gowns were clinging unashamedly to every one of their curves, seemed somewhat heightened by the fact that the stranger in question, with his sparkling navy-blue eyes and mop of thick light brown hair, cut short and expertly dishevelled in the very latest mode, was even more handsome than they had first realized. He was immaculately attired in blue velvet and, from the smug smile playing about his lips, appeared decidedly pleased with the sodden bounty of his rescue mission.

'I hope you will forgive my boldness, *mesdemoiselles*,' he said at length, 'but may I enquire as to your direction?'

The girls exchanged a dubious look.

'For the driver,' explained the man good-humouredly. 'Otherwise we shall have not the first idea where to deposit you.'

'Oh, of, er, course,' stammered Wilhelmina, chiding herself for being such a ninny. 'We are staying in La Rue de Charente, sir. Number 42.'

The man shouted up the direction to the driver who acknowledged it with a loud tap on the roof. He then turned his attention back to his travelling companions. Wilhelmina, in an attempt to ease her embarrassment, had opted to engage in an intense study of her fingernails whilst Lavinia stared miserably out of the steamed-up window.

'So,' said the gentleman, breaking the silence, 'may I ask what two such lovely young English ladies are doing wandering the streets of Paris unchaperoned and in such appalling conditions?'

Lavinia spoke first, oblivious in her misery to the fact that her wilting feather was creating a large puddle on the seat. 'We had meant to see the royal procession, sir,' she informed dolefully, transferring her gaze to a spot on the floor. 'However our own carriage was, er, undergoing some, er, repair; and we were unable to find a hackney. We found ourselves lost in the most odious part of the city possible; and then we missed the procession; and I broke the heel on my slipper; and then it started to rain; and I do believe this has been the most dreadful day of my entire life.'

The man cocked a surprised eyebrow. 'I see,' he declared, having obviously had not the least expectation of such a long, detailed and mournful explanation. Then, in an attempt to revive her spirits, he told her, 'But the exceedingly good news is, *mademoiselle*, that you have not missed the royal procession at all. It is, so I have it on the very best of authority, arranged to take place *next* week.'

'Next week?' repeated Lavinia with a glimmer of hope in her voice as she raised her eyes fleetingly to his. Then, obviously recalling the fact that she was extremely desirous not to remain in Paris for another week, she refocused on the spot on the floor, muttering a deflated, 'Oh.'

Seemingly undeterred by the subdued response to his revelation, the man continued amiably, 'Yes, indeed. I was talking to the queen about that very thing only yesterday – during my visit to Versailles.'

Conversely, the effect of *this* piece of news on Lavinia could not have been greater had the man informed her that she had just inherited the largest fortune in England. She regarded him directly now in wide-eyed fascination.

'You visited the *queen*?' she repeated incredulously. 'In *Versailles*? Oh, is it really as beautiful as they say, sir?'

'That I cannot deny, *mademoiselle*,' said the man, nodding his head earnestly. 'It is such a sight to behold that it quite puts my own chateau in the shade.'

'Ooh,' gasped Lavinia, not even attempting to conceal the excitement in her tone as she pressed a hand to her chest. 'You have your own chateau, sir?'

The man flashed a disarming smile. 'Indeed I do: le Chateau du Roxford.' He inclined his head graciously. 'The Comte de Roxford at your service, *mesdemoiselles*.'

'The – the Comte? de Roxford?' repeated Lavinia, flashing an incredulous glance at Wilhelmina whilst simultaneously making a futile attempt to rearrange her wilting tower of hair. 'What a great pleasure to meet you, my lord.'

'Oh, I can assure you, *mademoiselle* that the pleasure is all mine,' drawled the comte with a subtle smile. 'And if I may take another liberty, may I inform myself of the identity of my two charming travelling companions?'

'Oh, goodness,' flustered Lavinia, her previously dejected mood melting away to be replaced by a glow of enthusiastic confidence. 'Please do forgive my manners, sir. I am Lavinia. Lavinia Crump, er, *ington*. Smythe.' she added hastily.

The comte furrowed his brow. 'Lavinia *Cumperington* Smythe?' he repeated.

'No, sir,' corrected Lavinia, 'Lavinia, er, Crumpington-Smythe'.

'Ah!' said the comte, nodding his understanding. 'Lavinia *Ercrumptington*-Smythe?'

At the girl's unsuccessful attempt to elevate their ordinary surname, Wilhelmina choked back a snort of laughter.

Sensing her cousin's amusement, Lavinia shot her a reproving glare before stating definitively, 'No, sir, Lavinia *Crumpington-Smythe*.'

'Ah,' said the comte, nodding his understanding before turning his attention to Wilhelmina. 'And from the striking similarity am I correct in assuming that this charming lady is also a Crumpington-Smythe?'

'Yes, sir,' clarified Lavinia adroitly. 'My cousin, Delphine Crumpington-Smythe.'

Wilhelmina opened her mouth to protest but feeling Lavinia's sharp elbow suddenly nestled in her ribs, promptly closed it again.

'*Delphine?*' repeated the comte, narrowing his twinkling blue eyes. 'What a charming name – influenced by the *Française*, I think.'

'Indeed it is, sir,' said Lavinia, tossing Wilhelmina a victorious glance. 'Our family has a great association with France. In fact we are very distantly related to the king himself – on our fathers' side.'

At this fantastic proclamation, Wilhelmina almost slipped off the seat, but fortunately the driver chose exactly that moment to negotiate a sharp turn, the abruptness of which distracted her fellow passengers from the look of disbelief which had swept across her face. Lavinia, however, was carrying on gaily as if she had done nothing more than pass a comment regarding the weather.

The comte raised an impressed eyebrow. 'Relatives of the king?' he said, his tone one of the utmost interest.

'Yes, sir,' confirmed Lavinia. 'Although being brought up as two very refined young ladies of the highest class, we naturally do not like to boast of our noble connection.'

'Of course not,' agreed the comte, regarding the two girls now with an air of wonder.

'But pray, do tell me, sir,' carried on Lavinia levelly, 'what the queen was wearing yesterday, for we have heard that she is all that is elegant.'

'That I cannot dispute, *mademoiselle*,' said the comte ingenuously. 'Now, what was she wearing yesterday?' He cast his eyes skyward as though giving the matter a great deal of thought, before declaring, 'Ah yes! I do believe she was wearing a gown the colour of an unripe apple.'

Lavinia regarded him aghast. '*Green?*' she clarified, with a slight wrinkle of her nose.

'Very green. Yes, *mademoiselle*,' confirmed the comte, nodding.

'Oh,' she said, still taken aback. Then she tutted and declared, 'Well *of course* it was green. Why, there is simply no other colour to be seen in this Season. I, of course, have a number of green gowns, it being the most popular colour in London this year.'

'I am most pleased to hear it, *mademoiselle*,' said the comte, his lips twitching slightly. 'And may I ask if you reside in London?'

'But of course,' replied a now quite animated Lavinia. 'Although we do, naturally, divide our time between the great capital and our country estate – as do all upper-class English ladies, sir.'

Wilhelmina, who knew quite definitely that firstly, neither she nor Lavinia had ever been to London in their lives and secondly, that describing their unremarkable Chipping Sodbury garden as a 'country estate' was a gross exaggeration of fact, threw her cousin an admonishing glare, which was unashamedly returned with a beatific smile. The comte meanwhile, accepted the information graciously.

'How delightful. Why I am planning to visit London myself very soon. I find it a most interesting city.'

'One of the *most* interesting, sir,' concurred Lavinia without a moment's hesitation. 'Although, I confess, one can tire somewhat of the never-ending round of social engagements during the Season. Delphine and I are positively exhausted by it.'

Wilhelmina felt her eyes growing wide in her head as she wondered at the fickleness of her cousin's moods and her ability to lie so brazenly – and convincingly.

'So I can imagine,' said the comte, nodding his head sympathetically. 'I have no doubt that two such lovely ladies would be quite in demand. I do hope, however, that your fatigue will not prevent you from attending *Le Bal de Printemps* on Friday, *mademoiselle?*'

Having not the least knowledge of *Le Bal de Printemps* and guessing, by the puzzled look which swept momentarily over her cousin's face, that it was also the first time such an event had been brought to Lavinia's attention, Wilhelmina was more than a little amazed when her cousin declared merrily, 'Oh, of course not, sir. We would not miss it for the world, would we, Delphine?'

Scarcely believing that such words were being spoken by the same girl who, only minutes before, had wished herself dead rather than being in Paris, Wilhelmina's ability to do anything but gawp, deserted her.

The comte, however, sensing nothing at all untoward in the conversation, beamed at them. 'Excellent,' he announced before glancing out of window. 'Ah, but what a pity – I do believe the time has come for us to part company. It would appear that we have now reached La Rue de Charente.'

'Oh,' muttered Lavinia despondently as the carriage drew to a halt outside the Fitzgibbons' townhouse. 'That is a great pity indeed. How can we ever thank you for your kindness, my lord?'

'It was the very least I could do, *mademoiselle*,' replied the comte, as the sodden jarvey opened the door and pulled down the steps, with no less grace than he had performed the task several minutes before. 'And please be assured that your presence at *le bal* on Friday will serve as gratitude enough.'

'Oh, how very charming,' fluttered Lavinia, flashing him her most dazzling of smiles as she alighted from the conveyance.

Wilhelmina followed her cousin, after having expressed her own thanks to both the comte and the jarvey, who accepted his with a menacing dark scowl. The carriage was just about to pull away and the girls to mount the steps to the front door, when the comte pulled down the window and shouted, 'Until Friday, Miss Lavinia Crumpington-Smythe, Miss Delphine Crumpington-Smythe. I shall very much look forward to it.'

As Wilhelmina bounded up the steps to the door, which was now being held open by the Fitzgibbons' decrepit old butler, Lavinia, seemingly oblivious to the pouring rain battering her once again, stood and watched the conveyance until it trundled along to the end of the street and turned out of view.

'Oh my,' she declared dreamily, entering the hallway a few seconds later, 'was that not the most romantic way in which to meet one's future husband, Cousin? Why he was like a knight in shining armour rescuing us so – and quite, quite charming. I do believe that, with one or two minor embellishments and despite the fact that we are looking far from our best, we have managed to create *the* most favourable impression. Indeed I have absolutely no doubt that the man thinks us of the very highest class.'

'Those were not minor embellishments, Lavinia,' pointed out Wilhelmina, as she gratefully accepted a warm towel from one of the maids, 'those were downright lies.'

Choosing to ignore that too frank an observation, Lavinia gave a deep, contented sigh as she handed her soaking shawl to the servant. 'Oh, can you imagine,' she said, with a mischievous giggle, 'me – a Crump of Chipping Sodbury – becoming a comtesse? Why the look on Verity Drinkwater's face would be positively priceless.'

CHAPTER 3

'I HAVE a matter of great import to arrange tomorrow, Mrs Fitzgibbon,' announced Lavinia, as the three women were enjoying their dinner that evening.

Having some knowledge by now of Lavinia's theatrical demands and therefore fearing what was to follow this statement, an expression of dread began creeping over Mrs Fitzgibbon's kindly rounded face, framed by tight grey ringlets. She put down her glass of water and began dabbing nervously at her mouth with a crisp white napkin.

'Oh dear,' she murmured. 'Nothing to worry about, I hope?'

Lavinia did not raise her eyes from the slice of steak pie she was cutting. 'Well perhaps not at the moment,' she replied, 'but I am in need of a new gown and I fear that if I do not find exactly the right shade of green silk for it, then there may be a great deal to worry about.'

'Oh dear,' muttered Mrs Fitzgibbon again, beginning to tremble.

Wilhelmina was much less tolerant of her cousin's whims. '*Green?*' she repeated, holding a forkful of buttered beans before her mouth. 'But you abhor green.'

'Indeed I do not, Cousin,' countered Lavinia, a little sheepishly.

'Indeed you do,' replied Wilhelmina resolutely, lowering her fork. 'The last time I appeared before you in a green gown, you accused me of looking like a mouldy gooseberry.'

'Yes, well you did,' said Lavinia petulantly, raising her head to her cousin. 'However the charming Comte de Roxford, informed me that Queen Marie Antoinette was wearing green yesterday and one must follow her suit if one is to be accepted by Parisian society, Cousin. There can simply be no other colour to be seen in in Paris and I must therefore have a new green gown as soon as possible.'

'The-the Comte de Roxford, did you say, dear?' stammered Mrs Fitzgibbon who had only just returned to the house some thirty minutes before dinner and had therefore avoided having to suffer Lavinia's incessant ramblings about the man for much of the afternoon.

'Yes, indeed, Mrs Fitzgibbon,' confirmed Lavinia smugly. 'My cousin and I made the gentleman's acquaintance this very day. In fact he rescued us from a most dreadful situation. Of course, I hasten to add that, had we had the loan of your carriage today, Mrs Fitzgibbon, then we should not have found ourselves in such a dreadful situation. However, that point is now of no import for, had you seen fit to loan us your carriage, then we should not have made the acquaintance of the most charming, handsome man I have ever had the good fortune to meet.'

'I-er see,' said Mrs Fitzgibbon, as her fork slipped from her hand and landed on her lap.

Lavinia, ignoring the effect her ill-concealed grievances were having on her hostess, continued with her speech as the older woman retrieved her fork and began rubbing it vigorously with her napkin.

'Of course, we were looking far from our best, given that we had been soaked to the bone in the heaviest rain I have ever encountered,' continued Lavinia matter-of-factly. 'In fact, we may both die of pneumonia, Mrs Fitzgibbon, due to the fact that we were without a carriage – but pray do not let that concern you.'

Unable to hold it back, an ill-timed sneeze escaped Wilhelmina, which resulted in a look of horror spreading over Mrs Fitzgibbon's already anxious countenance. Lavinia meanwhile, continued.

'Nevertheless, I have no doubt that the man was positively enchanted by us, which is why he has requested our presence at *Le Bal de Printemps* on Friday.'

Mrs Fitzgibbon looked completely dumbfounded. '*Le-Le Bal de Printemps*?' she stammered. 'On Friday?'

'I can assure you there is no need to look so surprised, Mrs Fitzgibbon,' declared Lavinia. 'It has always been my intention to marry into the aristocracy and the Comte de Roxford fits the bill perfectly. He owns his own chateau, you know, which I shall enquire about in much more detail when I see him on Friday.'

Wilhelmina raised her brows questioningly. 'May I assume then, that your overwhelming urge to return to England has now passed?'

'But of course, Cousin,' declared Lavinia, in a tone which suggested her cousin was quite mad. 'Why on earth should I wish to return to boring old England, when there is a charming comte expecting me at a magnificent ball on Friday?'

'That is all very well, I am sure, Lavinia,' observed Wilhelmina, not without some irritation. 'However, it appears to have escaped your attention that you do not actually have an invitation to *Le Bal de Printemps*.'

Lavinia tutted dismissively. 'Of course, I am well aware of that fact,' she replied tartly, 'however, I am sure Mrs Fitzgibbon will have no problem in procuring us an invitation.' She raised her eyebrows optimistically to her mousy hostess. 'That will, I trust, not prove a problem, Mrs Fitzgibbon?' she added, more in the manner of a command than a question.

Mrs Fitzgibbon, whose face had now turned a worrying shade of puce stammered, 'Well, I, er, don't really think I, er know of anyone who attends such elaborate events.'

Lavinia was not to be deterred quite so easily. 'Well then perhaps you could think a little harder,' she pressed. 'It is, after all, a matter of the utmost importance. In fact, if I am not mistaken, I believe it is a matter upon which my entire future could depend. Not, of course, that I wish to place you under any pressure, Mrs Fitzgibbon.'

A horrified-looking Mrs Fitzgibbon slipped a shade lower in her chair giving Wilhelmina the distinct impression that she would quite happily have slid right off it and disappeared under the table.

Quite exhausted by the day's events, the girls retired a little earlier than usual, after drinking a warm glass of milk. Despite her previous proclamations that she was so excited she should not sleep a wink between now and Friday, Lavinia had fallen asleep the instant her head had touched the pillow. Wilhelmina, having read a little, had just blown out her candle and was on the verge of dozing off when she was alerted to the alarming sound of breaking glass, followed by a volley of loud, hysterical shouting. Both girls immediately jerked bolt upright in their beds.

'What's going on?' gasped Lavinia, looking wide-eyed at her cousin.

'I have no idea,' replied Wilhelmina, pulling back the coverlet and slipping out of bed. She padded over to the window and pulled back the wooden shutters.

'Oh my word,' she declared, clamping a hand over her mouth in horror as she shuddered at the terrifying sight which met her eyes.

'What? What is it?' demanded Lavinia impatiently, leaping up and joining her cousin at the window.

Wilhelmina could not reply but merely continued staring in awe at the terrifying scene below. The street which had been deserted during the downpour some hours before, was now flooded with a river of ragged-looking men, women and children – a strange, frightening medley of anger and exhilaration etched on their filthy, downtrodden faces. Some were striding purposefully along the cobbles, chanting to a deep ominous drumbeat, which echoed deep in the hollow of Wilhelmina's chest, as it grew increasingly louder. Others were dancing frenziedly – like lunatics freed from the asylum – screeching and shouting wildly. Many were carrying weapons in the form of swords or menacing-looking farming implements, whilst others sported burning torches, which cast an eerie orange light over their dirty faces and highlighted the malevolence shining brightly in their eyes.

Wilhelmina watched in stunned horror as two young boys threw rocks at the window of the linen-draper's opposite causing the glass to shatter into a thousand tiny pieces. The stooped old woman behind them opened her mouth to reveal a set of hideous black teeth before emitting a cackle of wicked laughter and tossing her burning torch into the shop. The flames claimed the cotton garments on display in the window and a waft of dirty black smoke began snaking its way out into the street. The woman stood surveying her handiwork for a brief moment before releasing another roar of laughter resonating with such evil that it pierced Wilhelmina's core and caused goose-bumps to break out all over her skin.

As the door to their bedchamber was suddenly thrust open, her heart froze in terror for a moment and she almost fainted with relief when she recognized the small, thin, unassuming figure of Mr Fitzgibbon whom she had not seen all day.

'What on earth is going on, Mr Fitzgibbon?' asked Lavinia, her voice quivering.

'It is just as I feared,' replied the man, looking grey and anxious as he walked over to the window to join them. 'The peasants have resorted to rioting and I must say I am not at all surprised. The tension in this city has been growing for months now and there has been a rumour circulating this week that Monsieur Reveillon intends to cut the wages of the workers at his wallpaper factory. If I'm not mistaken, that large fire over there could be the factory itself.'

All heads turned towards the area of Saint Antoine where the night sky glowed menacingly orange.

'But this is dreadful,' declared Lavinia, shaking. 'How dare mere peasants behave in such an unruly manner?'

'Oh they dare,' replied Mr Fitzgibbon. 'It is surprising what people will do when they feel they are being wronged. It is what else they may do that worries me.'

'Wh-what do you mean?' stammered Wilhelmina, feeling all colour drain from her face.

'I fear this is only the start,' replied Mr Fitzgibbon. 'There are a great many issues in this city which need to be resolved and I am anxious about the methods which may be employed to achieve results. I therefore think it wisest if you two girls prepare to take your leave of Paris immediately.'

'Take our leave of Paris?' repeated a stunned Lavinia. 'But we . . . we cannot. We have only just arrived. I mean what of . . . what of the comte . . . the ball . . . my *future*?'

Mr Fitzgibbon regarded her coolly. 'I fear you may not have a future if you remain here,' he said. 'The city is far too dangerous – especially for two young foreign ladies. Pack what things you need at once and I will arrange for the carriage to be outside in half an hour.'

'But I—' began Lavinia.

Mr Fitzgibbon shot her a warning glare. 'Do as I say, Lavinia,' he said, so unexpectedly firmly that Wilhelmina witnessed her cousin rendered uncharacteristically dumbstruck.

Regrettably for all those within earshot of the Fitzgibbon residence, Lavinia's silence did not last long.

'I have never heard the like of it, Cousin,' she expostulated as she stomped around the bedchamber, vigorously pulling out items of clothing from the commode and the armoire and flinging them onto the increasingly large pile on her bed. 'Absolutely no one seems to realize how important it is for me to stay here; no one at all. Why it is not every day that one makes the acquaintance of a *comte*, Cousin, and I dare not even contemplate what the man will think when I fail to turn up to the ball on Friday. I have a good mind to go out there and tell those wretched peasants exactly what I think of them creating such a fuss over nothing. A fuss that is set to ruin my entire future: my future as a comtesse.' Then, in a melodramatic gesture she flung herself on top of the large pile of clothes on the bed and began sobbing and wailing.

The commotion brought a perturbed Mrs Fitzgibbon scurrying along the corridor. Peeping around the doorframe and seeing what was amiss, however, she merely muttered a rather flustered, 'Oh my,' before turning on her heel and scampering away again.

Wilhelmina, meanwhile, much more accustomed to such exaggerated displays, calmly carried on stuffing various items of essential clothing into the small portmanteau she had unpacked only a few days before.

After several more minutes of sobbing and wailing, Lavinia, realizing that her performance was not having the desired effect, lifted her head and regarded Wilhelmina through red-rimmed, puffy eyes.

'I am doomed, Cousin,' she sniffed. 'Doomed to a life of boredom and marriage to a man without a title – for where else am I to meet a *comte*, Cousin? In Chipping Sodbury? No, I must resign myself to becoming a little drudge of a wife with a husband of absolutely no consequence. I must accustom myself to having no parties, no jewels, no grand houses, no servants, no – no – nothing. Indeed I must accept the fact that I am destined to be quite the most miserable girl on earth and I rather think I should prefer to be dead than—'

'Oh, for goodness sake, Lavinia,' berated Wilhelmina impatiently as she rolled up a chemise, 'do not be so dramatic. Now do hurry up. The carriage will be here in a few minutes and I for one cannot wait to be home safely.'

'That is because, unlike myself, you have absolutely no ambition, Cousin,' pronounced Lavinia sliding off the pile of clothes and smoothing down her skirts.

'Perhaps not,' replied Wilhelmina resolutely, turning her attention to a woollen shawl, 'but I think it perhaps better to be an unambitious living person than an ambitious dead one, don't you?'

Lavinia glared at her, which indicated that she was not necessarily of the same opinion.

CHAPTER 4

Calais, France

THE girls were accompanied during their journey to Calais – a distance of some two hundred miles – by both Mr and Mrs Fitzgibbon. For all that they had covered the same route less than a week before, their excitement at being on foreign soil for the first time in their lives had obviously made the journey appear much less interminable than this time. The matter was not helped at all by the fact that, wishing to make as much haste as possible, Mr Fitzgibbon allowed only the briefest of stops at the post-houses to change the horses and take some refreshment – very little of which, it had to be said, lived up to its name. Sleep, too, was proving unsatisfactory in the jolting carriage, as it bumped and trundled its way along the well-worn roads from the French capital to the country's busiest port.

It was almost eight o'clock the following evening when they eventually reached their destination and, understandably, not one of the party was in the best of moods. At least the rain had held off for their journey but the sky had retained its oppressive appearance and the air was heavy with the threat of a storm.

As the carriage drew closer to the port, it was obvious that the girls were not the only two people intending to leave France that evening and, from the sights they had seen on the journey out of Paris, Wilhelmina was not at all surprised. The city was ablaze with fires, shops were being looted and large, threatening gangs had convened outside the grand houses of the aristocracy, hurling stones at their windows and abuse at the no doubt terrified occupants. Even the Fitzgibbons' modest carriage had become a target of the mob's resentment at one point, albeit a very minor one, with driver, horses and passengers thankfully escaping any injuries from the few stones viciously cast their way.

Lavinia had spent the vast majority of the journey with her bottom lip stuck out petulantly and her arms rigidly crossed against her chest. She had uttered only a handful of words since they had left Paris – a circumstance about which none of her three travelling companions had the slightest inclination to complain.

'Now you girls must stay close to Mrs Fitzgibbon and me when we alight,' instructed Mr Fitzgibbon firmly as the carriage rolled into the port. 'It looks as though the place is a veritable hive of activity.'

Hive of activity was one description, thought Wilhelmina, as she observed the scene into which they were entering – total chaos was another. As soon as she stepped down from the carriage, her senses were immediately accosted by the magnitude of the activity. A barrage of shouting, mostly in languages she did not recognize, assaulted her ears, whilst the smell of rotting fish intermingled with that of the sea and fresh tar invaded her nostrils. Due to the threatening sky, night was falling rapidly, casting a shadowy gloom over the proceedings. Squinting out into the vast, dark expanse of sea beyond, she could make out the blurred outline of some half a dozen vessels departing the French shores, their bobbing lights giving them the appearance of skittish fireflies. On the land, meanwhile, the throng – made up of men – was scurrying around like a busy pack of worker ants.

Mr Fitzgibbon, seemingly more absorbed in his task to be rid of his charges than observing his surroundings, chivvied the proceedings along. 'Come now, girls,' he instructed briskly, once all four of them had alighted. 'Take only what luggage you need. We must waste no time in finding you a ship.'

Wilhelmina accepted her portmanteau from the driver of the carriage and made to follow Mr Fitzgibbon, the pair of them ignoring the fact that, from the large pile of baggage which the driver then proceeded to unload from the roof of the carriage, Lavinia's luggage reclamation was to take considerably longer than that of her cousin.

Taking extreme umbrage from the fact that not one offer of assistance was forthcoming from the plethora of men bustling around, nor indeed from the driver of their carriage, who had already informed her some three times now of his intention to move the conveyance away from the commotion as soon as possible to avoid further upset to the horses, Lavinia concluded, in a fit of pique, that there was nothing else for it but to carry the four band-boxes, a trunk, two battered brown leather valises and a portmanteau herself. Her undertaking did not get off to a particularly auspicious start, however, as, attempting to retrieve all four band-boxes at once, she discovered the wretched items to be remarkably cumbersome. Opting for an alternative strategy therefore, much to the bemusement of both the driver and Mrs Fitzgibbon, who had remained behind with her, she wasted no time in emptying the contents of each box and tugging the four hats – of quite varying shapes and sizes – onto her indignant head. At some point during this process, she had also decided that the maintenance of her vow of silence was not helping matters in the least and began employing a great deal of vocal activity in issuing instructions to a poor, terrified Mrs Fitzgibbon on how best the older woman might assist her with the transportation of the various items. The consequence of this tirade was that, a few short minutes later, Mrs Fitzgibbon found herself in an uncomfortable stooped position, dragging along a trunk with one hand and a battered leather valise with the other.

Mr Fitzgibbon, meanwhile, who was now standing alongside Wilhelmina, surveying the various vessels, turned to Lavinia and, adopting a disbelieving expression, shouted, 'Do hurry up, girl. And make sure you stay close. I am going to make some enquiries as to where the ships are bound.'

There was an eclectic mix of a dozen or so vessels in the port including a handful of schooners – of varying sizes – two cargo ships and a large imposing warship. Wilhelmina observed as Mr Fitzgibbon ran ahead and spoke to a man with swarthy skin, a large thick black beard and an enormous belly, avidly engaged in the task of unfastening the thick plaited ropes tethering a large schooner to the solid wooden mooring post. The man carried on with his task as Mr Fitzgibbon was talking and it did not take a genius to work out, by the vigorous shaking of his dark head, that the response was a negative one. After a few more minutes of animated conversation, Mr Fitzgibbon returned to Wilhelmina just as his laden wife and Lavinia also reached her.

'No luck, I'm afraid,' he informed, pulling a rueful face. 'This ship is heading for Spain and the sailor says most of the ships bound for England have already left. He also thinks it unlikely, given the current state of affairs, that there will be many more English ships docking here in the next few days.'

'Well, then we are quite obviously wasting our time,' pointed out Lavinia, injecting her tone with a degree of optimism. 'I suggest we turn around and go back to Paris this very instant.'

Mr Fitzgibbon shot her a reprimanding look. 'We will do no such thing,' he insisted. 'It is far too dangerous for you to stay in France. I shall see you off these shores if it is the last thing I do. Wait here while I make more enquiries.'

Now in high dudgeon, Lavinia watched through narrowed eyes as Mr Fitzgibbon marched over to the enormous, menacing warship and approached a tall, gangly young man who was engaged in rolling barrels up the gangplank of the craft.

'Hmph,' she huffed, crossing her arms over her chest. 'It is my opinion that we have placed ourselves in far more danger coming here. We should have been much better off staying in Paris,' she declared, tossing her head so violently that the precarious tower of hats perched upon it tumbled immediately to the filthy ground. 'Grrr,' she growled, bending down to retrieve them. 'Could this day possibly deteriorate any further?'

No sooner had the words flowed from her mouth, than the answer to her rhetorical question was revealed.

'We are in luck,' declared Mr Fitzgibbon, trotting briskly back to them. 'This Royal Navy ship is going to Bristol and will take you, but you must go this very instant. They are setting sail immediately.'

'Thank God,' muttered Wilhelmina, now feeling a desperate longing for the relative peace of her homeland.

Lavinia, on the other hand, made no attempt to disguise the fact that she was not in the least bit impressed by this news. 'Really,' she muttered, as she pulled the four hats back roughly on to her head and made to pick up her bags, 'this is positively outrageous. First we have to suffer that interminable journey with quite appalling sustenance and then I am ordered about as though I am nothing more than a mere serving girl. When my father hears of my treatment I have no doubt that heads will roll, sir.'

While Mrs Fitzgibbon, having stretched her weary back, made to resume her transportation of the trunk and valise, Mr Fitzgibbon, ignoring Lavinia's blusterings, placed a hand upon Wilhelmina's arm and steered her towards the ship where, with the barrel loading now complete, the crew were preparing to set sail.

'Wilhelmina,' he said anxiously, lowering his voice as they approached the foot of the gangplank.

'Hurry up now,' cried the gangly young man with whom Mr Fitzgibbon had just spoken. 'We'll be leaving in two minutes.'

Mr Fitzgibbon raised his hand to the man in acknowledgement of his words. Wilhelmina looked up at him, sensing the seriousness of his tone.

'Wilhelmina,' he said again, reaching into his jacket pocket and pulling out an envelope. 'This is a matter of the utmost importance; a matter, which you must speak to no one about – no one at all. If you do, you will be placing yourself in grave danger. Do you understand me?'

A stunned Wilhelmina wrinkled her forehead and gazed at the man in silent bewilderment.

Mr Fitzgibbon took hold of her right hand and pressed the envelope in it. 'You must take this letter to England with you,' he continued earnestly, closing her fingers about it. 'You will receive further instructions on what to do with it from our contact there known as The Stag. They will make themselves known to you when the time is right. In the meantime, you must keep the letter with you at all times.'

'But I-I don't understand,' stammered Wilhelmina. 'Why on earth are you giving this to me and who is this . . . this *Stag*?'

'Please do not ask me any more questions,' said Mr Fitzgibbon imploringly. 'I can tell you no more at this stage and quite frankly, the less you know, the safer it is for you. Do as you are instructed and I promise no harm shall come to you.'

Wilhelmina's eyebrows shot up to her hairline. 'Harm?' she repeated incredulously. 'You are asking me to do something where I might well be harmed? With all due respect, Mr Fitzgibbon, I really don't think you should be—'

'It is most unlikely that it will come to that,' assured Mr Fitzgibbon. 'However, should you at any point find yourself in an . . . an . . . *uncomfortable* situation, I have no doubt that with your level head and quick mind you will be able to remove yourself from it with ease.'

'But I . . . I have no wish to find myself in an uncomfortable situation, sir,' objected Wilhelmina her tone ripe with panic. 'Do I really have to—'

'Please be assured, Wilhelmina,' said Mr Fitzgibbon gravely, 'that I would not place this responsibility upon you unless there was a very real need. A great deal is resting upon you and I cannot stress enough that you must tell no one – no one at all – of your involvement. Do you understand me?'

Wilhelmina regarded him once again in astounded silence, desperately praying that she would wake up in a moment or two and all the pandemonium which seemed to have descended upon her so suddenly, would have vanished and the world reverted back to some kind of normality. It was not to be, however, and, aware of the man's expectant gaze upon her, she found herself incapable of doing anything more than meekly nodding her head.

'Good,' said Mr Fitzgibbon, his tone implying that he was satisfied she had fully comprehended her instructions. 'Then I wish you the very best of luck.'

Before another word could be said on the matter, the sound of a familiar voice remonstrating loudly, reached their ears. Wilhelmina quickly tucked the letter into her portmanteau as she and Mr Fitzgibbon turned around to face the complainant.

'I should like to make you aware, Mr Fitzgibbon,' declared a furious Lavinia as she struggled towards the gangplank with her luggage, 'that I have never been treated so appallingly in my entire life. If my father could see me now – loaded up with items like a . . . a donkey – I have no doubt he would have you and all these idle men strung up without a moment's hesitation.'

'Perhaps if you had not brought so much luggage, Lavinia,' pointed out Mr Fitzgibbon, going to her aid and relieving her of her cumbersome burden, 'then you would not find yourself in need of assistance.'

'I can assure you I have brought only my most essential of items, Mr Fitzgibbon,' she retorted defiantly. 'How any refined young lady could possibly travel with less is perfectly beyond me,' she said, casting a disdainful look at Wilhelmina's portmanteau.

'And I can assure *you*, Lavinia,' said Wilhelmina, still stunned from her conversation with Mr Fitzgibbon, 'that luggage is the very last thing on my mind at the moment.'

'Well, that's as may be,' declared Lavinia petulantly, 'however first and foremost on my mind is the ruination of my marriage to the Comte de Roxford and my entire future. Although nobody, including you, Cousin, seems in the least bit perturbed by that fact.'

Having had her fill of Lavinia's rants over the last few days, Wilhelmina rolled her eyes and went to relieve a perspiring Mrs Fitzgibbon, who had been trailing after Lavinia, of her heavy burden. Bidding the woman a fond farewell, and passing on her grateful thanks for her kind – and remarkably patient – hospitality, she then followed her cousin up the gangplank and onto the ship, dragging Lavinia's heavy trunk behind her.

CHAPTER 5

Aboard ship

IT was obvious to Wilhelmina, from the moment she set foot aboard the vessel, that it had undergone a great many long and arduous sea journeys. The wooden boards of the deck, although spotlessly clean, were bleached almost to white from the combination of hot sun, salt water and years of scrubbing. Above her, she noted the complex network of rigging supporting a host of dirty white, ragged sails, several of which had already been lowered in preparation for the forthcoming journey and were testing their roped constraints to the limit as they billowed in the wind. On the sides of the deck, skilful, painstaking craftsmanship juxtaposed alongside the cold, harsh face of war, as sections of the wooden sides had been decoratively carved out to allow eight menacing black-leaded cannon a first class view of their target. Wilhelmina's thoughts turned to the bloody scenes the craft must have witnessed throughout its long nautical career and she was still engaged in pondering this fact when her reverie was broken by the gangly man with whom Mr Fitzgibbon had spoken earlier.

'Now then,' he was saying in a broad London accent, 'we'd better be finding somewhere to put you two ladies. Could be a long journey by the look of that sky out there. My name's Peterson, by the way,' he announced, flashing them a broad toothy grin.

Lavinia said nothing as she continued to survey her surroundings with a disgruntled expression upon her face.

Wilhelmina, meanwhile, swiftly regaining a little of her equanimity and realizing that she ought to be showing the man at least some modicum of gratitude for his willingness to have them aboard, managed to stammer, 'Er, thank you for agreeing to transport us, Mr Peterson. I am Miss Crump and this is my cousin—'

'What's going on, Peterson?' suddenly roared a deep masculine voice from the other end of the deck.

Both girls whirled around and started slightly as they observed the approaching tall male figure whose booming voice complemented his intimidating physique perfectly. Indeed, with his wavy jet-black hair, hanging loose about his shoulders, and the thick dark stubble covering his chin, he put Wilhelmina instantly in mind of a terrifying, marauding pirate. He was dressed in a pair of tight-fitting black breeches and a grubby white shirt, whose rolled up sleeves displayed muscular, brown arms. Despite his overshadowing presence and threatening tone, however, it was the thunderous expression upon his face, which made Wilhelmina quake in her kid leather boots. She was thankful to see that Peterson appeared much more used to the man's manner.

'Two damsels in distress, Cap'n Tunbridge, sir,' he replied with another wide grin. 'Need to get back home so they do. Thought we could squeeze them in, given that they don't weigh much more than a sparrow between them.'

No grin – wide or otherwise – was forthcoming from the captain's face as he fixed the girls with dark piercing eyes. 'Perhaps *they* do not,' he said in a tone which made no attempt to conceal his contempt of his two new passengers, 'however I cannot say the same for this ridiculous pile of luggage. Get rid of it at once, Peterson, for it will prove nothing but a damned hindrance.'

'*Get rid of it?*' repeated Lavinia incredulously, the tower of hats on her head wobbling with indignation. 'Over my dead body.'

The captain threw her a look which left little doubt that that alternative would not be at all out of the question should she persist with her protestation.

'This is *my* ship, madam,' he stated so definitively that Wilhelmina stifled a gasp, 'and I will not be disobeyed. Get rid of it immediately, Peterson,' he ordered, 'before I throw it off myself.'

'Aye, aye, Cap'n,' said Peterson, bending down and placing his hand upon a brown leather valise. Before he had a chance to pick it up, Lavinia, who was not about to bow to the captain's authority quite so pliantly, jolted into action.

'Take your hands off that this instant,' she commanded, whipping the valise from him in a flash and causing the hats on her head to fall and scatter all over the wooden boards of the deck. 'This valise contains all of my lace-trimmed petticoats and in the trunk is my favourite sky-blue evening gown which, I can tell you, Captain, is most likely worth more than you could earn in an entire year.'

The captain's dark eyes clouded over with fury. 'I am warning you, madam,' he hissed, 'that if you do not release your hold of that valise by the time I count to ten, you will wish you had never set foot aboard this ship.'

His ominous tone caused Wilhelmina to gulp, but her cousin, now burning with rage, refused to be so easily daunted.

'I can assure you, Captain,' she declared, defiantly raising her chin to him as she clasped the handle of the case tightly with both hands, 'that I have wished that circumstance myself some two hundred times already and I have only been on your horrid ship for a matter of minutes.'

The captain's eyes narrowed. 'One,' he began frostily.

'And I can tell you, sir that when my father hears of the manner in which I have been treated—'

'Two.'

'—he will have you removed from your post immediately—'

'Three.'

'—and don't think for one moment that that is an idle threat, sir—'

'Four.'

'—for my father, Mr Crump – *ington, Smythe,* is an extremely influential man—'

'Five.'

'—and he will not take kindly—'

'Six.'

'—to his daughter—'

'Seven.'

'—his one and only daughter, I might add—'

'Eight.'

'—being spoken to in such an—'

'Nine.'

'—impudent manner.'

'Ten,' pronounced the captain before snatching the valise from Lavinia's hands, slinging her over his shoulder as easily as if she were a sack of potatoes, and carrying her off to the far end of the deck, seemingly oblivious to the fact that the girl was howling like a banshee and pounding furiously against his broad, muscular back.

Whilst the incident was obviously providing a great deal of amusement to the other crew members, a flabbergasted Wilhelmina found herself rooted to the spot, her mouth gaping open.

'Oh, Lord,' she muttered anxiously, turning her attention to the sailor. 'What on earth will he do with her?'

The sailor chuckled. 'Oh, don't you be worrying yourself about her, miss,' he replied, with another cheeky grin. 'Not one for hysterics is the cap'n. He'll be locking her in one of the storerooms downstairs till she calms down.'

'Oh,' muttered Wilhelmina. 'Well, if I know my cousin, that could be quite some time. I suppose I had better go to find her. What will you do with the luggage, Peterson?'

'Best get rid of it, miss,' pronounced the man solemnly. 'Those were the cap'n's orders and it's a brave man who disobeys them.'

'Oh,' said Wilhelmina again. 'Well, do you think he would, er, mind, if I just removed the blue evening gown from the trunk and took it to her?'

Peterson took a deep inhalation and scratched his head. 'Well, on your head be it, miss,' he said. 'But if I were you, I wouldn't be letting the cap'n know. He's a fair temper on him and you don't want to be getting on the wrong side of him an' all.'

'No,' murmured Wilhelmina, recalling with a shiver, the man's menacing expression. 'I most certainly do not.'

Having retrieved her cousin's four – now very grubby – hats from the floor and pushed all thoughts of rescuing the sky-blue evening gown from her mind, Wilhelmina followed Peterson to the end of the deck. From there, they climbed down three sets of wooden stairs into the bowels of the vessel, where she discovered a veritable labyrinth of rooms and narrow corridors dimly-lit by wall-mounted lanterns.

With Peterson leading Wilhelmina through the maze, they eventually located Lavinia in one of the many small storerooms which, from the overpowering stench inside, had recently housed a large quantity of extremely strong-smelling fish. The room was square in shape and about it were scattered a number of wooden crates. It was upon one of these that Lavinia was seated, her head miserably propped in her hands. She leapt to her feet as the door swung open and, just as Wilhelmina had predicted, did not appear to have calmed down one iota. Peterson, sensing this, wisely opted to make a quick retreat. Lavinia, meanwhile, pounced upon the hats with all the vigour of a starving lion on freshly killed prey.

'Oh, thank you, Cousin,' she said gratefully. 'But we must hide them all at once for I have not a single doubt in my mind that that dreadful captain man will throw them all into the sea before my very eyes, just to spite me. Did you ever meet such an odious creature?' she continued, lifting up an overturned empty box and placing a hat carefully underneath it. 'I own I have never been so humiliated in my entire life. That man is the most impudent, loathsome specimen I have ever had the misfortune to lay eyes upon. He should not be in charge of a ship. He should be—'

Suddenly the ship lurched violently to one side, causing Lavinia, in the middle of her hat hiding operation, to fall flat on her face, and the empty upturned crate upon which Wilhelmina was attempting to make herself comfortable, to slide rapidly along the wooden boards towards the opposite wall. She fortunately managed to avoid slamming directly into it by sticking out her legs in the most timely of fashions.

'What on earth was that, Cousin?' demanded Lavinia, with a slight tremble to her tone.

'I think the storm must have broken at last,' replied Wilhelmina, shuffling around on the crate so that her back was now towards the wall.

No sooner had she uttered the words, than the ship lurched to the other side, causing Lavinia – still flat on her stomach – to retrace the route she had just taken, and Wilhelmina and her crate to go hurtling towards the wall from whence they had just come.

'Oh my,' moaned Lavinia, still sprawled on the floor. 'This really is most unpleasant, Cousin. In fact it is so unpleasant, I am begin-

41

ning to feel quite out of sorts.'

As if mocking her discomfort, the ship began rocking vigorously from side to side.

Lavinia, gazing up at her cousin whilst simultaneously turning a rather worrying shade of green, emitted a low groan. 'I do believe I am going to be quite unwell, Cousin.'

'No!' countered Wilhelmina, struggling to her feet and attempting to reach for the door as the ship rolled in the opposite direction. 'Please do not be unwell, Lavinia. I shall go to seek help. Wait here.'

'Oh don't worry, Cousin – I shall,' came back the pitiful reply.

No sooner had the door swung shut behind Wilhelmina than there came a huge crack of thunder from directly above. She shivered involuntarily and began tentatively to retrace the route she had taken with Peterson a few short moments before. To her enormous relief, she managed to locate the stairs to the upper floors quickly and, clinging onto the banister for all her worth, mounted them cautiously. As she slowly approached the upper deck she became increasingly aware of a great deal of commotion taking place there: a volley of men's voices, splashing water and a huge amount of banging and clattering. She had only one more short flight of stairs to mount before she reached the deck, where she hoped she would locate someone who could help Lavinia. Just as she had managed to climb halfway up, however, the ship lurched violently, causing her to lose her hold of the banister and tossing her backwards. Bracing herself for a hard landing, she was amazed to find two strong arms at the most opportune of moments, reaching out and catching her. Her relief soon turned to horror, however, as she was spun around and found herself face-to-face with the formidable Captain Tunbridge who, she was aware, was continuing to hold on to her upper arms.

'Oh, er, thank you, Captain,' she muttered, not daring to raise her eyes to his but focusing instead on the bare triangle of brown skin, covered in dark hair, exposed above the two unfastened buttons of his shirt.

The man, just as she had expected, did not exhibit a great deal of pleasure at seeing her.

'What on earth are you doing wandering about, girl?' he snapped impatiently. 'Go back to your room at once.'

His patronizing tone had the effect of making Wilhelmina feel as though she were no more than five years old. 'Er, yes, sir,' she stammered, chiding herself for being so intimated by the man that she appeared to have lost the ability to construct a coherent sentence. 'That is I, er, will, of course. However, I was just, er, wondering, sir, if there was a, er, doctor on board. My cousin is not feeling at all the thing.'

He wrinkled his brow. 'Not feeling at all the thing?' he repeated in such a tone that not only did she feel like a child, but an incredibly dim-witted one at that.

Just then the ship swayed again, sending them both reeling. The captain, still retaining his hold of her, skilfully manoeuvred them both just in time to prevent Wilhelmina crashing into the stairs. Instead he bore the full blow himself whilst pulling her so tightly to him that she found her face crushed against the triangle of bare skin she had been studying earlier. His distinctly male odour tickled her nostrils for one brief, but disconcerting moment. In a flash, however, he set her apart from him and demanded tetchily, 'What on earth is wrong with her now?'

'She is, er, feeling somewhat, er, out of sorts, sir,' she stammered, embarrassed.

Unexpectedly and, from what she had witnessed so far, uncharacteristically, the captain released a sudden roar of raucous laughter, so loud that it almost made Wilhelmina jump out of her skin.

'Out of sorts?' he echoed. 'Well, she is not the first and most certainly will not be the last to suffer from sea-sickness. I'm afraid she will just have to get used to it, madam, for I have much more pressing matters to attend to – such as keeping the ship afloat – to worry about your chit of a cousin.'

Duly chastised and now ashamed of her behaviour, it was all Wilhelmina could do to mutter a feeble apology. 'Of, er, course, Captain. I am, er, extremely sorry to have bothered you. I shall return to my, er, the, er, room immediately.'

'Good,' pronounced the captain. 'And may I suggest that you stay there. You may also tell your cousin, madam, that I wish to hear no more from her until we set foot in Bristol.'

Wilhelmina gave an embarrassed nod accompanied by a fleeting, apologetic smile before swiftly taking her leave of the man and returning, in a shaken, tossed-about fashion, to the storeroom.

Upon reaching her destination, she hesitantly pushed open the door to find Lavinia still sprawled upon the floor, groaning.

'Please tell me you found a doctor, Cousin,' she whimpered.

In an attempt to cheer up the girl, Wilhelmina affected as bright a tone as she could muster. 'Alas there is no doctor, Cousin, but I did come upon the captain and he informs me that there is nothing to worry about for you are obviously suffering the effects of sea-sickness and should be as right as rain once we dock.'

Upon receipt of this news, Lavinia emitted such a loud pitiful moan that Wilhelmina flinched.

'Does that odious man think that I am stupid?' she groaned, before adding, 'No, pray do not answer that, Cousin. I am fully aware that I am suffering from sea-sickness but what I am desirous to know is how I am to cope with this affliction when it is a positive lifetime before we dock.'

The ship rolled once more, sending Lavinia sliding across the floor for the umpteenth time.

'Do you know, Cousin,' she whispered, 'I truly hope I shall die on this ship.'

'Oh, Lavinia, don't be ridiculous,' chided Wilhelmina, urgently looking around for a basin or some such, which, from the unbecoming shade of green which was spreading over her cousin's face, she feared they might need at any moment.

'I am not being ridiculous,' countered Lavinia tearfully. 'I hope I shall die right here, sprawled upon the floor of this stinking storeroom and that that wretched captain has my death on his conscience for the rest of his miserable life. That is assuming, of course, that such a loathsome creature has a conscience.'

'Oh, I can assure you I do, madam,' interjected the captain's voice from the doorway. 'Which is why I have come to remove you to more comfortable surroundings. Although, having just heard your wishes, it seems I may save myself the trouble.'

'Don't you dare, sir,' groaned Lavinia, looking boldly up at him. 'Why, if you allow me to suffer like this for the entire wretched journey I shall . . . I shall—'

'Tell your father?' enquired the captain coolly, as he knelt down and scooped her up in his arms as if she were a tiny babe. 'I confess I am quite looking forward to meeting this man, madam.'

'I doubt there will be little chance of that, Captain,' retorted

Lavinia frostily, as he carried her through the door with Wilhelmina bumping along behind them. 'It is after all hardly likely that our paths will cross again, sir—'

'A fact for which there is no one more grateful than myself, madam,' interpolated the captain, his steady gait as he negotiated the warren of corridors belying the fact that the ship continued to be tossed about like a cork in the wind by the inhospitable waves.

'—particularly,' continued Lavinia with considerable hauteur, 'as I am soon to be married into the French aristocracy.'

The captain stopped dead in his tracks. 'Good lord,' he exclaimed, 'do you mean to tell me, madam, that there is a man out there willing to take you on?'

All signs of her affliction momentarily forgotten, a wave of anger washed over Lavinia's green features. 'I will have you know, sir,' she retorted furiously, 'that there are a great many men out there who would be willing to take me on.'

The captain shook his head in disbelief. 'For all I am a captain in His Majesty's navy, Miss Crumpington-Smythe, and have fought in a great many battles around the world, I do not mind admitting that any man willing to carry out such an . . . an imprudent action, must be a damned sight braver than myself,' he proclaimed, resuming his march.

Lavinia gasped aloud. 'How dare you insult me, sir? Why I have never before experienced such insolence,' she began. 'And I should inform you that—'

'And I should inform *you*, madam,' cut in the captain, 'that if I hear one more bleat from you, I shall throw you overboard in an instant. And please be assured that I am not in the habit of making idle threats.' The sombre tone of his voice, confirmed this last statement – a fact which Lavinia, who immediately ceased talking – had also fully comprehended.

A few minutes later, having mounted two sets of stairs, they crossed an open, low-ceilinged space with yet more black cannon pointing outwards on either side. These were, Wilhelmina noted, substantially larger than their counterparts on the upper deck. Reaching the far end of this deck. the captain pushed open a door and strode into a comfortable room – some three times larger than the storeroom – with a window directly before them and polished boards upon the floor. It was furnished with only a single wooden bed, fixed to the left-hand wall and an uncomfortable looking wooden seat attached to the panelling in the bottom right-hand corner. Marching over to the bed, the captain deposited Lavinia upon it with a surprising show of gentleness. This insight into the more considerate side of the man's nature did not last long however.

'Now, madam,' he said, addressing himself to Wilhelmina who was, at that moment, clinging with all her might onto the door-frame as the ship began another vigorous rocking session, 'my own quarters adjoin this room.' He indicated his head towards a door on the left-hand wall, at the bottom of the bed. 'However, I have no wish to see either of you in there, or indeed in any other part of the ship, until we dock, which, I should inform you, may be some time yet, given the weather conditions.'

'Oh no,' sobbed Lavinia, clinging onto the wooden balustrade which had sensibly been placed around the bed in order to prevent its occupant being tossed out on to the floor. 'I shall die. I know I shall.'

The captain rolled his eyes and said, in the manner of one out of all patience, 'I thought perhaps you would have grasped the fact by now, Miss Crumpington-Smythe, that I find your melodramatics very tedious indeed.'

Lavinia opened her mouth to reply but, catching sight of the stony look upon the man's face, closed it again.

'Now,' he announced, once again addressing Wilhelmina, 'I have important business to attend to – such as keeping us all alive. May I wish you a pleasant journey, madam.'

'Er, thank you, Captain,' she stammered. 'This is most, er, kind of you.'

The captain inclined his head before turning on his heel and taking his leave of the room.

'Well,' exclaimed Wilhelmina, attempting to cheer up her cousin, as the door swung shut behind him, 'this is turning out to be quite an adventure. I would wager you are bursting to tell Verity Drinkwater all about it, Lavinia.'

Lavinia looked at her aghast. 'If you so much as breathe a word of this to Verity Drinkwater, Cousin,' she remonstrated with a slight hint of panic, 'I shall strangle you with my own bare hands.'

The bed of the cabin being infinitely more comfortable than the floor of the storeroom, Wilhelmina hoped that her cousin would fall asleep – which would result in a much more pleasant journey for both of them. What appeared to be keeping the girl awake however, was the ill-fitting catch of the window, which, with the incessant rocking motion of the ship, was making an irritating banging sound. Wilhelmina scanned her surroundings for something she could use to secure it. Apart from the chair upon which she was seated and the bed there was nothing else in the room, it obviously being used only for guests. She was about to admit defeat when, in a fit of inspiration, she remembered the blue silk ribbon providing a decorative lace-up effect on the bodice of her gown. Undoing it, she wrapped it around the catch, binding it as tightly as she could. The desired result was achieved in just minutes as Lavinia dozed off.

Wilhelmina wished that she could have done the same but the wooden chair was not at all comfortable. Instead, she attempted to distract herself with pleasant thoughts – none more pleasant to her at that particular moment, than being in her own bed in her own house in Chipping Sodbury. She had been staying with her aunt, uncle and cousin for some four weeks now while her parents were visiting her sick grandmother in Newcastle. She hoped, above all things, that they, too, were now making their return journey and that they would all be home together again soon. The ship reeled once more, jolting her from her musings. So violent was the jolt in fact, that it caused the adjoining door to the captain's quarters to fling wide open. To Wilhelmina's surprise, she found herself locked in an astounded gaze with an equally taken aback young red-haired woman whose exquisitely beautiful face was marred only by the fact that she had obviously been weeping. They looked at each other for a few short seconds – long enough for Wilhelmina to read the terror in the woman's eyes – before the ship lurched the other way and the door swung shut again. Within seconds, she was aware of heavy male footsteps and a key turning in the lock.

Some hours later, as the storm gradually began to subside, Wilhelmina realized that she was hungry. Indeed, having had nothing to eat for more hours than she cared to recall, her appetite could more aptly be described as ravenous. She pondered her situation for a few moments. The fierce captain had, of course, ordered her to stay in the cabin for the remainder of the journey but had that not been for her own safety whilst the storm had been at its very worst? Surely, he had not intended her to starve to death, although, recalling the man's terrifying manner, she would not have wagered more than a guinea on that assumption. Having eventually convinced herself that she was being silly and that of course he would not mind if all she was doing was going in search of a little bread and cheese, she summoned every ounce of her courage and slipped out of the room into the open deck with its rows of menacing cannons. Stumbling along towards the stairs, she realized that she had been mistaken in her assumption that the storm had abated for, yet again, there came an almighty sway. This time she was thrown forwards directly into the arms of an approaching cheeky young sailor with a freckled face and spiky red hair.

'Oh,' declared Wilhelmina with an apologetic smile. 'Thank you, sir. I was just going to the galley.'

'No need to apologize on my behalf, ma'am,' beamed the man, still with his arms about her narrow waist. 'Not often we have such prime articles as you on board. Fair made my day, so you have.'

'Has she indeed?' broke in the captain, his tone reverberating with disgust as he climbed down the stairs from the upper deck and began walking towards them. 'Well, if you have quite finished with her, Harley, may I suggest you get on with your duties?'

The sailor, looking petrified, muttered, 'Aye, aye, Cap'n,' and, flashing an apologetic look at Wilhelmina, scurried away as quickly as he could.

Wilhelmina wished that she could do the same but the captain, coming to stand before her and regarding her in the same manner as one would a criminal caught red-handed in the most unsavoury of acts, made it clear that he had not finished with her yet.

'May I suggest, Miss Crumpington-Smythe,' he began, his tone dripping with repugnance, 'that if you are finished "making the day" of able seaman Harley, you return at once to your cabin – where I recall ordering you explicitly to stay.'

Wilhelmina flushed to the roots of her hair. 'Of, er, course, Captain, I was just. er—'

'I can see perfectly well what you were "just" doing, Miss Crumpington-Smythe,' he remarked frostily, moving his hard gaze very deliberately from her face to her chest. Wondering what on earth he was referring to, Wilhelmina, following the path of his eyes, lowered her head and felt all the colour which had so recently flooded her face, immediately drain from it, as she noticed the bodice of her gown, where she had removed the ribbon some hours earlier, gaping brazenly open, allowing the captain – and indeed anyone else in her vicinity – a generous view of her chemise. Frozen with mortification, she could do nothing other than raise her eyes to his in utter dismay.

'I was just about to arrange some refreshment for you, Miss Crumpington-Smythe,' he continued icily, 'but you appear more than capable of satisfying your own needs. You may be in need of some – *stimulation* to relieve the tedium of the journey, but I would be grateful if you would refrain from distracting my men. Now if you will excuse me, I have my duties to attend to.'

And with that, he turned his back to her and strode away, leaving Wilhelmina feeling not like an idiotic five-year-old this time, but rather some three inches tall and a first-class, undisputed hussy.

What seemed like an eternity later, as land finally came into view and the two girls watched its welcome outline draw nearer from the window of their cabin, Lavinia, who, much to Wilhelmina's relief had remained asleep for the greater part of the journey, gave a huge yawn and stretched her hands over her head, declaring, 'Oh, I can scarcely wait to leave this ghastly ship, Cousin. And please do not forget that, should I ever express a wish to travel by sea again, then I should be shot immediately and hung up from a tree in nothing but my under-garments for I do believe that that fate should be far more pleasant than enduring another such hideous crossing.'

Wilhelmina's desire to have her feet on dry land again was no less great. She had, following her last humiliating encounter with the captain, stayed in the cabin for the remainder of the journey, having no wish to incur the wrath of the formidable man yet again nor even to see him. For some inexplicable reason, however, she found her good manners overriding her feeling of mortification and she found herself tentatively asking, 'Do you think perhaps we should find the captain and express our thanks, Lavinia?'

'Our thanks?' repeated Lavinia, regarding her dubiously. 'Whatever for? I certainly have nothing to thank the man for. He was perfectly odious to me.'

'But he did provide us with a most comfortable cabin.'

'Comfortable?' echoed the older girl, screwing up her nose. 'The fact that it has a bed in it, Cousin, does not, in my opinion, make it comfortable. Why, there is not even a solitary picture on the wall nor upholstered furniture to be seen anywhere.'

'Perhaps because it is a ship, Lavinia,' pointed out Wilhelmina a little tetchily, 'not an inn.'

'Well, whatever it is,' retorted Lavinia obdurately, 'I have no desire to see it or its wretched, insulting captain ever again. Now come, Cousin, let us gather our things. The sooner we are off this ghastly ship and away from that dreadful man, the better.'

Some thirty minutes later, not feeling at all comfortable with the situation, Wilhelmina followed Lavinia down the gangplank. With her feet, to her relief, once again on dry land, she turned back towards the ship and felt her heart skip a beat as she noticed the captain leaning over the side of the deck, observing her and her cousin. She gave a diffident smile and timidly raised her hand to him in a gesture of farewell. To her great chagrin, however, the man merely flashed a contemptuous glare before turning his back on her and vacating his spot.

CHAPTER 6

Chipping Sodbury, England

FOR all that it was unlikely that Chipping Sodbury would ever feature on the list of most interesting places in the world, the moment she set eyes upon the old weatherworn signpost engraved with the name of the small market town, Wilhelmina knew instantly that there was nowhere on earth she should prefer to be.

She gazed appreciatively out of the window as their hired carriage made its jolting way along the narrow country roads until, eventually, the welcoming sight of the new, honey-coloured house of her Aunt Clementine and Uncle Ernest came into view. So pleased was she to be home that even the property's entrance with its fussy, ornate pillars topped with two hideous gargoyles – of which her aunt was particularly proud – no longer appeared ostentatious, but quite one of the nicest things she had ever seen.

The conveyance came to a halt in front of the building and no sooner had its wheels ceased to turn, than its door was opened and Aunt Clementine's round, rouged face, complete with its row of wobbling chins, anxiously peered inside.

Upon discovering her daughter and niece exhausted, but otherwise quite well, her earnest expression was swiftly replaced with a wide smile, displaying two rows of tiny pearly white teeth. 'Oh thank the Lord you are returned – and safely, my loves,' she exclaimed, clasping both her hands to her ample bosom and raising her eyes skywards. 'We have been hearing of the most dreadful occurrences in Paris and I said to Mr Crump, "Mr Crump", I said, "I dare not even think what predicament those two lovely girls are in". We should never have let you go, my dears. I have not slept a wink since your departure and have been praying for your safe return every half hour. Now come, Lavinia. Give your poor mama a hug, girl, for I have been quite out of sorts with worry.' She then took a step back from the carriage and flung open her pale, podgy arms, awaiting the embrace of her daughter.

'Oh, Mama,' wailed Lavinia, stepping out the carriage and hurling herself straight into her mother's arms, 'we have had quite the most dreadful time of it. Do you know, I had only just made the acquaintance of a charming *comte* when—'

'A *comte*, dear?' repeated Aunt Clementine, hugging her daughter tightly to her, whilst her little round blue eyes grew large in her head. Then, being struck by a sudden thought, all hugging ceased as she stepped backwards and, holding her offspring at arm's length, enquired anxiously, 'Oh goodness. He doesn't know of our trading background I hope, my dear.'

Lavinia gave a dismissive tut. 'Of course not, Mama,' she replied smugly. 'I made no mention at all of merchants. In fact, I gave the impression that I was quite the upper-class young lady – just as you said I ought. I even mentioned that we were distantly related to the King of France himself – a fact which, of course, impressed the gentleman greatly.'

Aunt Clementine emitted a sigh of relief. 'Oh, well done, my dear,' she declared, encircling her daughter once more. 'Why, I can scarcely wait to meet the man. Imagine my daughter – a *comtesse*.'

Lavinia burst into a sudden flood of tears. 'But that's just it, Mama,' she wailed. 'I shall never be a *comtesse* now. It is all so positively ghastly. The comte obviously thought me worthy of his affections – indeed he invited me to a ball. Well, it was *almost* an invitation. And I am sure it would only have been a matter of time before he offered for me, had I attended, Mama. But I was unable to attend because then . . . then . . . those wretched peasants started creating such a fuss about not having food – or something equally tedious – and that boring little man, Mr Fitzgibbon insisted we leave and—'

'There is more?' interjected Aunt Clementine, still pressing her daughter to her whilst casting a look at Wilhelmina, which told her she was hoping there was not.

Wilhelmina nodded solemnly.

'—and then,' continued Lavinia, sniffing dramatically, 'we were put aboard this disgusting ship where the captain was the most odious, hateful man I have ever had the misfortune to meet and—'

Seemingly at a loss as to what to do with her hysterical daughter whose body was now racked with sobs, Aunt Clementine opted to engage in some rather tentative back-patting. 'There, there, dear,' she sympathized. 'Now I'm sure the man wasn't all bad.'

'Indeed he was,' countered Lavinia, her voice becoming more high-pitched with each remark. 'In fact I can scarce believe we have escaped his clutches relatively unscathed for do you know – he had one poor woman locked up in his cabin entirely against her will?'

Aunt Clementine raised a dubious eyebrow to Wilhelmina.

'The poor woman was quite beside herself was she not, Cousin?' continued Lavinia.

'Well she certainly appeared a little, er, upset—' began Wilhelmina.

'But the worst of it was,' interjected Lavinia, between a flurry of sobs and sniffs, 'he . . . he refused to let me have my luggage on board. He ordered the whole lot of it to be thrown overboard. Just like that. Without so much as a thought for any of it; not even my lace-trimmed petticoats.'

Finding this news of lace-trimmed petticoats infinitely more shocking than the news of the man having imprisoned a helpless woman in his cabin, Aunt Clementine let out a gasp of horror, released her hold of her daughter and clamped a hand to her mouth. 'He disposed of your lace-trimmed petticoats, my dear?' she repeated disbelievingly. 'Why I have never heard anything so outrageous. The man sounds a . . . a . . . veritable monster. Only wait until Mr Crump hears of this. I dread to think what the man will do.'

Not for the first time, Wilhelmina wondered at the impression Lavinia and her aunt had of her Uncle Ernest who, despite being rather 'careful with the purse strings' – as her mother always phrased it – was a man of great sensibility and easy-going disposition. Quite the opposite in fact, of the threatening, intimidating beast he was portrayed to be by his wife and daughter.

'Indeed he was a monster, Mama,' sobbed Lavinia, accepting the clean, white, lace handkerchief her mother had taken from her sleeve and was now offering her. 'And if I ever set eyes upon him again, I shall certainly tell him so.'

'Well, that makes two of us, my dear,' concurred Aunt

Clementine, as she ushered the two arrivals towards the house. 'Imagine disposing of a girl's lace-trimmed petticoats without so much as a by your leave. Why, the situation does not bear thinking about. Now let us go inside at once, for I have a sudden need of sustenance.'

'You are, of course, aware that this whole affair is Verity Drinkwater's fault, Mama,' sniffed Lavinia, marching up the garden path alongside her mother. 'Had she not concocted a whole heap of lies about what a wonderful time she had in Paris last year, then I should not have felt the slightest desire to visit the wretched place.'

'Well, that's as may be, my dear,' observed Aunt Clementine, 'but Verity Drinkwater was not pursued by a comte. Oh, can you imagine Venetia Drinkwater's face when I inform her that *my* daughter has caught the attentions of a member of the Quality? If I'm not mistaken, the nearest Verity has come to being pursued by an aristocrat was when Lord Farthington's dog chased her at the summer fair last July.'

Having followed the bustling figure of the older woman up the steps of the house, along the hall and into the pale blue drawing-room, they all now took their seats around the fire, which was merrily dancing in the grate.

The information regarding the Drinkwaters' likely reaction to the news of the comte, meanwhile, appeared to have restored Lavinia's spirits as, making herself comfortable in a high-back armchair, all sobbing ceased and a self-satisfied smile began to tug at her lips.

'Oh, I can scarce wait to tell them, Mama,' she declared excitedly. 'Let us send a message this very instant inviting them to take tea with us on the morrow.'

'Well,' muttered Aunt Clementine a little sheepishly, 'I'm, er, afraid we cannot, my dear. They are ... gone away for a few weeks.'

A wave of disappointment spread over Lavinia's tear-stained features, however, recognizing her mother's guilty tone, she enquired warily, 'To where are they gone, Mama?'

Aunt Clementine visibly tensed as she prepared herself for the response to her reply. 'To London, my love.'

As she had correctly anticipated, Lavinia's look of disappointment was swiftly replaced with one of outright dismay. 'To

London?' she repeated, her eyes flooding with a fresh onslaught of tears. 'Do not tell me they are there for the Season, Mama?'

Aunt Clementine pulled a rueful face. 'I'm afraid they are, my sweet,' she replied in an apologetic tone.

All at once, Lavinia thrust to her feet and began furiously stamping around the room.

'Oh no,' she exclaimed, the new flood of tears now streaming down her velvety smooth cheeks. 'Is it not bad enough that I have all these dreadful things happening to me in Paris, but I then discover that the wretched Drinkwaters are gone to London whilst I am doomed to spend the rest of the Season sitting here in the dullest place on earth. I might as well be dead.'

'Well, we did not expect you home so soon, my dear,' twittered Aunt Clementine looking anxious as she fiddled with a ribbon on her lace cap. 'We imagined your sojourn in Paris to last for a good many weeks yet.'

'Well, that's as may be,' retorted Lavinia petulantly. 'However, now that I am obviously *not* to spend a good few weeks in Paris, must I suffer the tedium of Chipping Sodbury? Oh, and what is more, Mama,' she gasped as realization overcame her and a look of panic spread across her countenance, 'the Comte de Roxford is planning on visiting London soon. Only imagine if he were to make the acquaintance of Verity Drinkwater. He might well fall in love with the odious girl, Mama and quite forget about me. What if he were to offer for her and she were to become a comtesse while the only offer I receive were from a boring, penniless Sodbury toad? It would be too much to bear, Mama – far, far too much. I might as well be dead as—'

At the news that the comte was planning a visit to the capital, Aunt Clementine's ears pricked up. 'The comte is coming to London, you say, my dear?'

'Yes, Mama. He informed us of his visit himself, did he not, Cousin?'

Wilhelmina nodded her tired, and now pounding head.

'Hmm,' mused Aunt Clementine, before announcing, 'then there is nothing else for it, girls. We shall simply *have* to go to London for we cannot pass up the chance of such a fruitful match. We will, of course, need to inform Mr Crump of our decision. Although quite what he will say, I have absolutely no idea. You know how infinitely stubborn the man can be.'

Just at that moment, the aforementioned man entered the room, looking his usual affable, portly self.

'Oh Papa,' pleaded Lavinia, rushing over to him and embracing him tightly, 'please can we go to London? Please, please, please?'

'Good lord, you're only just back from one trip, girl, and you're wanting to be off again,' exclaimed the old man, taken aback by this enthusiastic show of affection from his daughter. Having not the first idea how to deal with it, he too opted for the tentative back-patting action in which his wife had engaged a few moments earlier.

'Dearest, Papa,' pleaded Lavinia, squeezing him so hard, his face was turning puce, 'please may we go? You know how tedious I find it here and I have had the most dreadful of times. Why, I do believe I am quite fortunate even to be alive, sir.'

'Well, I'm not sure,' replied Uncle Ernest, managing to ease himself from his daughter's over-zealous clutch and making a quick dash for the mahogany sideboard, home to a number of crystal decanters. 'Can be a damned expensive business all that gadding about down there, you know?'

'Come now, Mr Crump,' asserted Aunt Clementine, matter of factly. 'You can see that the girl is positively distressed. I think a little jaunt to London is the least we can do to cheer up our only child and perhaps make an excellent match in the process.'

'Hmm,' mused Uncle Ernest, removing the stopper from one of the decanters and tipping its amber coloured liquid into a brandy balloon. 'Well, I suppose she must be dashed disappointed at having had to leave Paris so quickly.'

Lavinia gazed pitifully at her father through a fan of tear-soaked lashes. 'I can assure you I am, Papa,' she confirmed, dabbing the handkerchief at her eyes. 'I am quite devastated. As, of course, is Wilhelmina.'

There followed a brief pause while Uncle Ernest appeared to give the matter some thought. He turned to face them. 'Very well then,' he announced, a broad grin visible through his thick white beard. 'Can't have my girls upset, can we? Mind you, there'll be a whole host of arrangements to make. But don't any of you be worrying your pretty little heads about that, my dears. I shall get onto it this instant.'

'Oh, but pray do not concern yourself with me, Uncle Ernest,' interjected Wilhelmina from her fireside chair. 'I expect my parents shall be home soon and I shall be perfectly happy to remain here and await them.'

'Out of the question, I'm afraid, my dear,' replied Uncle Ernest, walking towards her, clutching his glass. 'We received a letter from your mother only yesterday. They are uncertain of how much longer they will stay in Newcastle – your grandmother, it seems, is not recovering quite as quickly as one would have hoped.'

Wilhelmina felt her heart sink which was, she noted with a large pang of guilt, more to do with the fact that she would now be forced to go to London, than the fact that her poor grandmother remained out of sorts.

'Oh,' she murmured.

'Now don't look like that, girl,' remonstrated her uncle genially, settling himself in a wing chair alongside her. 'You'll have a grand old time of it in London, I'm sure.'

After a total of some nine and a half short minutes in the hometown to which she had been so looking forward to returning, it was all she could do to manage a weak, unconvinced smile in response.

Unpacking her portmanteau in her bedchamber later that evening, Wilhelmina came across the missive Mr Fitzgibbon had given her. With all the dramas of the past few days, she was rather alarmed to realize that it was the first time she had given it a single thought. Perching on the edge of her bed, she examined it closely. It was formed from a single piece of thick white paper folded several times to conceal the words within, and sealed with a large red blob of sealing wax. She could not even imagine what was in the letter. She knew only from Mr Fitzgibbon's manner that its contents were important. But what on earth, she pondered as she flopped backwards onto the bed and gazed at the ceiling, was this all about and, more to the point, how had *she* come to be involved in it?

CHAPTER 7

'GOOD God. Three hundred people dead,' declared Uncle Ernest from behind his copy of *The Times* the following morning.

'What's that dear?' enquired a preoccupied Aunt Clementine, employing all the concentration of a skilled surgeon, as she removed the top from her boiled egg.

'Three hundred people,' came back Uncle Ernest's voice. 'Killed in the Paris rioting.'

Aunt Clementine gasped in horror as she put down her knife. 'Oh my goodness,' she declared, wiping her hands on her napkin, 'why I shall thank the Lord every hour for delivering you two girls home safely. Goodness only knows what would have happened to you if you had stayed there. It simply does not bear thinking about.'

'It certainly does not, Aunt,' concurred Wilhelmina, recalling with a shiver how terrified she had felt when their coach had been stoned *en route* to Calais. 'I own, however, that I am somewhat concerned about the safety of Mr and Mrs Fitzgibbon.'

'As indeed am I, child,' said Aunt Clementine, shaking her head despairingly. 'Goodness only knows why they are choosing to remain in such a dreadful place.'

'They are choosing to remain there, Mama,' pointed out Lavinia tartly, 'because for some reason that boring little man thinks the wretched insignificant insurance company he works for cannot survive a day without him. I am quite sure I should not risk my life for such a tedious cause.'

'Well,' puffed Aunt Clementine, 'I suppose one cannot call the man's dedication into question.'

'Dedication?' echoed Lavinia. 'I believe it is more suitably classified as downright stupidity. There are, of course, others of our acquaintance, who are remaining in the city for much more significant purposes. I have no doubt that the Comte de Roxford, for example, will be playing an extremely prominent part in the proceedings. Indeed, I would not be at all surprised if he is advising His Majesty himself on how best to handle the abominable situation. Did I mention, Papa, that the comte is on the very best of terms with both the king and the queen?'

'I believe you may have, dear,' muttered Uncle Ernest distractedly, from behind his paper. 'On one or two occasions.'

The following few days passed in something of a blur with Lavinia and Aunt Clementine intent on making the grandest impression on both the comte and London Society and ardently investing in an abundance of gowns, gloves, slippers, petticoats and reticules to aid them in their quest. Whilst Wilhelmina's interest in the shopping expeditions was limited, she was making a conscious effort to take more care of the letter entrusted her: it was safely tucked away in the bodice of her chemise during waking hours and just as carefully placed under her pillow each night when she retired.

Uncle Ernest's efforts, meanwhile, were fully engaged in finding a suitable property for the family to rent. With the Season already well underway and the most desirable houses being occupied for several weeks, the situation was not looking the least bit hopeful and the levels of hysteria in her aunt and Lavinia were increasing daily with the possibility that their planned sojourn in the capital might have to be denied them. This state of affairs had almost reached breaking point when they came to hear of a particularly prestigious residence – Number 22, Grosvenor Square – having been rather suddenly vacated due to the unexpected death of one of the current tenant's relatives in Yorkshire.

'Oh my, what a pity,' declared an unsympathetic Aunt Clementine upon hearing the reason for the sudden availability of the property. 'Still, God works in mysterious ways,' she continued matter-of-factly, 'and our Lord quite obviously wishes us to reside in one of the grandest addresses in London. I should point out, girls, that Grosvenor Square is infinitely more prestigious than Berkeley Square where the Drinkwaters are lodging and I own I am more than a little impatient to inform Venetia Drinkwater of the fact. Indeed that information, combined with the news of my daughter's aristocratic attentions, will undoubtedly make the woman green with envy. Oh, can you imagine, my dears, when the comte arrives in London and we are able to introduce him? The excitement will be too much to bear.'

'Indeed it will, Aunt,' muttered Wilhelmina, for whom the present level of excitement was already proving far too much.

London, England

'Why Clementine – what on earth are you doing here?' declared an astounded Venetia Drinkwater as Aunt Clementine and Lavinia swept into the garish yellow drawing-room of the Drinkwaters' enormous rented town house, with an infinitely less enthusiastic Wilhelmina trailing behind them.

'Venetia, my dear,' proclaimed Aunt Clementine, kissing the air on either side of Mrs Drinkwater's lined and heavily powdered cheeks, 'we simply could not stay away. Lavinia and Wilhelmina have just had the most exciting adventure in Paris and I was positively bursting to tell you that—'

'Oh, Paris,' sighed Verity Drinkwater, tossing them an uninterested glance, as she sat in a high-backed chair in front of the fire with her embroidery tambour. She was looking her usual radiant self in a day gown of worked muslin, her glossy light blonde hair gleaming in the light of the fire. 'It is a fine enough city I suppose, but I must confess I find it nowhere near as exciting as London. We have been having quite the most glorious time here, have we not, Mama?'

'Indeed we have, Verity,' concurred Mrs Drinkwater. 'However, do let our guests be seated before we tell them all our exciting news.' She gestured to the array of chairs and sofas arranged around the large marble fireplace.

'Well, I am very pleased indeed to hear that you, too, have been having a fine time of it, my dears,' said Aunt Clementine claiming the high-backed yellow armchair opposite that in which her hostess was lowering herself, 'but I doubt very much that your news can be quite as exciting as ours. You will never guess what has happened, Venetia. Why Lavinia has only caught the attentions of a *comte*. The Comte de Roxford, if you please. We are expecting the man in London any day now.'

Mrs Drinkwater's countenance displayed not a flicker of interest as she smoothed down her grey armazine skirts. 'Hmm, the Comte de Roxford?' she repeated, wrinkling her brow as though deep in contemplation. 'I am quite sure I have never heard of the man. Perhaps you happened upon such a gentleman when you were in Paris last, Verity darling?' she enquired, without a trace of enthusiasm.

Verity shrugged her shoulders in a dismissive gesture, her eyes steadfastly focused on her embroidery. 'I believe I may have,' she teased. 'Is he the short, fat comte with the pox-marked face and a rather poor excuse for a beard?'

'Indeed he is not,' countered Lavinia vehemently, from the small sofa alongside Verity and upon which Wilhelmina was also seated. 'He is exceedingly handsome and quite the most charming man I have ever met.'

'Really?' replied Verity disbelievingly, stabbing her needle into the square piece of linen stretched taut across its round wooden frame. 'Then I am obviously confusing him with another comte. I own one meets so many comtes when one is in Paris that one positively loses count. Oh, comtes and counts, Mama! Is that not witty?'

Mrs Drinkwater gave a little titter. 'Oh, is the girl not diversion itself, Clementine?'

Aunt Clementine, finding the remark not the least bit diverting, merely stared at her friend. Verity, meanwhile, made to continue her speech.

'Oh, but enough of boring old comtes,' she declared, raising her emerald eyes to her rival. 'Do you know, Lavinia, that I stood up last night at Almack's with the Earl of Thurlston – *three times*.'

Contrary to the girl's attempt at humour, this daring remark did evoke a response from Aunt Clementine, albeit not a particularly favourable one. '*Three times?*' sniffed the older woman disapprovingly. 'I'm not sure you should be boasting of such an occurrence, Verity dear. *Three times* is positively shocking.'

Verity, having refocused on her needlework, giggled roguishly. 'Oh, I am of course aware of that, Mrs Crump, but I was quite at a loss as to what to do. The man would scarce leave my side having obviously developed a *tendre* for me. Oh, he is terribly handsome, is he not, Mama? Not to mention, of course, heir to a substantial fortune.'

'Indeed, he is,' confirmed Mrs Drinkwater, flashing a satisfied smile at her daughter. 'We could not wish for a better match.'

Aunt Clementine did not look convinced. 'Hmm,' she mused aloud, 'perhaps not, though I always recommend that one should not jump ahead of oneself in such situations.'

'But I doubt very much that we are, Clementine dearest,' countered Mrs Drinkwater smugly as she gestured to the footman to bring refreshments. 'I consider that by standing up with the girl three times, the earl has made his intentions more than clear. I should expect an offer from him before the end of the Season.'

'As indeed should I, Mama,' confirmed Verity. 'Why, do you know what the earl said to me, Lavinia?' she enquired, casting a fleeting look in Lavinia's direction.

'I have no idea,' replied Lavinia uninterestedly.

'Well, of course you wouldn't,' giggled Verity, diverting her gaze once more to her tambour. 'Well, he said that he thought I had the face of an angel and the body of a goddess and he did believe he had quite lost his heart the moment he set eyes upon me.'

While Aunt Clementine, clearly taken aback at such shocking declarations, began fumbling in her reticule for her vinaigrette, Lavinia assumed the countenance of one not in the least impressed.

'Well, I'm afraid such proclamations would fail to inspire the least bit of enthusiasm from me, Verity,' she drawled blandly. 'I, for one, must have heard those very words spoken at least two hundred times.'

Verity, however, not in the least deterred by her rival's unimpressed response, continued.

'And that is not all, Lavinia. Why I have discovered that half the girls in London have set their caps at the man and indeed some poor little chit by the name of Octavia Harlington-Hartsworthy – she is one of the Harlington-Hartsworthys of Hertfordshire, you know – although I shouldn't of course expect you to be acquainted with the family given that this is your first time in London. . . .'

Lavinia cast her a disparaging glare.

'Well,' continued Verity, 'the poor girl was apparently under the impression that the earl was to make an offer for her. Although quite how she could possibly have thought such a thing is positively beyond me: the unfortunate little chit has the most dreadful case of freckles I have ever seen, has she not, Mama?'

Mrs Drinkwater shuddered dramatically. 'Quite, quite dreadful,' she concurred, with a shiver of revulsion. 'In fact, I do believe it would be impossible to put a pin between them.'

'Obviously, the poor girl is deluding herself,' carried on Verity gaily, 'for the Earl of Thurlston is so handsome one can only imagine him taking a wife of the very finest appearance.'

Lavinia said nothing but continued to regard her rival through narrowed eyes. Verity's emerald green pair, meanwhile, remained firmly focused on her needle.

'Why, can you imagine, Lavinia' – she continued, with a knowing titter – 'little old me a countess and mistress of Thurlston Hall? It is far too exciting for words, is it not?'

'Oh, I don't know,' muttered Lavinia archly. 'I am sure if I searched hard enough I could come up with several words.'

Verity chose to ignore the cutting remark. 'But enough of my boring old news,' she declared with an affected giggle. Lifting her eyes to her rival she arranged her expression into one of spurious concern. 'Now do tell me all about this Comte de Rottsville of yours, Lavinia. Are you expecting an offer yourself soon?'

Lavinia quickly managed to school her countenance into one of beatific contentment. 'It is the Comte de *Roxford*, Verity dear,' she pointed out, her tone hinting at irritation, 'and I am indeed expecting an offer any day now. In fact, it would not surprise me in the least if we were both to be married in the autumn?'

Verity's brow furrowed as she supposedly concentrated on her tambour. 'Hmm,' she replied unconvinced. 'Perhaps. Although I do suspect that the earl may not wish to wait that long. I would not be at all surprised if the man were to make his offer tomorrow evening at Lady Carlton's ball – particularly as it is one of the most prestigious events of the Season with the whole of the *haut ton* in attendance. You will be attending of course?' she enquired, raising her eyes momentarily from her needlework to gaze innocently at Lavinia.

Lavinia flashed a disingenuous smile. 'But of course,' she replied blithely, 'we wouldn't miss it for the world would we, Mama?'

Aunt Clementine took another deep inhalation of her salts, before declaring, with some alacrity, 'Absolutely not. I should rather die than miss Lady Carlton's ball.'

'Hmm,' said Verity, going back to her sewing. 'But what a pity we shall not be able to make the acquaintance of your comte tomorrow evening, Lavinia. When did you say you were expecting him in London?'

'Oh, very soon,' said Lavinia, waving her hand dismissively. 'Very soon indeed. Why the man cannot bear to be apart from me. Alas, however, one cannot make definite plans at the moment with all this dreadful upheaval going on in France and I have no wish for him to endanger his life just because he is impatient to see me,' she pronounced with a virtuous smile.

'Really,' mused Verity, seemingly focusing on a particularly difficult needle manoeuvre. 'One would have thought that if the man had such a *tendre* for you then he would think nothing of risking his life to see you. I have no doubt the Earl of Thurlston would do such a thing for me. In fact . . . what was it he said to me the other day. . . ?' She raised her eyes to the ceiling for a moment as if attempting to recall a piece of long-forgotten information. 'Oh yes,' she continued brightly, 'he said that should I wish him to do so, he would climb the highest mountain in England to win my heart – wearing only his carpet slippers. Can you imagine?' she added, with another irritating titter.

'I would much rather not,' muttered Lavinia, her eyes now narrowed to two slits. Then, in a brighter tone, she announced, 'Well, if the Earl of Thurlston is a man of such heroic tendencies, Verity, perhaps you should send him to France. The country is in such turmoil that that should be a much better test of the man's commitment than merely wandering up a mountain in slippers. The Comte de Roxford is of course, playing a very large part in helping the king sort out the rabble and I can assure you, Verity, that the place is not for the faint-hearted. Indeed, Wilhelmina and I only just managed to escape with our lives.'

'Really?' muttered Verity in the most jaded of tones.

'In fact,' affirmed Lavinia, 'were it not for my actions, then we should most likely be dead now.'

'Oh my,' gasped Aunt Clementine, waving the vinaigrette frantically below her nose.

Verity, contrarily, appeared not the least impressed, as she cast a surreptitious look in Lavinia's direction.

'Do you know,' continued Lavinia earnestly, 'that the ship in which we crossed the Channel would most likely have sunk had I not single-handedly climbed the highest mast to unfurl its sail – and in the most dreadful storm the captain said he had ever encountered in over ten years at sea. The whole experience was positively exhausting, was it not, Cousin?'

Wilhelmina, her mouth gaping open, found herself devoid of speech. In spite of such a fantastic story, however, Verity's gaze remained firmly fixed on her embroidery.

'Well,' she said blandly, holding up the tambour before her eyes and making a great show of studying her efforts so far, 'it all sounds positively ghastly, I'm sure. How fortunate you are such a good sailor, Lavinia. I confess I should most likely have been quite ill.'

'Yes, well there is no time for such indulgences when one is saving both one's own life and that of fellow crew members. Am I right, Cousin?' she said turning her head once again to Wilhelmina.

Without even attempting to search for any words this time, Wilhelmina merely nodded her flabbergasted head.

CHAPTER 8

HAVING not the least desire to attend Lady Carlton's ball, Wilhelmina chose to play no part in the frenzy which began as soon as they returned from the Drinkwater residence. Her aunt and cousin, however, were relentless in the pressure they piled upon poor Uncle Ernest and, following several bursts of tears, much pleading and begging, and one threatened suicide, an extremely harassed Mr Crump, using every one of his contacts, eventually succeeded in procuring the much coveted invitations.

On the evening in question, it became obvious that Lavinia and her mother's tireless shopping efforts had not been in vain for they both looked quite splendid – Lavinia in green taffeta trimmed with silver spangles and Aunt Clementine in fetching crimson satin. Wilhelmina, for her part, had donned one of her favourite gowns of rose pink silk, looped over a silver underskirt.

The ball was being held at Lady Carlton's grand town house in Piccadilly and, upon their arrival, they found the Drinkwaters already in attendance with Verity as stunning as ever in turquoise chenille. No sooner had the trio stepped through the door, than Mrs Drinkwater whisked Aunt Clementine away saying that there was someone to whom she simply had to introduce her. This left the three girls standing on the black-and-white chequered floor of the spacious hallway.

'So, Lavinia, you achieved it after all,' said Verity, making no effort at all to hide her surprise. 'And looking so . . . green,' she remarked, her eyes travelling slowly, and somewhat disdainfully, down the length of Lavinia's exquisite gown.

'Green is all the crack in Paris,' countered Lavinia adroitly. 'In fact, it was the only colour to be seen in.'

'How very strange,' mused Verity with affected bewilderment, 'that fashions can vary so between countries. That was of course the case here *last* year. But don't worry, my dear,' she continued, patting Lavinia's arm. 'We must make some concessions for you given that this is your first time here.'

Lavinia glared at her and was searching for a cutting retort when a deep male voice suddenly interrupted.

'Ah, Miss Drinkwater. How delightful to see you again. If you would do me the great honour, I should be delighted to dance with you again this evening.'

All eyes turned towards the slim, handsome gentleman standing before them dressed in immaculate evening dress of frilled shirt, knee breeches and tail-coat. His dark-blond hair cut short enough to allow only the hint of a curl. A slightly mischievous expression was hovering over his countenance.

Verity sank into a deep curtsy. 'Of course, my lord,' she replied, a smug smile playing about her pretty lips. 'However, please do let me introduce you to my two friends. They are newly arrived in London. This is Miss Lavinia Crump and her cousin, Miss Wilhelmina Crump. This, my dears, is his lordship, the Earl of Thurlston.'

Both the girls dropped into a curtsy while the earl bowed graciously.

He fixed Wilhelmina with a playful gaze as she rose. 'Wilhelmina?' he repeated, his blue eyes twinkling. 'That was my late grandmother's name, you know?'

'My,' exclaimed Wilhelmina, somewhat taken aback. 'You do surprise me, sir. I know not of anyone with the same name as myself.'

'Then you should consider yourself quite unique, Miss Crump,' declared the earl teasingly.

A stunned Wilhelmina flushed to the roots of her hair.

'Ahem,' interrupted Verity, whose forced smile failed to conceal her annoyance. 'I am sorry to interrupt, my lord, but you did mention a dance. I believe I am free for the cotillon, sir.'

'Oh, of, er, course,' said the earl, inclining his head, 'if you would allow me that pleasure, ma'am, I shall be over to claim you then.'

Verity inclined her head to him in acceptance, before flashing

Lavinia a victorious smile.

As he then took his leave of the group, Lavinia declared impishly, 'My, my Verity, it appears you may well have a rival for the earl's attentions. The man appeared positively smitten with Wilhelmina.'

Although she had not thought it possible, Wilhelmina felt her flush deepen.

'Don't be ridiculous, Lavinia,' snapped Verity. 'One cannot help but comment on Wilhelmina's name. It is after all, a little . . . *eccentric*. Although I must confess I am somewhat surprised to learn that it belonged to a member of such a prestigious family.'

'And it may yet belong to another,' remarked Lavinia with a supercilious smile.

Verity said nothing but glareed at her rival before folding her arms rigidly across her chest and petulantly sticking out her bottom lip, in the most familiar of manners.

While her cousin and Verity were vying with one another for the attentions of their many male admirers, Wilhelmina opted to keep her distance from the squabbling pair, having discovered a relatively quiet spot behind a marble pillar in the corner of the ballroom. She had accepted only two offers to dance: one from a pleasant looking young marquis of somewhere or other, and the other from a distinguished widower of some middle age, who still retained the shadow of the handsome man he had undoubtedly been in his youth. Despite their pleasing appearances, however, Wilhelmina had found the conversation of both partners not in the least stimulating and had been relieved when the dances had ended and she could return to her corner.

Having vacated her spot very briefly, a half hour later, in order to partake of a glass of orgeat, she was surprised to find, on her return, that it was now occupied by Lavinia who was looking hot and bothered and making a futile attempt to conceal herself behind the slim marble column.

'On my word, Cousin,' she gushed, grabbing hold of Wilhelmina's arm and pulling her behind the pillar with such haste that Wilhelmina almost collided with a footman bearing a tray of full champagne glasses, 'you will never guess in a million years, who is just about to enter the room.'

Wilhelmina, in no mood for Lavinia's dramatics, replied wearily, 'I confess I have absolutely no idea, Lavinia.'

'Then think of the most odious, most rudest, most arrogant man on earth,' instructed Lavinia briskly.

Realizing that she would not have a moment's peace until she made at least some show of participating in the drama, Wilhelmina furrowed her brow whilst thinking for a moment, then declared, 'Old Doctor Leonard. I must confess I always found him to be most dreadfully rude and arrogant.'

Lavinia rolled her eyes and tutted dismissively. 'No of course not old Doctor Leonard,' she sniped back tetchily. 'The man has been dead some two years. I am naturally referring, Cousin, to Captain Tunbridge: the captain of that dreadful ship in which we were forced to return from France. I own I almost did not recognize him upon first viewing, for he has at least made some attempt to smarten himself up. However, I fear that if he hopes such a gesture will result in him being accepted by the upper classes, then he is most definitely mistaken.'

Feeling a large bubble of what she could only describe as dread, expanding in the pit of her stomach, Wilhelmina stuck her head tentatively around the side of the pillar. Having held onto a brief glimmer of hope that Lavinia had been mistaken in her identification, she unfortunately found it not to be the case for there, standing under the arch of the entrance to the ballroom was none other than Captain Tunbridge. Carrying out a rapid visual appraisal of the man, she was not in the least surprised that her cousin had almost failed to recognize him for the thick dark stubble, wild hair and working clothes of the ship had been replaced by a clean-shaven face, gleaming, unpowdered hair, neatly tied back at his neck, and immaculate clothes of the very latest mode. The entire transformation had the effect of making him appear not only several years younger, but also disconcertingly handsome. He was deep in animated conversation with the evening's hostess, the rotund and heavily bejewelled Lady Carlton and, as he laughed politely at one of the woman's humorous sallies, his face took on a startlingly different air from the dark menacing aura he had maintained on the ship.

Retreating quickly back behind the pillar before he had a chance to spot her, Wilhelmina could not help but observe that she was not the only female carrying out a surreptitious inspection of the hand-some late arrival. Indeed she sensed an almost palpable buzz of admiration snaking its way around the room as a large number of female heads turned towards the captain – some more discreetly than others. In fact, the only female who did not appear the least bit impressed by the man's appearance was Lavinia who was continuing her disparaging tirade without a single pause for breath.

'Obviously,' she now sniffed, 'he is attempting a feeble endeav-our to crawl up the social ladder and improve his lowly status. Well, he needn't think *I* shall be assisting his pitiable cause, Cousin, for I wish never to speak to the odious creature ever again and I shall make sure he and everyone in this room, is aware of my reasons why. Indeed, if the ladies here were to learn of the manner in which he discarded my lace-trimmed petticoats – as if they were no more than—'

Just as Lavinia was launching headlong, yet again, into her favourite petticoat diatribe, the two girls were joined by the Drinkwaters and Aunt Clementine, newly returned from the supper-room.

'Goodness,' gushed a flustered Mrs Drinkwater, whipping out her fan and fluttering it furiously as they came to stand before Lavinia and Wilhelmina, 'have you seen who is just about to enter the room? Oh, is he not the most handsome of men? And what a surprise to see him here. He is apparently rarely seen in London these days.'

With perfect accord, Lavinia and Wilhelmina peeped out once again from behind the pillar, observing the spot Mrs Drinkwater was indicating. They could see no one, however, other than the captain and Lady Carlton.

'I confess I have no idea to whom you are referring, Mrs Drinkwater,' said Lavinia, her tone impatient as she retreated back behind the pillar.

'Why the Duke of Linthorpe of course,' declared Mrs Drinkwater matter-of-factly. 'He is standing right there in the doorway talking with Lady Carlton.'

'The Duke of Linthorpe?' repeated Lavinia with a scornful laugh. 'Forgive me, ma'am but I think you may need to apply your spectacles. The only person standing in the doorway speaking to Lady Carlton is none other than the odious Captain Tunbridge –

the dreadful man who captained the ship which transferred Wilhelmina and me from France.'

Mrs Drinkwater gave a knowing titter. 'Captain Tunbridge is his working title, my dear. He is William Tunbridge, Duke of Linthorpe, and is, I own, not the most conventional of dukes. Indeed I know of none other who would risk his life gadding about here, there and everywhere when there is absolutely no need of it. Particularly when he is in receipt of forty thousand a year.'

This information evoked a strange strangled sound from Aunt Clementine who now began wafting her own fan with energetic fervour. 'A duke? In receipt of forty thousand a year?' she repeated, her eyes as wide as saucers. 'And you are already of his acquaintance, Lavinia?'

Lavinia nodded miserably.

'Well, what are you waiting for, girl?' Aunt Clementine demanded, regarding her daughter as though she were a dimwitted imbecile. 'Go over and speak to him at once.'

Lavinia, however, was exhibiting none of the enthusiasm so apparent in her mother and Mrs Drinkwater. 'I will not, Mama,' she protested. 'The man is perfectly odious.'

'Odious or not, my girl,' countered Aunt Clementine with equal resolution, 'he is in receipt of forty thousand a year.'

'But he is so odious, Mama, that even forty thousand a year fails to make him appealing.'

'Don't be ridiculous, girl. No man could ever be that odious!' countered Aunt Clementine. 'Now go over and speak to him at once.'

'But you said yourself, Mama,' protested Lavinia again, 'that any man who throws a girl's lace-trimmed petticoats overboard can be nothing but a monster.'

'Yes, well,' flustered Aunt Clementine a little sheepishly, 'that was before I knew of his station, my dear. As far as I am concerned, any man in receipt of forty thousand a year can do what he likes with a load of old lace-trimmed petti—'

All at once their wrangling was interrupted by a familiar deep male voice. 'Good evening, ladies. What a pleasant surprise to see you all again.'

The bickering immediately ceased as all five heads turned in remarkably measured unison to discover the Duke of Linthorpe standing directly before them. In an extremely exceptional occurrence, the entire group of women were, for the very briefest of moments, rendered dumbstruck: Wilhelmina cringed with embarrassment as she recalled their last encounter; and her aunt and Lavinia were visibly mortified at being caught in the act of discussing his credentials in such mercenary fashion – a fact which was also causing a great deal of discomfiture to Mrs Drinkwater and Verity. It was Mrs Drinkwater, however, who was the first to gather her composure.

'Good, er, evening, your grace,' she stammered, dipping a curtsy. 'I must say we did not expect to see you here this evening. One always imagines you to be off on some heroic adventure or other,' she added with an affected titter.

'Even we heroes make time for some pleasures, Mrs Drinkwater,' replied the duke with a disarming smile.

'Oh, of, er, course you do,' said Mrs Drinkwater flushing slightly at the inference. 'Now you must excuse me, your grace, I am quite forgetting my manners. You know my daughter, Verity of course—'

Verity shot the man her most charming of smiles before sinking into a deep curtsy.

'And this is my dearest friend, Mrs Clementine Crump, who is newly arrived in London, together with her daughter Miss Lavinia Crump and her niece Miss Wilhelmina Crump – who, I believe, are, er, already of your acquaintance, sir.'

All three women sank into a curtsy while the duke bowed graciously. As Wilhelmina rose, her gaze momentarily fused with his and she was uncomfortably aware of her heart skipping a beat and colour flooding her cheeks. They held one another's regard for the very briefest of seconds, long enough for the message to be conveyed that he had neither forgotten nor forgiven her apparent behaviour on the ship. A pang of resentment pulsed through her as he then, coolly and deliberately, averted his regard from hers and proceeded to address himself to her aunt and Lavinia, leaving Wilhelmina feeling, yet again, like an errant, berated child.

'Forgive me, ladies,' he said, affecting a much more pleasant countenance, 'but I was under the distinct impression that your family name was Crumpington-Smythe.'

A rush of pink now began stealing up Lavinia's neck while

Verity, with a knowing, condescending smile, announced, 'Oh no, sir. I have known the girls for over ten years and I can assure you they have always gone by the name of Crump – however much they wish they did not.'

'I see,' mused the duke. 'Then please do forgive me. I must be mistaken.'

'I very much doubt it, sir,' said Verity, throwing a disingenuous smile at Lavinia. 'Lavinia has something of a . . . fertile imagination. In fact, she was just telling me the other day of her . . . *eventful* journey across the Channel, your grace.'

Lavinia tossed Verity a chilling glare.

The duke, meanwhile, raised his brows in surprise. 'Was she indeed?' he enquired, one corner of his mouth tilting upwards.

Lavinia, looking decidedly uncomfortable, was rapidly turning a similar shade of crimson to that of her cousin.

'Indeed she was, sir,' continued Verity, revelling in an opportunity to make her rival squirm. 'I own I had no idea she was such a good sailor. Imagine her climbing single-handedly up the highest mast like that to unravel a sail. One would never have thought her capable of such bravery.'

'One certainly would not,' agreed the duke, his dark brows creeping a little further up his smooth forehead, 'however, it is surprising how people react when there is a crisis afoot, Miss Drinkwater.'

'I believe I should have been no use at all,' giggled Verity girlishly. 'In fact I should probably have spent the entire journey flat on my back.'

At this naïve confession, the duke regarded Verity with a strange look on his face for several long seconds before saying, 'Indeed, ma'am. There is, of course, always that . . . temptation.' He threw an accusing glare at Wilhelmina. 'I am afraid, though, that in this case, there was no time for such luxuries, Miss Drinkwater. Miss Crump has no doubt informed you that we required all hands to the deck?'

'Indeed she has, sir,' replied Verity, disappointed not to have caught out Lavinia.

'And has she also told you how she single-handedly rescued our first-mate who was thrown overboard in the storm?' enquired the duke, assuming the most earnest of expressions.

Lavinia's eyes grew wide in her red face while Aunt Clementine gasped aloud and resumed her frantic fan-fluttering which had momentarily ceased with the shock of finding the man before them.

'No, she has not, sir,' replied a miffed Verity.

'Really?' exclaimed the duke, regarding Lavinia with a look of astonishment, 'you do surprise me, Miss Crump. Perhaps you would like to recount that story to your party now, for I for one should never tire of hearing it.'

Lavinia, now as red as the very ripest tomato, gulped before waving a hand and saying, 'Pray, not this evening, your grace. I do not wish to bore my company with yet more sea-faring exploits.'

The duke nodded understandingly. 'As considerate of others as always I see, Miss Crump,' he observed, smiling. 'And may I enquire if we have the pleasure of the company of your betrothed at this evening's ball?'

'Your *betrothed*?' repeated Verity incredulously. 'Why you said that—'

'I'm afraid we do not, sir,' countered Lavinia. 'He has been detained. In France.'

'What a pity,' declared the duke with feigned regret. 'I do so hope I shall have the pleasure of meeting the man at some point during my stay in London. I am sure we shall have a great deal to talk about.'

Lavinia cast him a look, which left no doubt that she could happily have strangled him. The duke, meanwhile, returned the glare with the most engaging of smiles.

'Now if you will excuse me, ladies,' he announced smoothly, 'I must pay my regards to old Lady Falmouth. Do enjoy the rest of your evening.'

Observing the usual formalities, he took his leave of the group, leaving in his wake, a remarkable disparity of opinions: an impressed Aunt Clementine; seething Lavinia; and Wilhelmina who, she was quite sure, should have found the scene wholly amusing had she not, at that moment, been suffering from a severe case of humiliation intermingled with a large dash of anger at the man's arrogant treatment of her.

'Goodness,' exclaimed Aunt Clementine, still fluttering her fan as they all stood observing his broad retreating back. 'What a perfect gentleman and so devastatingly handsome.'

'No, he is not, Mama,' countered Lavinia, with a distinct catch to her voice. 'He is not a perfect gentleman at all, nor is he the least bit handsome. He is a heartless, cruel monster and you said you were going to tell him so.'

'And so I should have done, my dear,' explained Aunt Clementine, 'if I had found that to be the case, but I confess I found him both exceedingly charming and quite the most good-looking young man I have ever set eyes upon. Apart from your father, of course,' she added hastily. 'Although that was several years ago now.'

'But the duke kidnaps women and imprisons them in his room, Mama,' protested Lavinia. 'Surely you would not wish your only daughter to be acquainted with such a brute.'

'Don't be ridiculous, Lavinia,' remonstrated Aunt Clementine. 'Why on earth would such a handsome man in receipt of forty thousand a year need to kidnap women and imprison them in his room? You do let your imagination run a little wild sometimes, my dear.'

'A fact which I simply must endorse,' interpolated Verity. 'Please do clarify for me, Lavinia dear, for I am a little confused, whether or not you are actually betrothed to the Comte de Roxton.'

'It is the Comte de *Roxford*,' corrected Lavinia crossly, 'and of course I am betrothed to the man – almost.'

While Verity flashed her the same pitying smile that she might have employed when encountering a person of significantly below average intelligence, who was using everything possible not to appear so, Aunt Clementine was occupied in the plotting of one of her cunning schemes.

'Well,' pronounced the older woman, resolutely snapping shut her fan, 'what we must first do, Lavinia, is waste no time in clearing up this silly misunderstanding regarding your betrothal to the comte. The duke is such a gentleman it is unlikely he will pay you even the slightest attention if he thinks you are promised to another.'

'Oh, I really shouldn't bother, Mrs Crump,' cut in Verity with a knowing smile. 'Whether Lavinia is betrothed to her comte or not will signify little to the duke for it is rumoured the man has a beautiful secret lover.'

Lavinia gave a scathing snort. 'Oh, believe me, Verity, I would not set my cap at the Duke of Linthorpe if he were the last man on earth and was in receipt of eighty thousand a year. As far as I am concerned the man's poor lover – beautiful or not – is quite welcome to him.'

While Aunt Clementine shot her daughter a look which strongly implied that she had other ideas, Wilhelmina's mind flashed back to the image of the beautiful red-haired woman she had seen in the man's quarters on the ship. Could she be the woman to whom he had reputedly lost his heart and, if so, why was she being kept a secret?

CHAPTER 9

FOLLOWING the duke's departure from their party, Aunt Clementine began a vigorous grilling of Mrs Drinkwater regarding the Tunbridge lineage. Lavinia and Verity, meanwhile, having engaged in a heated argument regarding a pimple which Verity had discerned beginning to flourish on Lavinia's unblemished chin, had now moved on to discuss that debated topic of whether protruding teeth were a worse affliction for a young lady than a case of the freckles – the poor Octavia Harlington-Hartsworthy, who actually looked to Wilhelmina to be quite a pretty little thing – being held up as an example of the latter condition.

Opting to keep out of either conversation, Wilhelmina had been dwelling on the matter of the duke's shameful behaviour towards her and had succeeded in working herself into such a state of agitation that she desired to return to Number 22, Grosvenor Square, thereby removing herself from the man's supercilious presence. She was in the process of contemplating this possibility still further and wondering what tactics she could employ to bring it about, when a distinctive teasing voice behind her broke her reverie by pronouncing, 'Ah, the unique Miss Wilhelmina Crump. I wonder if you would do me the honour of the next dance, madam?'

Somewhat startled, she span around to find herself face-to-face with the Earl of Thurlston, an impudent grin playing upon his handsome face.

'Wh-what,' stammered a perplexed Wilhelmina, aware that all conversation regarding the Tunbridges and dental deformities had abruptly ceased and Lavinia and Mrs Drinkwater's eyes were now boring into her like red-hot pokers, 'I, er, don't really think I, er—'

'Nonsense,' said the earl, taking her arm, 'there is no need to be nervous, Miss Crump: Miss Drinkwater will, I hope, assure you that I am an expert dancer, will you not, Miss Drinkwater?'

'I most certainly will, sir,' gushed Verity, plastering a false smile onto her miffed countenance. 'Indeed, if I may be so bold, my lord, I should say that your quadrille is second to none I have encountered to date.'

The earl smiled. 'There now, Miss Crump,' he declared proudly, 'surely you are not about to refuse me, given that I come with such a glowing accolade?'

Wilhelmina, having not the slightest idea what to make of the offer, looked first at the earl, then at Verity, whose warm pretended smile belied the glacial look in her green eyes.

'Oh, don't be such a blushing ninny, Wilhelmina. Go and enjoy yourself, girl,' she suddenly directed, in a tone which left little doubt that she should have been much happier had Wilhelmina announced that she was going off to boil her head in oil.

'Well – I—' stammered Wilhelmina.

The earl, however, used to having exactly his own way, gave her no chance to continue as he took hold of her arm and began steering her towards the dance floor.

'Please do excuse us, ladies,' he announced to his astounded audience. 'I shall return her directly.'

'So, Miss Wilhelmina Crump,' he began, as he held her in his arms and whisked her around the polished marble floor in as expert a fashion as he had boasted, 'where has such a charming creature as yourself been hiding all this time?'

'Chipping Sodbury, sir,' muttered Wilhelmina, feeling decidedly uncomfortable with the man's attentions.

'Chipping Sodbury, eh?' mused the earl. 'I should not have credited such a place with the production of such beautiful women.'

'Oh, well, there you are quite wrong, sir,' corrected Wilhelmina frankly. 'My cousin and Verity are two of the most beautiful women there and there is also a young lady by the name of Catherine—'

'I can assure you I was not referring to any of them, madam,' interjected the earl, gazing down at her.

Wilhelmina gulped and averted her eyes to the floor.

In no mood for the subsequent frosty reception she was certain to receive from Verity upon returning from her dance with the Earl of Thurlston, Wilhelmina retired immediately to the ladies' withdrawing-room overcome by a strong urge for a little peace and quiet. She was therefore relieved to find the room empty upon her arrival and sank down gratefully on to one of the little velvet stools in front of a dressing-table. Gazing at her reflection in the looking-glass, she noted that she was somewhat wan. She pinched her cheeks hoping to bring a little colour to them and searched in her reticule for a spare hairpin to fix a wayward curl. Rather than coming upon either a pin or her handkerchief, which were the only items in the purse, she was astounded when her fingers came into contact with a thick piece of paper. Slowly pulling out the item with trepidation, her heart skipped a beat when she saw what it was. Both the edges of the note were highly curved, indicating that whoever had had the audacity to slip it into her reticule – which she had retained about her person the entire evening – had rolled it up to make the insertion easier and less noticeable. The perpetrator had succeeded in this mission, for she had discerned nothing at all untoward during the evening and had not the faintest idea who could be responsible.

As she smoothed out the note on the dressing table, she noted that there were only five lines of text on the paper, written in a very neat hand, in black ink. They formed a short list of instructions on what she was to do with the envelope given her by Mr Fitzgibbon. The instructions were concise and directly to the point:

Deliver the note for The Stag
THIS EVENING
Leave underneath the sack in the fruit boy's barrow at
the bottom of St Stephen Street.
Tell no one!

She was aware of blood pumping around her veins and her heart beating fast. There was nothing she wanted more than to be rid of the note and the responsibility she had been burdened with ever since it had been entrusted to her. At the same time, however, she had a burning urge to know what it was she was involved in. How had the deliverer of the note known she was in London? And what was the whole mystery about? For all she knew, the whole thing could be someone's idea of a prank. But whose? With the exception of the Drinkwaters, she knew no one in the capital. She was overcome by a crushing urge to rip up both wretched notes and pretend she had never set eyes upon them. What's more, the note explicitly said that she was to tell no one. She could not therefore risk asking a footman to accompany her. She certainly had no inclination at all to wander the streets of London alone at night. Was the note really so important that she should risk her own safety? The only way she was going to know, she concluded, was if she opened it. She pulled the crumpled envelope from her bodice and stared at it. Should she open it? The instructions did not say, after all, that she should not. She was not in the habit of reading other people's mail but, on the other hand, nor was she in the habit of having complete strangers deposit secret notes into her reticule. Gazing at her pale reflection in the looking-glass again, she failed to notice her wayward curl, but recalled, with an involuntary shiver, the earnestness of Mr Fitzgibbon's words before she boarded the ship. She heaved a deep sigh. There was nothing else for it, she concluded, staring at first the sheet of instructions and then at the envelope. She would have to deliver the note. And she would have to do so alone.

With both notes deposited in her reticule, she fastened the purse tightly around her wrist, took her leave of the withdrawing-room and, having obtained directions from the butler, slipped out of the house as soon as the man's back was turned. The only palliative she could derive from the operation was that St Stephen Street was but a few short minutes' walk away, the servant having informed her that it was the second street on the left from Lady Carlton's residence. Turning right at the bottom of the townhouse steps just as she had been instructed, she then marched briskly past the rows of carriages waiting outside, ignoring the inquisitive glances of the drivers. Her heart was pounding louder with each stride she took. Eventually, upon reaching the end of Lady Carlton's street, she turned left, continuing her hurried pace. She crossed the cobbled road of the first street and mounted the pavement on the other side. In less than a minute, she found herself at the entrance to St Stephen Street. She stopped and looked about her. There was not a soul to be seen. The street itself was quite unremarkable, resembling many others in the city, its cobbled road flanked on either side by a row of fashionable, five-storey houses with their symmetrical floor-to-ceiling windows. To her greatest dismay, however, there was no sign at all of a fruit boy's barrow and, with a pang of annoyance and apprehension, she realized that the barrow must be located at the other end and that she was therefore going to have to walk the entire length of the street in order to carry out her task. Attempting a deep reassuring inhalation, she resumed her walk, not daring so much as to glimpse at any of the houses *en route*, but keeping her eyes focused a little way ahead of her. As she approached her destination, she was aware that the flambeaux were not lit and that she was walking into pitch darkness. Biting her bottom lip, she stuck out her chin defiantly. She *could* do this. She *would* do this. If nothing else, just to rid herself of the wretched note.

As her eyes adjusted to the darkness she was soon able to discern the outline of the barrow parked against the wall. Slipping the note from her reticule with hands that were both shaking and clammy, she then rooted around inside the barrow for the sacking. As her fingers happened upon the coarse material, she almost cried out with relief. Pushing the note swiftly underneath, she turned around at once to retrace her steps. As she did so, however, out of the corner of her eye she caught sight of a tall dark figure slowly approaching the barrow from the opposite direction. Too terrified even to scream, she span around, picked up her skirts and flew back up the street as fast as her legs would take her. Once back in the reassuringly safe orange glow of the flambeaux, she dared to stop for a brief moment and turned to look behind her. As she did so, she noticed the outline of the figure slip back into the shadows. Her skin prickled at the realization that someone had been watching her. Feeling another stab of panic, she gathered her skirts once more and sprinted as hard as she could along the pavement back to the ball, caring not one jot what the curious carriage drivers made of her unconventional behaviour.

81

Bounding up the stairs to the Carltons' townhouse two at a time, she bowled into the black-and-white chequered hall and came to an immediate, panting standstill as she found herself face-to-face with the Duke of Linthorpe who, in a most untimely coincidence, had appeared, by the sound of the door closing behind him, just to have taken his leave of a room on the right.

He came to a standstill the moment he saw her, his cold eyes travelling the length of her dishevelled figure. 'Miss Crump,' he enquired, with no hint of concern, 'what on earth have you been doing, madam?'

Wilhelmina, panting heavily as a result of her exertions, found herself devoid of speech and could only manage to stare unblinkingly at the man as her heart pounded wildly against her ribcage. At that very moment, though, she became aware of another person entering the hall behind her. She span around and was amazed to see that it was the Earl of Thurlston, whose earnest expression as he entered the building melted into one of confusion as he happened upon his unexpected spectators.

As the duke's gaze settled upon the earl, his own grave countenance visibly hardened. 'I see,' he declared coolly, his contemptuous gaze flitting from first the earl to Wilhelmina and then back again as his mind evidently drew yet another erroneous opinion. 'I should have known. Please do excuse my naïvety, *madam*.' And, with those caustic words, he wheeled around and headed back into the ballroom.

The earl, meanwhile, inclining his head to her, attempted to discard the disconsolate air he had had about him upon his entry into the building. He said nothing but threw her a half-hearted, fleeting smile before following the duke into the ballroom, leaving her, still panting, alone in the hall. Her head was reeling with a confusing combination of anger at the earl for choosing that particular moment to appear and furious resentment at the duke for casting her as a harlot yet again.

She was still attempting to regain both her breath and her equanimity when the same door which she had observed swinging shut behind the duke a few short moments before, was thrust open and through it slipped a ravishing beauty with a mane of glossy chestnut hair, dressed in a gown of shimmering burnt amber. Without so much as glancing at Wilhelmina, the woman swept straight past her, out of the house and down the steps to the street, leaving in her wake a trail of exotic, expensive perfume.

CHAPTER 10

'MORE trouble among those damned Frenchies,' muttered Uncle Ernest from behind his copy of *The Times* the follow-ing morning. 'Peasants creating havoc again by all accounts. Shunning the queen at some procession or other and favouring this Duc d'Orléans chap instead, although who he is, I have no idea.'

'Really, dear?' muttered Aunt Clementine in an uninterested tone, as she attempted to squeeze an ambitiously large bunch of spring flowers into an unyielding crystal vase at the sideboard.

'I do believe the Duc d'Orléans is something of the people's champion, sir,' informed Wilhelmina, pouring herself a cup of chocolate.

'Well, whoever he is, I think it is an abomination,' declared Lavinia stoutly. 'Whoever heard anything like it – peasants taking over the place? It is about time the wretches were put in their place once and for all.'

'Quite right, my dear,' concurred Aunt Clementine as she forced a reluctant hot-house lily between two pink tulips. 'Quite why people cannot be content with their station in life is beyond me. They should learn to accept that some of us were simply born to be Quality whilst others were quite obviously not.'

Uncle Ernest lowered his paper and peered studiously at his wife and daughter for a moment, before retreating back behind it.

Early that evening, despite Wilhelmina's protestations that she was not feeling at all the thing – which indeed she was not, having spent the entire night before and all of the present day so far, anxiously pondering the issue of delivering mysterious notes to dark streets with lurking strangers – Aunt Clementine insisted they take a turn around Hyde Park which was, she informed, apparently *the* place to see and be seen.

Having not the slightest desire to engage in either of the afore-mentioned activities, Wilhelmina found herself, as usual, reluc-tantly swept along on the tide of preparations for the excursion. Surprisingly, after having spent the previous evening in the pres-ence of Verity Drinkwater, Lavinia had demonstrated exceptionally good spirits all day which seemed, in no small part, correlated to the girl's opinion that Verity's intended Earl of Thurlston appeared to have developed a definite *tendre* for Wilhelmina.

Although these perceived attentions did not interest Wilhelmina in the least, they had aroused much stronger sentiments in Verity who, obviously of the same opinion as Lavinia, had made a great show of ignoring Wilhelmina for the remainder of the evening, following her dance with the coveted earl. As if to exacerbate matters still further, the man had danced only once with Verity all evening and had demonstrated no sign at all of his intention to make the offer so eagerly awaited by the girl and her mother. The combined effect of all this was that Lavinia was positively glowing with delight.

It was a perfect spring evening with the sun still high in the clear blue sky and not the slightest hint of a breeze. Not wishing to miss out on the clement weather, the park was thronged with ambling bodies, trotting horses and an array of conveyances.

Seated in their open-topped landau, Aunt Clementine, Lavinia and Wilhelmina had just completed one turn around the grounds and had exchanged pleasantries with a great many of their new acquaintances, much to Aunt Clementine's delight, when, having instructed their driver to engage in yet another turn, she gasped loudly and pressed a hand to her chest.

'Oh my word,' she declared, looking for all the world as if she had just witnessed the most wonderful of occurrences. 'There he is. Right there. Heading directly towards us. Oh, is this not fate itself taking a hand in the proceedings?'

'To whom are you referring, Mama?' asked Lavinia brightly, screwing up her eyes against the sunlight as she scanned her surroundings.

'Why the Duke of Linthorpe, of course,' replied Aunt Clementine, in a tone which suggested there was no other man on earth. 'Stop the coach at once, man!' she commanded their driver and then, turning her attention to her travelling companions, 'Come now, girls, we must present the most charming of appearances.'

Following the direction of her aunt's round blue eyes, Wilhelmina saw that she was not mistaken. There, atop a jet-black stallion with a distinctive white flash running down its right hind leg, was the Duke of Linthorpe, attired in immaculate riding wear and steering his mount directly towards them.

All at once, Lavinia's gleeful mood disappeared as she crossed her arms tightly over her chest and stuck out her bottom lip. Wilhelmina's enthusiasm, although not demonstrated in such a petulant pose, was no more zealous.

'Really, Mama,' remonstrated Lavinia, 'you are positively wasting your time in attempting to interest me in the man. I own he does appear much better than he did on that stinking ship of his but he is still nowhere near as handsome as the Comte de Roxford and not even half as amiable.'

'Do be quiet, Lavinia dear,' said Aunt Clementine, affecting her most welcoming of smiles as the duke reached them and drew his horse to a standstill.

'Good evening, Mrs Crump, Misses Crump,' he said, inclining his head in a gesture which encompassed all three ladies. 'I trust you all enjoyed the ball yesterday evening?'

Lavinia said nothing but turned her head deliberately away from him, as if already bored to distraction. Wilhelmina, meanwhile, felt herself shrinking to the usual thumb-size proportions she was now accustomed to adopting in the Duke of Linthorpe's intimidating presence. Despite the lack of enthusiasm being demonstrated by the two younger girls, however, Aunt Clementine could not disguise her own elation at the man's attentions.

'Oh, indeed we did, your grace,' she gushed with a knowing little titter. 'And Lavinia was just telling me how much she enjoyed seeing you again. She was so hoping to renew your acquaintance after having spent such an, er, interesting time on your ship.'

Lavinia turned her head just long enough to shoot her mother a reproving glare.

'Was she indeed?' enquired the duke, astonished.

'Oh, she was, sir. Why she has scarce stopped speaking of her little adventure since she arrived home,' continued Aunt Clementine, with her broadest of smiles.

The duke's eyebrows crept up his forehead. 'Really?' he said, making no attempt to conceal the surprise in his tone. 'I would have thought it was not an experience she would have cared to recall.'

'I can assure you it is not, sir,' muttered Lavinia sullenly, not even bothering to look at him.

Aunt Clementine glowered at her daughter before schooling her features into a perfectly serene countenance.

'Do you often take a ride around the park, your grace?' she enquired innocently.

'Whenever I am in London, ma'am,' he replied. 'Which is, I must confess, becoming a rare occurrence. I find the atmosphere here quite stifling at times.'

'Oh, I couldn't agree more, sir' concurred Aunt Clementine. 'Why, I was just saying to Mr Crump this morning, "Mr Crump," I said, "I do believe the atmosphere here is quite stifling at times." We have recently taken up residence in Grosvenor Square, you know, your grace,' she added, not without a degree of pride.

'Then you are just round the corner from myself, ma'am,' informed the duke. 'My own house is in Bourdon Street.'

Aunt Clementine emitted a squeal of delight and clapped her hands together. 'Why, what an amazing coincidence,' she declared jubilantly. 'We are almost neighbours.' Then adopting a more earnest tone. 'We must, of course, not waste such an unexpected opportunity, your grace. No, indeed. Why, what is the point of having such gracious neighbours, I ask myself, if one cannot engage in the most neighbourly of activities? There is absolutely nothing else for it, sir: you simply must come round to us for dinner. Would that not be delightful, Lavinia dear?'

The menacing scowl which Lavinia threw towards her mother, left little doubt as to her opinion.

'Tomorrow evening,' pronounced Aunt Clementine, with a decisive nod of her head.

'Tomorrow?' repeated the duke, a little taken aback at the invitation. 'But I'm afraid I have a previous—'

'At seven of the clock sharp,' continued Aunt Clementine, urging their driver on before the duke could make his excuses. 'We shall very much look forward to it, your grace, will we not, girls?'

A stunned Wilhelmina and a furious Lavinia did not reply but merely stared at the nobleman open-mouthed, leaving the duke, in a similarly bewildered state, staring directly after them.

Arriving back at Number 22, Grosvenor Square, Lavinia, in high dudgeon, retired immediately to her bedchamber, declaring that she had no appetite at all for dinner and that it was all the fault of her mother for having offered 'that invitation'. Aunt Clementine, meanwhile, visibly trembling with excitement at the thought of 'that invitation', rushed down to the kitchens to speak with Cook about the menu for their distinguished dinner guest.

It was not the matter of the duke's invitation that was weighing heavily on Wilhelmina's mind, however, but rather the incident with the note yesterday evening. For all she had always credited herself as being of above the average intelligence of most of the women of her acquaintance, the more consideration she gave to the ridiculous situation in which she had become unwittingly embroiled, the more she realized she did not have the first clue as to how to start making sense of it. A million questions were buzzing angrily around her head, battling with each other like a swarm of angry wasps: who had put the note into her reticule yesterday evening? Was she likely to receive any more like it? What was in these notes? What had Mr Fitzgibbon meant when he said she could find herself in 'uncomfortable situations'? And who was this infamous Stag person? Concluding that she should feel much better and much less worried if she had some answers to these questions, she decided to carry out a subtle investigation of her own starting with the only clue she had – the pseudonym of 'The Stag'.

'Uncle Ernest?' she enquired, upon eventually locating the man in the library. 'I, er, don't suppose, sir, you know of anyone who has a special interest in, er, deer here in London?'

'Huh?' replied Uncle Ernest, jerking his head up from the book he was reading. 'Deer, did you say, girl?'

'Yes, sir.'

'Hmm,' he mused, rubbing his white beard, 'can't say I do, child. Not wanting to join that hunting set are you? Damned expensive business, so I hear.'

'No, sir,' replied Wilhelmina.

'Jolly glad to hear it,' he declared, going straight away back to his book.

Wondering how she could now return to the subject without appearing ridiculous, Wilhelmina then enquired, 'Well, I don't suppose then that you are acquainted with anyone whose name has anything to do with, er, deer, Uncle?'

Uncle Ernest peered at her from above his spectacles. 'You feeling all right, my girl?'

'Perfectly, sir. I am just attempting to solve a riddle.'

'A riddle, eh?' he said. 'Don't care for them myself. Damned poor use of brain power if you ask me. Far better off learning the names of capital cities, I always find. Never know when you're going to need the name of a good capital city.'

'No indeed, sir,' muttered Wilhelmina with forced enthusiasm. 'Perhaps I shall do that.'

'Jolly glad to hear it,' declared Uncle Ernest again. 'Never did me the least bit of harm and I can tell you there are not many people who know the capital of Finland, my girl.'

Just as she was concluding that, unless she wished to appear a complete and utter dimwit in front of her uncle, she had better say no more on the matter, the library door was flung open and, on a cloud of excitement, in sailed a radiant Aunt Clementine.

'Oh, Mr Crump,' gushed the older woman, bustling over to the leather wing chair opposite that in which her husband was seated. 'Can you believe it: we, the Crumps of Chipping Sodbury, entertaining a duke? We must congratulate ourselves on our elevation in society, sir. We are indeed part of the Quality now and I can only guess what Venetia Drinkwater will say when she hears of it. I own she will be so jealous she may never speak to us again.'

Uncle Ernest raised his head momentarily from his book. 'I doubt anyone could ever be blessed with such good fortune, my dear,' he muttered, before calmly flicking over a page.

The following evening, at seven of the clock sharp, the Duke of Linthorpe, appeared promptly upon the doorstep of Number 22, Grosvenor Square.

Despite the sumptuous feast which Cook, under Aunt Clementine's rigorous and excitable supervision, had taken all day to produce, dinner was a strange affair. Lavinia was silent and morose, preferring to focus all her attentions on the silver pepper pot she insisted on studying, rather than their guest. Having received nothing more than a courteous, cool greeting from the duke, Wilhelmina, feeling both dejected and indignant, was also in no mood to exchange pleasantries. Aunt Clementine, on the other hand, apparently oblivious to the discomfort of the two younger women, was merrily waxing lyrical on a whole host of subjects ranging from the merits of the muff to the uses of leeches. Uncle Ernest, exploiting the fact that his wife would not dare chastise him in front of such an esteemed visitor, was joyously downing as much of the best burgundy as possible. The duke, meanwhile, with his impeccable manners, slipped comfortably into the role of perfect dinner guest, listening with polite intent to Aunt Clementine's incessant ramblings and engaging in a range of appropriate noises on the rare occasions she paused for breath.

The footmen were just in the process of serving a dessert of lime jelly when there was an almighty knocking at the door.

'Who on earth can that be at this time of night?' tutted Aunt Clementine, visibly put out that her diatribe on the colouring of lips had been interrupted. 'If it is that tabby, Venetia Drinkwater, who has got wind of our gathering and come to intrude, then I shall—'

'A Mr Tipping, ma'am,' announced the butler, Hodge, gravely from the open doorway.

'Tipping? Tipping?' repeated Aunt Clementine tetchily. 'I know no one of that name, Hodge. Send the man away immediately. Now, what was I saying, your grace? Oh yes – now I do believe—'

'Please do forgive me for interrupting, madam,' interjected the duke, folding his napkin into a small triangle and placing it on the table, 'but I believe the man at the door may be my valet.'

An expression of incredulity washed over Aunt Clementine's countenance. 'Oh,' she muttered, clearly taken aback. Then, regaining her composure, she turned her attention to the butler, who was continuing to hover undecidedly in the doorway, and snapped impatiently. 'Well what on earth are you waiting for, Hodge? Show his grace's valet in immediately, man.'

Nodding his acquiescence the butler left the room and returned a few seconds later with a wiry looking man of some forty years, dressed in burgundy livery and looking extremely dishevelled.

'I am so sorry to disturb you, your grace,' he flustered. 'However, I'm afraid there has been quite an incident.'

'An incident?' repeated the duke, wrinkling his brow. 'What sort of an incident, Tipping? There's no one hurt is there?'

'Fortunately not, sir,' informed the man, 'however, there has been a fire at the house, which has ruined all of the rooms on the first three floors.'

At this news, Aunt Clementine emitted a shrill shriek, which caused all persons present to rise a number of inches from their seats. 'A fire?' she repeated. 'How dreadful. Why thank the Lord that you were absent, your grace. It simply doesn't bear thinking what could have—'

'But no one is hurt?' enquired the Duke of his servant again.

'No one at all, sir,' informed Tipping. 'We think it was one of those cats from next door, sir, got in through a window and knocked over a candle. Mrs Potts had called one of her staff meetings in the kitchen, so fortunately we were all down there. But when we came back up after the meeting, sir, it had taken quite a hold.'

'Well, I think for the first time in our lives we may all be grateful to Mrs Potts for her staff meetings,' said the duke, with obvious relief. 'What state is the house in, Tipping?'

'All of the rooms on the ground floor are ruined, sir and those on the first and second floors are filled with smoke. The attic rooms have escaped with the least damage,' informed an earnest Mr Tipping.

'Hmmm,' mused the duke. 'Well, at least that solves the problem of having to rehouse the servants. I, on the other hand, shall have to find alternative accommodation until I can resume some kind of order. Arrange for the coach to be brought round at once, Tipping and—'

'Nonsense, nonsense,' boomed Aunt Clementine, so loudly that Uncle Ernest emitted a hiccupping sound and Lavinia dropped the silver pepper pot. 'There is no need for any of that gadding about at this hour of the evening, your grace. And I know Mr Crump would never forgive me if I did not offer you the most obvious solution, would you not, Mr Crump?'

'Indeed, I would not, Mrs Crump,' slurred Uncle Ernest, 'had I the first idea what you were talking about.'

Aunt Clementine shook her head despairingly. 'Why the solution is staring us all in the face, Mr Crump. There is absolutely nothing else for it: his grace must stay here.'

'But I couldn't possibly—' began the duke, with just the slightest hint of panic.

'We have more than enough room,' continued Aunt Clementine undeterred by both the duke's protestations and the stream of objectionable looks which were being thrown towards her from all corners of the table. 'Indeed you can have the Chinese room which, if I may say so myself, will suit you quite splendidly: it has an interesting scene regarding nymphs engraved about the fireplace, you know?'

The duke raised a doubtful eyebrow.

'And,' continued Aunt Clementine, obviously interpreting this eyebrow raising as the gesture of one impressed by the information regarding the nymphs engraved about the fireplace, 'we could even see fit, I am sure, to squeezing a couple of your men into the servants' quarters upstairs.'

The duke looked askance. 'That is extremely kind of you, ma'am,' he stammered, 'but I couldn't possibly impose on you so, and particularly not at such short—'

'Fudge!' declared Aunt Clementine, slamming a fist onto the table so hard that all the crockery flew up in the air and the lime jelly began quivering tremulously in its serving dish. 'It will prove no imposition at all. In fact it shall be most enjoyable having such an esteemed houseguest. Now, as it is quite late already I suggest we waste not another moment in making you comfortable, sir.' Turning her attention to the man standing in the doorway, she said, 'Tipping, see that his grace's belongings are brought here immediately and don't forget his carpet slippers, man. These marble floors can be dreadfully cold first thing.'

Tipping cast an imploring look at his master, who merely shrugged his shoulders in the manner of one well and truly defeated.

92

CHAPTER 11

WILHELMINA awoke the next morning to find the spring sunshine streaming through her bedroom window. She had had a fitful night's sleep which, for some unfathomable reason, seemed due to the fact that she had been acutely aware of the presence of the Duke of Linthorpe in the bedchamber directly above her own.

Hoping that a splash of cold water on her face would make her feel a little more refreshed, she slipped out of bed and padded over to the wash-stand in the corner of the room. When she noticed with a start what was sitting on the top of the blue-and-white water jug, however, the blood froze in her veins. There, as bold as brass, gazing directly at her without even the hint of an apology, was yet another note. Horrified, she stood stock-still staring aghast at the missive as a worrying thought hit her: having washed her face just before she had retired the previous evening, she knew definitely that the envelope had not been there then, which brought her to the very unsettling conclusion that someone had been in her bedchamber whilst she had been sleeping. The realization caused an icy shiver.

Tentatively picking up the offending item, she walked slowly back to the bed and sank down upon it, her knees giving the impression that they could not have held her upright for a single second longer. The instructions, printed in the same neat hand as the previous missive, said:

Deliver to Madame Montreau's Milliner's shop, Oxford Street
before 11 o'clock TODAY.

Place it under the black hat in the window.
Tell no one!

Wilhelmina glanced at the ormolu clock on the mantelpiece. It was already nine o'clock and she wasn't even dressed. She knew where Oxford Street was, of course, but it was a long street and she had no idea whereabouts on it one was to find Madame Montreau's Milliner's shop. And what on earth was she going to say to her aunt and Lavinia, who would undoubtedly think it the oddest thing that she had suddenly taken it into her head to go haring off to a milliner's in Oxford Street when, despite all their best efforts, she had shown not the slightest interest in shopping during their sojourn so far.

Deciding it best not to waste yet more time deliberating, she quickly pulled on a blue muslin walking dress, splashed some water onto her face and hastily threaded a blue riband through her hair. She then made her way downstairs with as much discreet haste as possible. Absorbed in the task of concocting a credible excuse for her outing, she was caught wholly off-guard when she entered the breakfast-room to find no one present except the Duke of Linthorpe. He was seated at the table staring into space, deep worry lines etched upon his forehead. Quite the opposite, in fact, to the jovial persona he had demonstrated the evening before. He started as she entered the room, fixing her with his usual frosty gaze, which inspired in Wilhelmina a strong urge to turn around and leave without exchanging a single word with him.

It was while she was summoning up the courage to take such action, however, that the opportunity was snatched away from her by the duke saying, with unconcealed forced politeness, 'Good morning, Miss Crump. I trust you slept well.'

Recalling some of the more shocking images which had pervaded her mind whilst she'd lain abed, Wilhelmina attempted to control the colour, which rushed to her cheeks. Concluding that she now had little choice but to exchange civilities with the duke, she walked over, a little shakily, to claim the chair opposite his, whilst replying with what she hoped was equal coolness, 'Thank you, sir. I slept very well indeed.'

'I am very pleased to hear it,' replied the duke in a tone so caustic, that it suggested quite the contrary. 'In my opinion, there is nothing to compare with a good night's sleep to help one through the important business of the day.'

At this proclamation, Wilhelmina flinched. Whatever did he mean by that? Had he some knowledge of the note? Reaching for the silver coffee pot, she concluded that the most cautious way to proceed was to feign ignorance. She therefore replied, with a great deal of forced equanimity, 'I have no idea to what "important business" you are referring, sir.'

'Why your preparations for Lady Pontington's musical soirée tomorrow evening, of course,' he replied in a tone which had the no doubt intended effect of making Wilhelmina feel she was the dimmest girl alive. 'You ladies do place great importance on such events, do you not?'

She eyed him suspiciously. 'I can assure you I do not place any importance at all on such occasions, sir,' was her rejoinder as she poured the coffee into the floral Sèvres cup and willed her hands to stop shaking.

'Of course you don't,' he concurred, his voice reverberating with such a scathing tone that she almost dropped the pot. 'It had quite slipped my mind for a moment that you derive *your* pleasures from other . . . *activities*.'

Wilhelmina set down the pot as a renewed wave of colour rose in her cheeks – this time, she was glad to note, that it resulted more from anger than embarrassment. The man was obviously referring to the incident with the shipman on the boat and the unfortunate timing of the Earl of Thurlston's appearance at Lady Carlton's ball. Feeling incensed that she had not been granted an opportunity to explain either situation, she determined that she should waste not a moment longer in defending herself. Opening her mouth to do so however, she found, rather frustratingly, that her ability to speak had entirely disappeared, to be replaced by a rather strange squeaking sound.

Hoping desperately that the squeak would somehow metamorphose into a string of coherent, cutting words, a mixture of both disappointment and relief pulsed through her when the duke pushed back his chair and rose to his feet.

'Please do excuse me, Miss Crump,' he said, 'but I myself have a great many important matters to settle today.'

And with that he took his leave of the room leaving behind a stunned and still squeaking Wilhelmina.

★

Her ragged nerves in even more of a tattered state following the Duke of Linthorpe's scathing comments, Wilhelmina was only grateful that her aunt and Lavinia had already left the house on yet another shopping trip. With her stomach churning uncontrollably, she had not even had the appetite to finish her cup of coffee and had vacated the breakfast-room only minutes after the duke. Donning her bonnet and cloak and, with the note tucked in her reticule, she slipped out of the house the moment the hall was clear of servants and trotted swiftly to the end of the road in search of a hackney cab.

Accompanying her on her journey was the worrying sentiment that everyone – including the duke, the butler, and the young girl standing at the end of the street selling wilting bunches of daffodils – was observing her movements, which were all the more suspicious given the fact that she was, once again, walking out without a chaperon. She was amazed, therefore, when the red-haired jarvey of the hackney she flagged down regarded her perfectly normally when she informed him of her desired destination. Accepting it with a toothless grin and an enthusiastic nod of the head, he created the impression that there was nothing at all untoward in an unaccompanied lady requesting he transport her to such an establishment. But after all, she considered as she climbed into the conveyance, such establishments were in the main patronized by women so why on earth should the man perceive anything at all suspicious in her request? Chiding herself, she made yet another attempt to quell her mounting nerves. Gazing unseeingly out of the window she noticed nothing of the hustle and bustle of the streets through which they passed but was instead lost in her thoughts which were, yet again, revolving around the topic of how on earth she had managed to become involved in such a mysterious coil and, more importantly, what it all signified?

Failing to derive a solitary answer to any of her questions in the short time it took the jarvey to reach her destination, she was shaken from her reverie when the carriage jerked to a halt and she found herself staring directly into a curved shop window in which three hats were displayed, each perched upon its own stand. There was a fetching pink bonnet, adorned with tiny pink and cream silk rosebuds and a lilac creation trimmed with lace. It was undoubtedly the black hat, however, sitting smartly between the other two, on a stand elevated some three inches higher, which was the *pièce-de-résistance* of the display: an enormous wide brimmed creation complete with gold silk ribbon and a huge black plume – it epitomized the style of the fashion icon, the Duchess of Devonshire. Could this be the hat then, under which she had been instructed to place the note?

In search of further confirmation, she looked away from the window and glancing upwards detected a brass sign affixed above the door, engraved with the words *Madame Montreau, Milliner.* She needed nothing further – this was indeed her destination.

She alighted from the carriage somewhat shakily, paid the driver and as he bid her a courteous good day and spurred on his horses, found herself standing on the pavement, unable to move a single limb. Her despair at her immobility was nevertheless tempered with some relief as she took stock of her surroundings and spotted a large ornate gilded clock suspended above the doorway of a jeweller's, two doors up. It was some twenty minutes before eleven. Twenty minutes should, she concluded, be sufficient time to carry out her instructions given that she was now standing directly outside her destination – if only, of course, she could bring herself to enter it. Warily regarding her fellow pedestrians, she noticed a nanny pushing a pram, an old woman hobbling across the road on a stick and a young man opposite, polishing a shop window. None of the trio appeared to be paying her the slightest interest but all three were instead giving the impression of being preoccupied with their own business. Attempting to convince herself that no one could possibly be aware of her reasons for visiting the shop, she started slightly as she suddenly noticed a young lady of some similar years as herself, dressed in a fashionable gown of peacock blue, push open the door to *Madame Montreau, Milliner* and step inside to, what seemed to Wilhelmina, the rather alarming sound of a tinkling little bell. Not wishing to cause any more ringing activity than necessary, she concluded that she should follow the girl and sprang into action, bounding into the shop directly behind her.

'*Bonjour, bonjour,*' drifted out a high-pitched voice from behind a curtain as the door swung shut behind her. 'I will be with you in *un moment.*'

Whilst the fashionable young lady glided gracefully over to the last dressing-table in a row of four placed along the right hand side of the wall, Wilhelmina took the opportunity to gather her bearings. The shop was surprisingly small inside and, from the large towers of hat boxes crammed into every conceivable space, evidently doubled up as a store room. The left-hand corner, in which Madame Montreau herself was lurking, had been curtained off diagonally and from the evidence peeping out from the bottom of the curtain, was home to yet more hat boxes. Directly facing her meanwhile, to the right of the curtain, was a wooden table crammed with all sorts of decorating paraphernalia, including several pairs of scissors and a plethora of little straw baskets overflowing with ribbons, pins, pearls and silk flowers. She recognized the tiny pink rosebuds, some of which were randomly scattered about the surface of the table, as being those belonging to the pink bonnet in the window. Oh Lord! The window! She realized, with a stab of panic that, in her efforts to compose herself, the reason for her visit had temporarily slipped her mind. The fashionable young lady seated herself on the little red velvet stool at the dressing-table, having removed her own chip hat, and replaced it with a fetching cream feathered creation which she had evidently dug out from one of the boxes under her dressing-table. She was engrossed in admiring her perfect profile in the gilded mirror, paying Wilhelmina not the least attention.

Experiencing a pang of hope that she could simply place the note under the black hat and slip away without even having to encounter Madame Montreau, Wilhelmina attempted a little graceful glide herself, which, given her shaking legs, did not come off quite as elegantly as that carried out by the fashionable young lady. She did, nonetheless, manage to manoeuvre herself slowly over to the window display. Feigning an impression of being undecided as to which of the three hats to try, she first picked up the rosebud bonnet, examined it and returned it to its stand. She was just about to pull the note surreptitiously from her reticule and carry out a similar action with the black hat, when a tiny little body, with a halo of orange hair burst out from behind the curtain with all the zeal of an actress about to give a much acclaimed performance. This, Wilhelmina assumed, was Madame Montreau.

'*Bonjour mesdemoiselles,*' she boomed loudly in a French accent which Wilhelmina, having returned from France only a few weeks before, recognized as having its roots more in Yorkshire than Paris. This fact, however, did not deter the *patronne* from her enthusiastic greeting.

'Ah, how delightful having two such pretty ladies to assist today,' she exclaimed with a broad grin. 'Now you, *mademoiselle*,' she declared, turning her attention to a startled Wilhelmina. 'I see you are liking the hat *noir, non*? Why I think it would suit you perfectly. Come, come, *asseyez vous* here and we shall have a look, *n'est ce pas*?'

At a loss as to what else to do, Wilhelmina meekly allowed the woman to lead her to one of the red velvet stools, where she reluctantly sat down and permitted the woman to remove her bonnet. Having then deposited the black creation on her head, the woman stood back to admire the effect in the looking glass.

'*Voilà*! It looks perfectly *charmant, n'est ce pas*? What do you think, my dear?'

There was no doubt that it did look quite charming. Indeed it had the effect of transforming Wilhelmina into an elegant young lady about town. She had no doubt that had Lavinia set eyes upon it, she should have purchased it immediately.

'It is indeed charming, ma'am,' she began, 'but I didn't really, er—'

'And only sixty guineas,' declared Madame Montreau proudly.

Wilhelmina almost fell off the stool. 'Sixty guineas. But I don't think I can— I mean I haven't— That is, I didn't really come here to—'

'Hmm,' sighed Madame Montreau, narrowing her eyes, 'perhaps this is a little . . . too elaborate for one so young. Now let me see what else I have. . . .'

'May I suggest this one, *madame*?' proposed the fashionable young lady, proffering the older woman a strange shaped creation in green. Wilhelmina, who wasn't at all certain whether that was the actual colour of the hat or if it was mould, watched aghast as it was lowered on to her head.

'*Parfait*,' pronounced Madame Montreau, clasping her hands in front of her bosom in a manner of pure delight. 'And I have another one of a similar style which will also suit just fine, *n'est ce pas*?'

Strutting over to the other side of the room, she rummaged about in a box before pulling out with a great deal of ceremony, a hideous brown hat which, by the overpowering smell of mothballs which accompanied it, had not seen the light of day for some time.

'Is that not the prettiest thing you have ever seen?' enquired Madame Montreau, gazing at Wilhelmina in affected awe.

'Quite the prettiest, *madame*,' agreed the fashionable young lady whom Wilhelmina was beginning to dislike.

'When one finds two quite perfect hats, *mademoiselle*,' declared Madame Montreau earnestly, 'it is always my recommendation that both are purchased, for one can spend months, indeed years, trying to find something similar to that which one did not purchase but which one has never forgotten.'

'I couldn't agree more, *madame*,' concurred the fashionable young lady, whose facial features, Wilhelmina was beginning to notice, bore a strong resemblance to those of Madame Montreau.

'But I didn't really want—' began Wilhelmina.

'I shall put them both into boxes for you, *mademoiselle*,' pronounced Madame Montreau, giving her no chance to finish her sentence. 'And you do, of course, qualify for a small discount, given that you have purchased two items. That will in fact, be only forty guineas, *n'est ce pas?*' she announced proudly with a smile.

'*Forty guineas?*' repeated Wilhelmina, her eyes almost popping out of her head. 'But I don't have forty guineas.'

'Thirty-five?' suggested Madame Montreau optimistically, raising her brows.

'I think I may have, er, fifteen,' admitted Wilhelmina, opening her reticule, 'but that is my entire allowance for—'

'Fifteen it is then,' pronounced Madame Montreau, holding out her upturned palm.

A dismayed Wilhelmina reluctantly retrieved the money from her reticule, which was snatched from her hand by the eager proprietor. The fashionable young lady, she noticed, had now disappeared behind the curtain and appeared to be making herself quite at home.

'Is that young lady related to you by any chance, *madame?*' enquired Wilhelmina suspiciously.

'Related?' repeated Madame Montreau innocently. 'Good heavens, no. Whatever gave you that idea?'

Wilhelmina flashed her an accusing glare before realizing with a stab of horror that the clock above the wooden table showed it was now some two minutes to eleven and she had still not placed the note under the black hat in the window. Indeed, she noted with increasing panic, that it would not now be possible to place the note under the black hat in the window as the black hat was no longer in the window but was languishing, quite comfortably, on the dressing table at which she had been seated. What on earth was she to do?

'I don't suppose,' she enquired innocently, observing the woman as she lowered the hideous green creation into its box, 'it would be possible to add a little, er, blue ribbon to the brown hat?'

'Blue ribbon?' echoed the woman, wrinkling her face in distaste. 'To a brown hat?'

'Of course,' replied Wilhelmina, matter of factly. 'It is my favourite combination of colours. In fact I am just returned from Paris where brown and blue are quite the colours to be seen in. I would have thought that you would have been aware of that fact, *madame.*'

'How on earth would I know— Oh, of course,' replied the woman. 'Why they are quite in vogue, *n'est ce pas*? Let me see what I can do for you, *mademoiselle.*'

'How kind,' replied Wilhelmina, unable to conceal the sardonic lilt in her tone.

As the woman took the hat and strutted over to the table containing all the bits and pieces, Wilhelmina watched the long hand of the clock move slowly onto the number twelve. Realizing that she had little choice but to make the most of this opportunity, she casually picked up the black hat and, carrying it over to the window, slipped the note from her reticule and deposited both on the hat stand, just as the clock outside chimed eleven o'clock.

'*Voilà,*' pronounced Madame Montreau, holding up the hat for Wilhelmina's inspection. 'Looks all the crack, *n'est ce pas?*'

Wilhelmina noted that the woman had randomly stuck onto the brim a few pieces of blue ribbon making the creation appear even more hideous.

'Beautiful,' she agreed, now feeling an overwhelming urge to escape the shop. 'Now if you wouldn't mind putting it into its box, I must be on my way.'

'With pleasure,' said the woman gleefully.

Two minutes later, having disposed of fifteen guineas and

acquired two of the ugliest hats she had ever set eyes upon, Wilhelmina strode out of the milliner's shop accompanied by an enormous sense of relief.

So intent was she on congratulating herself on the successful completion of the task, that she almost collided head on with a large, stout woman dressed all in black who was heading towards the shop. Wilhelmina muttered an apology and carried on walking. A little way down the street, however, she realized that she had not the first idea what she should do now. Having briefly contemplated her options, she concluded she had best return to Number 22, Grosvenor Square, before her absence aroused too much suspicion. She was on the verge of hailing another hackney when a voice behind her said, 'Good morning, the unique Miss Wilhelmina Crump. What an absolute pleasure to see you again – and so unexpectedly.'

Having had not the slightest expectation of running into anyone of her limited acquaintance, Wilhelmina almost jumped out of her skin.

Whirling around she found herself face-to-face with the Earl of Thurlston, who was just taking his leave of the jeweller's shop and looking a great deal chirpier than when she had last encountered him in the hall at Lady Carlton's ball.

'Oh,' she muttered, feeling a guilty blush steal across her cheeks. 'Good, er, morning, my lord, I was just—'

'Enjoying this fine spring morning,' interjected the man brightly. 'As indeed am I, Miss Crump. But wherever is your chaperon?'

Wilhelmina's flush deepened. 'There was, um, no one available to, er, accompany me, sir.'

The earl regarded her quizzically for a few moments before pronouncing, 'Well, then I consider it my duty to accompany you. You will join me on a stroll, I hope.'

'Well,' muttered Wilhelmina, the very thought filling her with a sense of dread, 'that is very kind of you, I am sure, my lord, but I. . .I couldn't possibly.'

'And why not, may I enquire?' he asked in a teasing tone.

Wilhelmina sought frantically for a reason which was guaranteed to rid her of his company. 'Because I have to, er, go to the . . . linen draper's,' she blurted out. 'To buy some, er, petticoats.'

To her intense mortification, however, the earl appeared not the least bit discouraged. 'How very interesting, Miss Crump,' he rejoined with a beguiling smile. 'Why, I myself have a great need of some new petticoats and I could not possibly allow you to wander the streets alone. May I suggest then, that we go together?' He proceeded to take the hat boxes from her and offer her his well-clad arm.

Realizing that she could not possibly escape the humiliating situation without appearing rude, Wilhelmina accepted the tendered arm and found herself being marched along Oxford Street, feeling decidedly uncomfortable and praying that no one of any note should see her.

The pair had just reached a crossroads when a large black dog hared out of one of the side streets directly into the oncoming traffic. Wilhelmina and the earl stopped dead in their tracks, the girl's hand flying to her mouth as they observed the potentially perilous scene. Fortunately, the driver of the elegant bottle-green carriage under whose wheels the dog very nearly ended, managed to pull the four perfectly matched bays to an abrupt halt just as the animal dived nimbly between the wheels and sprinted off. Wilhelmina emitted a huge sigh of relief. She and the earl were just about to walk on when she noticed the occupant of the carriage staring at the two of them from the window. Her heart plunged to her feet as she recognized the observer as none other than the Duke of Linthorpe. Their eyes met for the briefest of seconds but, yet again, that was more than sufficient time for her to feel the full, chilling impact of the man's disapproval.

CHAPTER 12

WITH a parcel containing two unwanted petticoats added to her purchase of two superfluous hats, Wilhelmina returned to Number 22, Grosvenor Square some two hours later, grateful that she had at last managed to shake off the unwanted, but extremely persistent, attentions of the Earl of Thurlston. Not only had the man insisted on accompanying her to buy the petticoats but he had, to her shock and amazement – and indeed to the shock and amazement of all those present in the establishment – quizzed the poor, blushing assistant on every possible detail of the lace petticoats versus the gauze, before making an unabashed purchase of three of each.

Praying that she had arrived home ahead of all other members of the household, allowing her the opportunity to secrete her purchases without the need to explain them, she managed only a curt nod at the butler who opened the door to her, before making an unladylike dash for the stairs. She had just placed one foot on the bottom step when out drifted the unmistakable voice of her aunt from the crack in the drawing-room door opposite.

'Wilhelmina, is that you, my dear? Do come and join his grace and me in a cup of tea.'

Unable to move, Wilhelmina felt the blood freeze in her veins. 'I'm, er, afraid I can't, Aunt,' she stammered. 'I am, er, busy . . . extremely busy.'

'Don't be silly, my girl,' commanded her aunt. 'What on earth can you be busy with? I was just telling his grace how the Crumps of Chipping Sodbury are one of the most influential families in Chipping Sodbury, my dear. I'm sure he would love to hear more from you, would you not, sir?'

'Oh, most definitely, ma'am,' floated out the deep, well-modulated voice of the duke.

With her foot seemingly now glued to the stair and the butler eyeing her strangely, Wilhelmina racked her brain in search of a more convincing excuse. Unfortunately, not one excuse – convincing or otherwise – was forthcoming and, admitting defeat, she slowly peeled her foot from the stair and made her way, rather sheepishly, into the drawing-room, oblivious to the fact that she was still carrying her parcels.

Her aunt and the duke were sitting in two armchairs on either side of the white marble fireplace. Between them was a round ormolu-decorated table on which sat a tray containing a silver tea service and a plate of sweet biscuits. Both heads turned towards her as she entered the room.

'Here she is,' announced a beaming Aunt Clementine, with such fervour that one could have imagined Wilhelmina a soldier newly-returned from the war. 'Now where on earth have you been, my dear? No one seems to have seen hide nor hair of you this morning.'

Aware of the duke's eyes burning into her, Wilhelmina used all her resolve not to look at him, whilst simultaneously chiding herself for the flush creeping over her face and chest. She seated herself on the small sofa directly in front of the fire, placing her purchases alongside her.

'I had need of a little air, Aunt. I had a the, er, headache,' Wilhelmina replied.

'Oh, you poor girl,' fluttered Aunt Clementine sympathetically. 'But I see that you have been shopping. Marvellous remedy for the headache I always find. And you have bought hats. How terribly exciting. Do try them on for us, my love.'

'I would rather not, Aunt, if you don't mind,' muttered Wilhelmina, her cheeks now burning.

'Oh, come now, my dear. You know how new purchases always excite me so,' urged Aunt Clementine.

'I can assure you that they are most definitely nothing to excite oneself about, Aunt,' confessed Wilhelmina.

'But I do so adore new hats,' enthused her aunt. 'A girl can never have too many hats. Isn't that right, your grace?'

'I'm quite sure it is, ma'am,' agreed the duke.

'There you are, Wilhelmina,' declared Aunt Clementine. 'Why even the Duke of Linthorpe is eager to see your new purchases. Don't be a spoilsport, my dear: let us see them.'

Reluctantly, Wilhelmina opened the hat box and retrieved the brown creation, complete with its newly attached blue ribbons. She placed it, somewhat despondently, on her lap for her audience and awaited their reaction.

'Oh,' murmured Aunt Clementine, then, injecting a little more enthusiasm into her tone, 'well, I'm sure it looks so much better when it is on. That is quite often the case, you know, your grace.'

'Is it indeed?' said the duke, not looking at all convinced as he regarded the offending item with a dubious air.

'Well, come along then, girl,' chivvied Aunt Clementine. 'Don't dilly-dally. Try it on for us.'

Doing her utmost to avoid looking at the duke, Wilhelmina unwillingly removed her own bonnet and replaced it with the new one.

Aunt Clementine narrowed her eyes as if making a great study of the hat, before emitting a rather unambiguous, 'Hmmm.' There then followed another brief pause where each one of the trio appeared to be at a loss for words. All the while, however, Wilhelmina was aware of the duke regarding her curiously.

'Well,' declared Aunt Clementine at length. 'I am sure the other one is far more. . . . Why don't you try the other one on for us, my dear?'

Not wishing to prolong the agony by once again objecting to the request and being overruled, Wilhelmina reluctantly repeated the same process with the mouldy green hat. The response was just as she had suspected. After another, 'Hmmm,' from Aunt Clementine, followed by another brief silence, the older woman suddenly declared, 'Still there are always gloves. I always think that gloves do so often make an outfit. Do you not agree, your grace?'

A rather strange snort came from the duke, which Wilhelmina was almost certain was the sound of laughter. 'Oh, indeed, I do, ma'am,' he replied with a distinct twitch of his lips.

Hoping desperately that that was to be the end of the embarrassing interrogation, Wilhelmina realized with a sharp stab of disappointment that it most definitely was not.

'So what else have you bought, dear?' enquired Aunt Clementine brightly, now eyeing the brown parcel.

'Petticoats, Aunt,' muttered Wilhelmina.

At the mention of petticoats, Aunt Clementine winced slightly, obviously recalling the uncomfortable situation Lavinia had reported when the duke had thrown her petticoats overboard on their journey from France.

'Oh,' she flustered, evidently caught a little off-guard. Then affecting a dismissive laugh. 'Well, such things are of no import at all, are they, your grace? I am sure the world would continue to function quite swimmingly without our obsession for petticoats.'

'Perhaps, ma'am,' replied the duke, his lips still twitching, 'however I fear not half so prettily.'

An instant flush was evident under Aunt Clementine's rouged cheeks. 'Oh my, sir,' she giggled girlishly, patting her lace cap. Then, not wishing to appear too coy in front of her niece, 'Now do have a cup of tea, Wilhelmina dear,' she offered, gesturing to the tray. 'You are looking a little peaked, child. I do hope you are not coming down with something before the musical soirée this evening.'

Before Wilhelmina could reply, her aunt abruptly changed the direction of the conversation by announcing: 'Now where on earth is that girl, Lavinia? She was supposed to bring me my lorgnette some ten minutes ago. Please do excuse me, your grace, while I go to seek out the wretched child.'

The duke inclined his head politely as Aunt Clementine rose to her feet and waddled off towards the door. Wilhelmina, meanwhile, had the greatest wish that she could shrivel up and disappear in a puff of smoke rather than be left alone with the man. Unfortunately, however, her wish was not granted.

'So, Miss Crump,' he said evenly, setting down his teacup on the table, 'I take it you had an enjoyable trip to Oxford Street this morning?'

Wilhelmina said nothing, but stared glumly at the flickering flames of the fire. The message had given explicit instructions that she must tell no one of her reason for visiting Oxford Street but how on earth was she to explain her outing without making the entire episode with the earl appear much more than it actually was. Deciding there was nothing else for it but to broach the subject

107

head on, she took what she hoped would be a deep calming inhalation and, meeting his hard, dark gaze, said, 'I would be grateful, your grace, if you could refrain from mentioning my trip to Oxford Street to anyone else. And not, I may add, for the reasons you no doubt suppose I say that.'

Leaning back in the chair, the duke steepled his fingers over his chest and stretched out his long legs, regarding her studiously all the while. 'And for what reasons do you suppose I suppose you say that, Miss Crump?' he enquired coolly.

Wilhelmina felt a wave of irritation wash over her. 'You may well be under the impression that I had a liaison with the Earl of Thurlston, sir. I can however assure you that that was most definitely not the case.'

'I see,' he said, with infuriating neutrality. 'And why do you think I should care for one moment if you had a liaison with the Earl of Thurlston?'

'I do not care if you care or not, sir,' retorted Wilhelmina hoping, as the words tumbled from her mouth, that they were making sense. 'I do however, have no desire at all to be the subject of gossip, particularly when there is nothing to gossip about.'

The duke sprang to his feet and regarded her from above, making her feel, once again, like a very small child. 'I can assure you, madam,' he began frostily, 'that I have never gossiped in my entire life. I would however suggest that if you wish to carry on such clandestine meetings in the future that you do at least make some attempt to make them just that,' and with that he strode from the room, leaving Wilhelmina feeling as stung as if he had slapped her across the face.

CHAPTER 13

'GOOD lord, those Frenchies are still at it,' announced Uncle Ernest from his usual position behind the newspaper the following morning. 'Some blasted pamphlet campaign in Paris now.'

'Pamphlets, dear?' repeated Aunt Clementine, engrossed in the delicate operation of removing the bones from her kipper.

'Pamphlets indeed,' confirmed Uncle Ernest. 'A load of them. All attempted to disgrace the queen. Why it appears the place is quite out of control.'

'Respect, Mr Crump!' declared Aunt Clementine vehemently, looking up from her kipper. 'That is what is missing.'

'It would appear so, Mrs Crump,' concurred Uncle Ernest, the up and down movement of the newspaper providing a good indication that the man behind it was nodding his head.

'It does appear that events are indeed becoming more serious in Paris,' pointed out Wilhelmina concernedly, 'and I have still not received a reply to the letter I forwarded the Fitzgibbons some two weeks ago.'

'Hmmm,' mused Aunt Clementine. 'Well the French certainly do appear to have got themselves in quite a pickle and I own it does seem a little odd, when Ermintrude is normally so meticulous with her correspondence. I, however, have the solution, my girl,' she proclaimed jubilantly. 'I shall write to the Fitzgibbons myself this very day instructing them that they are to leave behind that dreadful disorder and return to England at once. They must come immediately to London – as our guests.'

Lavinia pulled a face, which indicated she was not in the least impressed by this suggestion, but before she could express her opinion, Aunt Clementine pushed aside her coffee cup and announced – with all the triumph of one having made a miraculous discovery – that she was going to speak to his grace's man and ascertain a list of the duke's favourite dishes. This announcement was greeted with the same amount of enthusiasm from Lavinia as that of the Fitzgibbons' invitation.

Thanks to her aunt's tireless efforts, the news that the Crumps of Chipping Sodbury had an eminent new houseguest was soon brought to the attention of all the most prominent persons in Society. This had, judging by the sudden flood of invitations delivered to Number 22, Grosvenor Square, the much-desired effect of not only dramatically raising the family's profile but also of pushing out of joint the much-peered-down nose of Mrs Venetia Drinkwater.

'Well, quite obviously, Clementine, the man must be desperate,' Mrs Drinkwater remarked, as they made their way to Lady Pontington's music room, inclining their heads in greeting to Mrs Harlington-Hartsworthy and her daughter, Octavia, as they passed by.

'Oh, I shouldn't have thought so, my dear,' replied Aunt Clementine brightly. 'I am quite sure a man as charming as the Duke of Linthorpe would never be short of offers of places to stay.'

'Hmph,' huffed Mrs Drinkwater. 'Well, nevertheless I find it decidedly odd that he should wish to lodge with people significantly below his own station. Now do let's take our seats, my dear. I believe the performances are about to begin.'

Wilhelmina's only experience of a musical soirée to date had been back in Chipping Sodbury and had involved one of her contemporaries, poor Penelope Prestwick. The girl's mother, Mrs Ophelia Prestwick – to whom Aunt Clementine always referred as 'that ghastly ambitious woman' – had taken it upon herself to invite the most prominent persons of the town to a 'musical soirée' in which poor Penelope's extensive repertoire of musical accomplishments was to be demonstrated. Being such a 'ghastly ambitious woman', however, Mrs Prestwick had a somewhat glorified view of her daughter's musical achievements – a view which was certainly not shared by poor Penelope nor indeed by anyone else. On the evening in question, with all guests gathered in the Prestwick's fussy drawing-room, the pressure on Penelope's young shoulders was all too obvious when, during her first recital on the pianoforte, the poor girl, so overcome with nerves, had deserted her post and fled into the hall, where she had emptied the contents of her stomach in an elephant-shaped plant pot, brought back from India some years previously by the former Mr Prestwick.

So far, it had to be said that Lady Pontington's musical soirée was demonstrating all the signs of being less eventful. Indeed the music was so dreadful it was having a soporific effect on Wilhelmina who, thanks to yet another erratic night's sleep the evening before, was quite exhausted and not in the best of humours. She was grateful when Mrs Pontington announced a short interval for refreshments – not because she was in any particular need of refreshments, but because it indicated that the evening was some halfway through.

'Oh, was not the Italian ballad quite delightful,' trilled Verity Drinkwater, helping herself to a cream puff. 'Why, I may even have one sung at my own wedding.'

'What a marvellous idea, my sweet,' declared Mrs Drinkwater, enthusiastically. 'You could well set a most fashionable trend among the *ton*, Verity. Particularly when there will be so many of them in attendance at the marriage of the Earl of Thurlston.'

Verity gave a contented sigh as she leaned over a plate of cucumber sandwiches, popping two onto her plate. 'Well, as we are all aware, Mama,' she pointed out, with a large dose of hauteur, 'aristocratic women do have a most important role to play in society. Why without them, nobody should have the first idea which fashionable direction to take. Of course, once I am Countess of Thurlston, I myself shall be burdened with such responsibilities. However, I shall bear them stoically and shall do my utmost to serve my country well. Indeed, in doing so, I may even take over the role of fashion leader from the Duchess of Devonshire who will, of course, be receiving an invitation to my wedding given that she is, I believe, somewhat distantly related to the earl.'

This dialogue, which would not – with one or two alterations – have sounded incongruous had it been uttered by the mouth of Mr Pitt himself, had been listened to by an evidently astounded Lavinia. The girl wasted no time in expressing her own opinion on the matter.

'I am quite sure, Verity, that the Duchess of Devonshire is *distantly related* to a great many people,' she pointed out with some condescension. 'That does not mean, however, that she will grace them all with her presence at their weddings. Why, I am sure if that were the case, the woman would do nothing *but* go to weddings.'

Verity regarded her as she daintily held the triangular sandwich between her slender fingers. 'La, do I declare a hint of envy in your tone, Lavinia dear?' she enquired, raising her perfectly arched brows.

Lavinia arranged her own exquisite features into a rueful expression. 'I'm afraid not,' she replied, injecting an apologetic tone to her voice. 'I am simply pointing out what is a quite obvious fact.'

'Oh really?' replied Verity, replacing the sandwich onto her plate. 'And we all do know, Lavinia, how much you value facts. Although, I confess I am beginning to doubt the *fact*, my dear, that there is such a man as the Comte de Rottingsford in actual existence.'

Lavinia instantly lowered the macaroon which had been *en route* to her mouth. 'It is the Comte de Roxford and what exactly are you implying?' she challenged.

'Nothing at all, I am sure,' replied Verity, feigning innocence. 'I am merely pointing out the *fact*, my dear, that no one other than your cousin – who, by definition, cannot be classed as impartial – appears to have set eyes upon the man.'

Lavinia's eyes grew wide at the impertinent implication. 'Are you suggesting that I have . . . I have . . . *invented* him?' she spat.

Verity affected a compassionate smile. 'Well, it would not be the first time, my dear.'

Lavinia's eyes were now giving the impression of being on the verge of popping right out of her head. 'How dare you suggest for one moment that I would make up such a thing?' she demanded.

'Well I have known you for some years now, dear,' observed Verity.

Wilhelmina held her breath for a moment as the two girls regarded each other in threatening silence: Verity's countenance, one of pure innocence; Lavinia's, apoplectic with rage. But all at once, the latter's fury melted with amazing seamlessness into the most charming of smiles as she became aware of a young gentleman approaching the group.

'Oh look, Wilhelmina,' she declared brightly, 'here is the Earl of

Thurlston coming to see you.'

Whisking around, Verity affected a similarly dazzling smile as she, too, spotted the rapidly approaching earl. She immediately pushed her plate onto the table behind her and whipped out her fan.

'I think you will find, Lavinia *dear*,' she snarled through gritted teeth, 'that the man is coming to see *me*.'

'We shall see soon enough, *dear*,' replied Lavinia gaily.

Upon reaching the group, the earl, looking as dashing as ever, flashed them all a mischievous grin before bowing graciously. 'How rare to see such a bevy of beauties together,' he pronounced. 'I am come to see how you lovely ladies are enjoying the music.'

'Oh, it is quite delightful, my lord,' cooed Verity, flirting her fan at the man. 'I particularly enjoyed the Italian ballad.'

'Did you indeed?' he said blandly. 'And what is your own opinion, the unique Miss Wilhelmina Crump?'

Wilhelmina flashed him a warning glare. 'I, er, must confess sir, that I much prefer ballads when they are sung in tune.'

The earl gave a snort of laughter. 'How delightful and how exactly like my own sentiments, Miss Crump,' he added with a chuckle. 'Now please do excuse me, for I am afraid I am required to leave somewhat earlier than I had hoped. May I wish you all a very pleasant evening.' And with that comment, he executed another bow before turning on his heel and striding from the room.

Lavinia cast Verity a pitying look. 'Well, my dear,' she sighed. 'I'm afraid the *fact* of the matter is that it does not appear that your proposal of marriage will be forthcoming this evening.'

Verity glared. 'Perhaps not,' she said, 'but at least the earl is flesh and blood. If your comte does not appear within the next se'enight, one can only assume that he is indeed yet another figment of your fertile imagination.'

A seething Lavinia clenched her fists as Verity span around and made off in search of her mother.

Wilhelmina, meanwhile, thanked God that the earl had not thought fit to mention their shopping expedition the day before. She had quite enough to cope with at the moment without incurring the redoubtable wrath of Verity Drinkwater.

Following the interval for refreshments, which had proved less tedious than the performances, the party resumed their seats for the second half of the proceedings during which they were not only forced to endure a painful Beethoven bagatelle, but also an embarrassingly out-of-tune soprano. Wilhelmina was beginning to feel the will to live slowly slipping away from her. Her despondent mood was not helped by the fact that the room was so stuffy, there appeared to be no air at all circulating. Deciding to ask a footman to rectify the situation, she slipped quietly out of her seat and padded over to one of the windows which faced out onto the street below. She watched as he unfastened the brass catch and was about to pull up the pane when, out the corner of her eye, she spotted a black stallion clattering furiously down the cobbles of the street towards a stylish burgundy carriage parked directly below. As the occupant of the carriage alighted, Wilhelmina immediately recognized her as the woman who had been in the room with the Duke of Linthorpe at Lady Carlton's ball. She looked no less beautiful this evening, dressed in a deep red, low-cut gown, her rich chestnut hair arranged in an elaborate cascade of curls. She remained standing on the pavement as the rider of the horse drew to a halt alongside her. Wilhelmina almost gasped in amazement when she saw that the person in question was none other than the Duke of Linthorpe – attired in entirely black riding wear. As he leapt down from the horse the woman handed him something. The two of them then engaged in a short but intimate exchange before the duke leapt back on his horse and galloped away again at breakneck speed. A dazed Wilhelmina, being so engrossed in the drama below that she had completely forgotten to breathe in the fresh air, slipped back into her seat just as the performance ended. As the lethargic audience made their polite applause, the doors to the salon were suddenly pulled open and in swept the woman who, just moments ago, had been talking to the duke.

'Ah, the Baroness Beaumont,' sighed Mrs Drinkwater, regarding the female with some awe. 'And looking as stunning as ever although I own the woman does make a dreadful habit of being rather late for events.'

The Baroness Beaumont must be exceedingly clever as well as incredibly beautiful concluded Wilhelmina, wishing that she too had been able to arrive with only minutes of the evening's proceedings remaining. But if Baroness Beaumont was, as she appeared to be, the duke's 'beautiful secret lover', why were they so intent on keeping their affair secret and who then was the woman he had locked in his cabin on the ship? With this whole new set of questions beginning to whirl around in her head, she was only too grateful when the final precarious note had been warbled and they could, at last, take their leave of the Pontington residence.

CHAPTER 14

WILHELMINA awoke the following morning in a state of considerable trepidation; weighted down by the nagging presentiment of discovering another strategically placed note. She had taken several measures to discourage any further nocturnal visitors to her bedchamber by wedging a chair against the door handle, ensuring all the windows were well and truly closed, and jolting awake every half hour. Although this latter measure could, she reluctantly admitted, be more attributed to the resident of the room above, whose behaviour was rapidly becoming as puzzling as that of her mysterious message deliverer.

Concluding, after three long minutes that, as tempting as the thought was, she could not possibly languish in bed all day, she plucked up courage to prise open her eyes and peep about the room. No unwanted communication being visible, she released a sigh of relief and hoped that perhaps she could look forward to a somewhat calmer day than those she had experienced in London so far.

A little over half an hour later, however, and it became evident that her optimism had been misplaced. Her initial good spirits upon entering the breakfast-room and not encountering the Duke of Linthorpe, evaporated rapidly upon discovering the furious mood that had apparently overtaken her cousin.

'I do declare, Mama,' expostulated Lavinia, stabbing her fork viciously into the unsuspecting piece of ham on her plate, 'that if Verity Drinkwater makes one more remark about my having invented the Comte de Roxford, then I shall . . . I shall—'

'Language, dear,' came the command from behind *The Times*.

116

'Sorry, Father,' apologized Lavinia, now angrily using her knife to saw off a piece of the meat, 'but that girl really is insufferable.'

Aunt Clementine sighed heavily, her huge bosom, cased in layers of Belgian lace rising up and down quite magnificently as she did so. 'I must agree, my dear,' she observed wistfully, as she spooned a small mountain of sugar into her coffee cup, 'that the girl can indeed be quite tiresome at times.'

' "Tiresome" was not the word I had in mind, Mama,' muttered Lavinia.

'I do think however,' continued Aunt Clementine, ignoring her daughter's remark, 'that regarding the comte, we should not be placing all our eggs in one basket and closing off other, perhaps more lucrative . . . *avenues*,' she said, placing a particular knowing emphasis on the word 'avenues'.

Lavinia groaned and set down her knife and fork. 'I do hope you are not referring to the Duke of Linthorpe, Mama. Why I can scarcely bear to be in the same room as the man. Quite what enticed you to invite him to stay here is positively beyond me.'

'My dear, he is quite, quite charming,' enthused Aunt Clementine, stirring her spoon around the floral coffee cup, 'and that is without the influence of his forty thousand a year. Why, imagine Verity Drinkwater's face, my love, if you were to marry him. A duke is infinitely more Quality than a comte or indeed an earl.'

'I'm afraid even that thought does not tempt me, Mama,' declared Lavinia stoutly.

'Good God,' pronounced Uncle Ernest suddenly from behind the newspaper.

'Well, I'm sorry, Father,' stated Lavinia tetchily. 'But I do possess certain standar—'

'The world has gone quite mad,' interjected the old man disbelievingly. 'It would appear that a young lady by the name of Catherine Cavendish was kidnapped last night in London – in the city in which we are currently residing, I might add,' he pointed out, rather unnecessarily. 'Beggars left a ransom note. Says if they don't pay up, they'll remove both her thumbs and post them back to her parents.

Lavinia gave a gasp. 'Catherine Cavendish? Oh no, Mama – why we were introduced to her at Lady Carlton's ball. She was the blonde young lady with the prettiest hands I ever saw.'

'Good lord,' declared a dismayed Aunt Clementine. 'Indeed she was, my dear – a cousin of Lady Harcourt and quite one of the daintiest little things at the ball if I do recall.'

'Well, it looks as though her days of having pretty hands could well be numbered,' said Uncle Ernest. 'Shocking business if ever I heard any.'

'Greed, Mr Crump!' suddenly declared Aunt Clementine, so vehemently that all her fellow breakfasters started slightly. 'That is the cause of it all. People always wanting more than they have. Quite why people cannot be satisfied with what they have is positively beyond me.'

Uncle Ernest regarded his wife, who was busy adding another spoonful of sugar to her cup, in bewildered silence for a few moments, before once again retreating behind his paper shield.

'Well now, let us not dwell on such unpleasant matters,' pronounced Aunt Clementine brightly. 'Who is for a spot of delicious strawberry jam?'

No sooner had the words left her mouth, than the door swung open and in came, much to Wilhelmina's chagrin, the Duke of Linthorpe, looking wan.

'Ah, now I'm sure you would not say no to a little strawberry jam, your grace,' said the older woman. 'Particularly as I have it on extremely good authority that the strawberries used in the making of this very preserve were cultivated in the gardens of Chatsworth House – with the specific aim of being enjoyed by the Duke and Duchess of Devonshire themselves. Such Quality people.'

The duke's anxious expression melted into one of amusement as he observed Aunt Clementine stroking the pot of the prestigious preserve. 'Well I own that I am partial to berries of the straw variety, Mrs Crump,' he admitted, his lips twitching slightly as he slipped into the chair opposite his hostess and Lavinia.

'Oh my,' giggled Aunt Clementine, patting her cap. 'You are amusing, your grace. Is not his grace amusing, Lavinia dear?'

Glowering at her mother, Lavinia said sardonically, 'Indeed he is, Mama. In fact he is so amusing I can scarce contain myself.'

Throwing her daughter a glower which told her she was not in the least bit impressed by her cynicism, Aunt Clementine arranged her features into an expression of deep concern before enquiring of their houseguest, 'Now we did not see you at the musical soirée yesterday evening, my lord. I do so hope you will not permit this dreadful business with the fire to play havoc with your social life.'

'No indeed, ma'am,' replied the duke, shaking out his napkin and proceeding to smooth it over his lap. 'I had other plans yesterday evening.'

'Oh, but what a great pity,' pronounced Aunt Clementine. 'It was most delightful, was it not, girls?'

Neither of the girls replied. Lavinia, sitting in brooding silence glowering at the pot of coveted jam and Wilhelmina, having witnessed the man's apparent haste yesterday evening and his intense exchange with the beautiful Baroness Beaumont, wondering what on earth these 'other plans' could have involved.

Later that morning, all members of the household – with the exception of Uncle Ernest – were to be found in the long crimson drawing-room. The ladies were seated around the crackling fire engaged in their embroidery while the duke was scribbling what appeared to be a mound of correspondence at the writing bureau at the back of the room. It was Hodge who interrupted Aunt Clementine's inane and incessant ramblings, by entering the room bearing a silver tray on which lay a white calling card.

Having snatched the card from the tray and informed herself of the caller, Aunt Clementine pressed a hand to her chest and declared breathlessly, 'Oh my word. You will never guess who has come calling, my dears. Why, none other than the Earl of Thurlston himself. Oh, wait until Venetia Drinkwater hears of it. Well, what are you waiting for, Hodge. Show him in at once, man.'

As the butler nodded his acquiescence and left the room, Lavinia set down her embroidery and clapped her hands together in delight. 'Goodness, is this not marvellous, Mama. The man is quite obviously coming to see Wilhelmina. In fact, it is my sincere opinion that he has no intention at all of offering for Verity Drinkwater but for Wilhelmina instead. Imagine, Cousin, you too could be marrying into the aristocracy. We shall both be grand ladies, mistresses of enormous houses, wives of—'

'Do be quiet, Lavinia,' implored Wilhelmina. 'As I have already informed you on several occasions, I have no interest at all in the Earl of Thurlston.'

No sooner had the words left her mouth than a rather strange strangled sound came to their attention from the area of the writing bureau. All three women immediately turned concernedly towards the scribbling duke, convinced that the man was suffering a fit of some nature. To their surprise, they found him looking perfectly well, if perhaps a little piqued.

'If you will excuse me, ladies,' he suddenly announced, bundling up his correspondence and rising from his chair, 'I shall leave you to your visitor.'

'Oh, please do stay, your grace,' pleaded Aunt Clementine. 'It would be quite delightful having two such dashing gentlemen in our drawing-room.'

The man threw her an apologetic smile. 'As much as it would give me the greatest of pleasure, madam,' he confessed, 'I'm afraid I have a prior appointment. I am quite sure, however, that my absence will not detract in the least from the charms of the Earl of Thurlston.' He tossed a knowing glance at Wilhelmina.

Feeling a wave of anger wash over her at his unwelcome inference, Wilhelmina sat silently seething as the duke strode with great purpose from the room to be replaced some thirty seconds later by the earl.

In contrast to the Duke of Linthorpe, the Earl of Thurlston was in high spirits and made no disguise of his delight at seeing the Crumps once again. For all the man's indisputable charms however, Wilhelmina could not help but feel that there was something disingenuous about him – a fact which evidently occurred to neither her aunt nor her cousin, as they revelled in his amiable presence.

'Is this not the most pleasant of surprises, my lord,' flustered Aunt Clementine, busily tucking her loose curls under her cap.

'My dear, Mrs Crump,' declared the earl, bowing graciously over her plump hand, 'you were the very first people I thought of today and I was overcome with a burning desire to call upon you and assure myself of your good health this fine morning.'

'Ooh,' cooed Aunt Clementine delightfully. 'How very gracious of you, sir. Indeed we were only saying how delightful it was to see you again yesterday evening. Was not Lady Pontington's musical soirée quite ... um... ?'

'Indeed, it was, ma'am,' concurred the earl, nodding his head earnestly as he settled himself on a stool. 'Very much so.'

'Quite ... in fact,' added Lavinia enthusiastically. Then, clearly eager to maximize the advantage of the earl's visit, but the art of subtlety being as foreign to the girl as the Chinese language, she wasted not a moment in steering the conversation around to her own means. 'So, my lord,' she pronounced innocently, 'we were just discussing the subject of marriage before you arrived.'

The earl cocked a surprised brow. 'Were you indeed?' he enquired, amusement lilting his tone.

'In the most general sense, of course, sir,' clarified Lavinia with some alacrity. 'It is my opinion, my lord, that the ideal age at which a gentleman should engage in marriage is not less that eight-and-twenty years. Do you agree, sir?'

The man affected a charming smile. 'I shall be exactly that age myself in two weeks' time, ma'am, and I can confirm that the subject is never far from my mind.'

'Ooh,' cooed Lavinia excitedly, 'then do you mean to say, my lord that, should you encounter the lady of your dreams, then you should be only too prepared to wed now?'

'Indeed I should, Miss Crump,' he confirmed. 'I should waste no time at all in sweeping the young lady off her feet and making her my wife.'

Lavinia flashed him her most beatific smile. 'And would it be impertinent to ask if you have any inkling if that young lady has come along yet, sir?'

A bemused smile tugged at the man's lips. 'Time will tell, Miss Crump,' he said, casting a sly glance in Wilhelmina's direction. 'Time will tell.'

Satisfied that she had her answer and that she had been quite correct in her assumptions, a delighted Lavinia spent the following thirty minutes of the man's visit in witty, animated conversation before he announced that he ought to be on his way.

'Oh, so soon, my lord,' regretted Aunt Clementine.

'Alas, I have a great deal to attend to today, ma'am,' informed the earl. 'I do hope however, that I shall have the pleasure of seeing you all at Lady Ormiston's Spring Ball this evening.'

'Oh, indeed you will, sir,' confirmed Aunt Clementine. 'Why we are all so looking forward to it.'

'Then I can assure you that you shall not be disappointed, Mrs Crump. Whitlock Castle is quite the most extraordinary place. I am sure you shall enjoy it immensely.'

'We have no doubt of that, my lord,' confirmed Lavinia, winking slyly at Wilhelmina.

The remainder of the day having consisted principally of Aunt Clementine and Lavinia analysing the earl's conversation and the intentions of his visit, Wilhelmina was only too glad when it was time to go upstairs to begin their preparations for the evening.

'Ah, Tipping,' enquired Aunt Clementine of the man, as the three of them encountered his grace's valet on the sweeping staircase. 'Do you know if his grace will be attending Lady Ormiston's Spring Ball this evening? I own he was rather vague on his plans when I spoke to him earlier today.'

'As far as I am aware, his grace will be attending, ma'am,' replied the valet, heading down the stairs carrying a pair of muddy top boots. 'Although I confess he has developed a tendency of late to change his plans at rather the last minute.'

'Goodness,' fluttered Aunt Clementine with more than a hint of anxiousness. 'Then we must hope he does not do so this evening. Now come along, Lavinia. You must look your very best for the ball. I thought perhaps your dove silk and your. . . .'

Whitlock Castle, the scene of Lady Ormiston's Spring Ball, was situated some ten miles outside of London and Wilhelmina found the journey most agreeable as the bustle and dirt of the grimy city melted into the tranquillity and fresher air of the countryside. A pleasant feeling of relaxation had just begun to envelop her, when a strong cloud of pollen from the orchards on either side of the narrow country lane along which they were trundling, wafted in through the open carriage window and tickled her nostrils. Having the sensation of quite the most enormous sneeze forming in the depths of her nose, she immediately whipped open her reticule to retrieve her lace handkerchief. It was not her handkerchief, however, which she set eyes upon as she drew open the strings of the purse: it was something altogether quite different, the startling shock of which caused her to gasp aloud. How on earth had yet another confounded note found its way into her reticule and, more to the point, who had put it there? She drew the reticule quickly shut again.

'Something wrong, my dear?' enquired Aunt Clementine concernedly, upon hearing her niece's gasp and observing the look of horror spreading across her countenance.

'Er, no, Aunt,' replied Wilhelmina, managing a feeble smile. 'I have just discovered that there is a, um, spider in my reticule.'

At this piece of information Aunt Clementine shrank back against the squabs, her eyes bulging in a most unattractive fashion whilst tiny drops of perspiration appeared on her forehead.

The news was received with no less horror by Lavinia who took a long deep inhalation and clasped a hand to her throat. 'Did you say *a spider*, Cousin?' she asked, with rather a large dose of anxiety.

Wilhelmina gave a reluctant nod, harbouring a strong feeling that whatever was to follow next was not to be at all pleasant. She was not mistaken in her assumption.

'Stop the coach at once, Jenson!' screeched Lavinia at the top of her voice.

'Wh-what?' spluttered a perplexed Wilhelmina. 'What on earth is wrong?'

'Have you forgotten Mama's dreadful aversion to spiders, Cousin?' enquired Lavinia, whipping out her own handkerchief and dabbing furiously at her mother's glistening brow. 'You must remove it from the carriage this very instant.'

With Aunt Clementine looking for all the world as if she was about to have an apoplexy, the coach drew to a shuddering standstill and Wilhelmina, not wishing to cause her aunt any further distress than she already had, wasted not a moment in hastily removing herself – and, more importantly, her reticule – from the carriage. Turning her back to the coach, she walked a little away from it and then proceeded to make a great display of emptying the silk purse of its contents before vigorously shaking out the imaginary insect. As she did so, she allowed herself the opportunity to sneak at look at the envelope. The instructions this time read:

Deliver THIS EVENING
after 11 o'clock.
Hide under the barrel in the barn at Fowler's Field.
Tell no one!

Her heart sank. She had certainly had not the slightest expectation of finding another envelope this evening and she was most definitely devoid of all desire to go exploring fields – Fowler's or otherwise – in the dead of night, on her own and attired in her silver evening gown. She chewed her bottom lip as she contemplated the situation, staring unseeingly at the envelope.

She was jolted from her thoughts by the sound of her cousin's concerned voice.

'Have you found it yet, Cousin?' enquired an anxious Lavinia hanging out of the carriage window.

At this enquiry, a strange moaning sound floated out of the conveyance.

'Wh-what?' stammered Wilhelmina, hastily pushing the letter back into her reticule before spinning around to face her cousin.

'The spider?' clarified Lavinia, a fretful look darkening her perfect features. 'Is it still in your reticule?'

'Er, no,' replied Wilhelmina, attempting to smile as she picked up her skirts, turned around and headed back to the coach. 'It scurried away quite happily once I set it free.'

'Ugh!' shuddered Aunt Clementine, her tone dripping with a combination of disgust and terror. 'Such hideous creatures. Hideous,' she declared somewhat shakily. She was slumped against the golden squabs of the carriage, holding her vinaigrette and looking deeply distressed. Wilhelmina chided herself for having momentarily forgotten her aunt's phobia and for having blurted out the first thing that had come into her head.

In an attempt to at least make some amends for her impromptu invention, she instructed Jenson to carry out a very thorough inspection of the carriage for any more unwanted visitors. With the man declaring that he could find not so much as a single hairy black leg, Aunt Clementine's concerns were allayed and the man subsequently ordered to drive on. It was some thirty silent minutes later that the party eventually arrived at their destination, Aunt

Clementine, by this time having recovered something of both her equanimity and her colouring.

Set amidst extensive grounds, Whitlock Castle was a huge, imposing building, the oldest segment of which dated back to the days of King John. Throughout the centuries, various generations of Ormistons had made attempts to leave their own distinctive mark on the property with the addition of another wing or turret or – much to Aunt Clementine's joy – gargoyle. The Earl of Thurlston had certainly not exaggerated when he had described the place as extraordinary. Indeed the eclectic result, glinting in the bright evening sunshine was, Wilhelmina concluded, so enchanting, it was almost magical.

She was also delighted to discover that the castle was no less impressive inside, housing a wealth of fascinating – and no doubt priceless – antiques, whilst the ballroom itself was the most enormous room she had ever set eyes upon, already swarming with a glittering, dazzling array of bodies, chattering and laughing gaily. When she set eyes upon Verity Drinkwater, resplendent yet again, this time in blue sarcanet, Lavinia, having not forgotten the girl's scathing comments regarding her alleged invention of the Comte de Roxford, returned Verity's dazzling smile with a dark glower, sticking out her bottom lip and folding her arms over her chest.

'Oh, my,' muttered Aunt Clementine dolefully, as they hovered at the doorway to the room, observing the proceedings. 'I fear I cannot see the Duke of Linthorpe. I do so hope this evening is not another of those instances where he has changed his mind at the last moment.'

'With a bit of luck, he may have decided to go and throw himself headlong off a cliff instead, Mama,' suggested Lavinia facetiously.

'Don't be silly, dear,' chided Aunt Clementine. 'How on earth would we be able to marry you off to him if the man were lying in a crumpled heap at the bottom of a cliff?'

Lavinia tutted irascibly. 'That, Mama, is precisely the point I am trying to make.'

Aunt Clementine, now lifting onto her tiptoes in order to gain a better view of the proceedings, chose to ignore her daughter. 'No,' she concluded with a deep sigh as she resumed her normal stance.

'The man is most definitely not here. Oh, I fear this evening has not got off to an auspicious start at all, girls.'

Wilhelmina, thinking of the task looming dauntingly ahead of her, wholeheartedly agreed with her aunt but for a completely different set of reasons.

CHAPTER 15

FOR all Lady Carlton's ball had been an undisputed impressive event, it was obvious from the effort made by Lady Ormiston, that her reputation as one of London's leading hostesses was completely warranted. For Wilhelmina, however, anxiously observing the hands of the great grandfather clock in the enormous entrance hall slowly crawl around to the allotted eleventh hour, the evening was proving not the least bit enjoyable.

Lavinia, meanwhile, appeared to have cheered up immensely due to the fact that not only was the Duke of Linthorpe absent, but so too was the Earl of Thurlston. A fact which had evidently not escaped Verity Drinkwater's notice, judging by the way in which the girl had spent most of the evening hovering expectantly at the entrance to the room.

Having the sensation of being at the castle for several days, not hours, Wilhelmina experienced a strange combination of relief and apprehension as the great clock chimed the hour of eleven – a chime which, undoubtedly because of the significance of the hour, seemed to her to appear ten times louder than all those struck previously. Slipping away whilst her aunt and Lavinia were deep in conversation with old Lady Falmouth, she made her way out of the ballroom and into the great entrance hall where, completely absorbed in her thoughts, she avoided a near collision with Mrs Harlington-Hartsworthy and her freckle-faced daughter, Octavia.

Having not the first idea where Fowler's Field was to be found, she decided that, as there were unlikely to be a great many people wandering about outside the gates of the castle at such an hour, it would be much more prudent to make her enquiries before taking her leave of the building. With this in mind, she approached the footman standing on guard at the main door and enquired of him, adopting as nonchalant a tone as she could summon, the location of her required destination. The servant in question, having a pounding headache from the barrage of requests for directions he had received throughout the evening, mostly to the withdrawing-rooms, the card tables and the supper-room, found the fact that an exceptionally attractive young lady was brazenly asking him the way to Fowler's Field, undeniably refreshing and could not help but envy the young man with whom she must have an assignation there.

Having satisfied herself that she knew exactly where she was heading, Wilhelmina thanked the man for his assistance and was a little taken aback when, as she made to take her leave, he threw her a disconcerting wink. Feeling so nervous that she could not even begin to think what he intended by such a gesture, she returned it with a slightly baffled smile, before pulling her wrap tightly around her shoulders and with her head held high, exiting the castle. The impressive long gravelled drive which she followed was lined on either side by rows of exceedingly tall yew trees. A full moon was suspended in the sky, casting long, wavering shadows across the gravel as the trees' branches moved gently in the breeze. Wilhelmina was aware that she was shivering and attributed this more to the jumble of nerves welling in her stomach, than the slight nip in the air.

Upon reaching the bottom of the drive, she turned right and began her march along the country lane which ran parallel to the castle grounds, this time delineated on both sides by thick, prickly hedgerows. Apart from the crunching of her slippers underfoot and the fierce pounding of her heart, there was not a sound to be heard – a fact which she found disconcerting, particularly given that she had just left a room full of some hundred people laughing, chatting and dancing.

In a short while, having walked approximately a quarter of a mile, she happened upon a stile – exactly as in the footman's meticulous directions – and, hoisting her skirts to her knees, managed to negotiate it with ease. She landed, on the other side, in a flat, grassy meadow. According to her directions, this should be Fowler's Field and the building in the bottom left-hand corner, which she could see quite clearly in the bright moonlight, should be the barn in which she was to deposit the note.

Keeping her skirts held high so as not to soil the hem on the damp grass, she began making her way tentatively across the field towards the barn. She was some halfway across when a large, silent owl suddenly swooped in front of her, almost brushing her face with its wide wings. Her heart froze in terror and she stood still for a moment, attempting to calm her agitated nerves with the thought that the task should be completed in a few, short, uncomplicated minutes. Holding that in the forefront of her mind, she spurred herself on towards her target.

Close up, the building appeared much larger than she had first thought. It was rectangular in shape, the large arched door being on one of its shorter sides. Having no desire at all to prolong her mission, she quickly sought out the large brass ring, which served as a handle, and made to open the door, anxious now to be inside. She pulled it. Nothing. She pushed it. Nothing. She twisted and kicked and pummelled it. Nothing. The door obstinately refused to budge a single inch. With a large surge of frustrated annoyance, she eventually, and rather reluctantly, concluded that it was well and truly locked. She took a few steps back and regarded it in the dusky light. How could it be locked? How could whoever it was who had arranged for her to be out in the middle of a field in the middle of the night, have led her to a locked barn? Ice-cold shards of panic began to spear her. What on earth was she to do now? She considered her options: one – she could push the note under the door. That, however, was not what she had been instructed to do and could mean the note might well fall into the wrong hands. Two – she could simply return to the castle, taking the note with her. But what if someone were depending upon it? Sighing, she realized that her only real choice was option three – to try to gain entry to the building and place the note under the barrel as instructed. Wondering for the umpteenth time, and with a decidedly heavy heart, how on earth she had come to be involved in such a mysterious – and undoubtedly perilous – state of affairs, she began to walk slowly around the construction, scouring the wooden walls for alternative access.

Having completed a thorough but unfruitful inspection of two sides of the building she discovered nothing to assist her in her quest, other than a wooden ladder, lying on the ground, propped up against one of the walls. All hope of accomplishing her task was deserting her when she spotted it: a hatch door in the back of the building, propped slightly ajar, some eight feet from the ground. She concluded that it was so high up it must lead directly into the hayloft. Her spirits lightening, she marched briskly back to the side of the barn, picked up the ladder and carried it around to the hatch wall. Placing it in position and having assured herself, to the best of her ability, of its safety, she then climbed it – with shaky legs.

The hatch, designed for large bales of hay, was more than wide enough for her slim frame to crawl through. Once inside, however, she found the barn darker than she had expected, with only a handful of thin strips of moonlight filtering through the gaps in the boards of the roof. To maximize the light, she propped open the flap as wide as it would go. Guardedly moving to the edge of the hayloft, she peered into the murky light below and was relieved to make out the outline of a lone barrel standing to the right of the door. Using another ladder, already in place for the purpose of accessing the loft, she made her descent to the ground floor and, upon reaching what she hoped was the designated barrel, drew the note out of her reticule.

Crouching down, she eased up the bottom of the cask a little and slipped the envelope underneath. As she did so, a large black rat, surprised at having its comfortable hiding place disturbed, darted out, brushing against her hands. She squealed in horror and leapt to her feet. Overcome with a burning urge to be out of the building that very instant, she ran to the large arched door and, using the handle on the inside frantically attempted, any way she could think of, to open it. Yet again, however, it did not yield an single inch.

With tears of panic and frustration now welling in her eyes and an icy hand of terror clutching at her heart, she turned and ran back to the ladder, mounting it awkwardly in her haste. Her relief at reaching the hayloft, though, was short-lived as three energetic bats chose that very moment to make their own departure from the building, emitting a high-pitched squeal as they swept past her head towards the open hatch. Wilhelmina let out another scream and, unable to hold back the tears a moment longer, they began streaming down her face.

She bounded over to the hatch as quickly as she could and turning around began her clumsy descent to the ground outside. In her longing to escape the field and return to the safety of the castle as quickly as possible, she caught the heel of her slipper in the hem of her gown, causing her to fall from the fifth rung and land in a heap. Not wasting a second, however, she was immediately back on her feet, sprinting with all her might across the field back to the stile, not daring for one moment to look behind her. Frantically clambering over the stile she landed on the other side and continued her running back along the hedgerowed lane towards the castle.

The sound of rattling carriage wheels behind her reached her ears but, with Mr Fitzgibbon's last words to her ringing alarmingly in her head, the noise only served to spur her on still faster. She did not even stop when she heard someone calling her name.

'For God's sake, Miss Crump,' exclaimed a man as the carriage eventually drew up alongside her. 'What on earth are you about?'

Recognizing the voice now, a stunned Wilhelmina stopped in her tracks and span around to face the caller. Through her bleary eyes, swimming with tears, she could make out the handsome face of the Earl of Thurlston, as he hung out of his carriage window.

'Good lord, Miss Crump,' he commiserated, as his eyes took in her bedraggled appearance, 'look at the state of you. Get in the carriage at once.' He threw open the door of the conveyance with great assertiveness.

Wilhelmina stared at him vacantly, aware of nothing other than the fact that she was panting wildly and that some sense of relief was beginning to flow through her veins at the realization that she was safe.

As she climbed into the carriage and seated herself opposite him, the earl surveyed her appearance with wide-eyed surprise. 'What on earth have you been doing wandering about alone?' he demanded.

Now feeling both embarrassed and awkward, Wilhelmina focused her eyes on her hands clasped in her lap, not having the first clue how to explain herself. 'I, um, went for a, er, walk, my lord, and I – that is a – er, I mean I got lost and I—'

'Got lost!' he repeated, concern shining in his eyes. 'Good lord, girl, anything could have happened to you. Why the countryside is crawling with bandits and I dare not even hazard a guess as to what they would have done with such fair prey as yourself. Have you no sense at all?'

As Wilhelmina was not feeling at all in the mood for remonstrations, the tears renewed their journey down her cheeks. 'I'm beginning to think not, my lord,' she confessed, as she despaired of her miserable situation.

'Oh, come now,' urged the earl, just as the carriage pulled up outside the castle. 'Let's get you inside and sorted out.'

'No!' exclaimed Wilhelmina, gazing at him imploringly. 'I cannot go inside like this, sir. My aunt will wish to know where I have been and I couldn't possibly tell her.'

'Well, that is perfectly understandable,' concurred the earl, 'given your irresponsible behaviour. I will have my driver deposit us at the stable block and he can arrange for some soap and water and a glass of ratafia to be brought out in order that you can compose yourself before you see your aunt.'

'I should be much obliged to you, sir,' murmured Wilhelmina gratefully.

The stable block was to be found at the back of the building and upon their arrival in the yard, the earl alighted from the carriage first, before lifting out Wilhelmina with perfect ease and depositing her on the ground.

'The unique Miss Wilhelmina Crump,' he tutted, with his arms upon her waist. 'What on earth am I to do with you?'

Wilhelmina said nothing but stared miserably at the cobbles of the stable yard.

At that very moment, a black stallion clattered into the courtyard. Startled, the two turned towards its rider. So despondent was she however, that she could do nothing more than merely blink at the Duke of Linthorpe as he observed the scene from his saddle with his usual haughty air. Let the man think what he liked, she concluded. She was, for that evening at least, completely past caring.

Lying exhausted in her bed some hours later, having abolished all hope of sleep, Wilhelmina gazed at the ceiling and found her thoughts turning once again to the Duke of Linthorpe in the room directly above. Thanks to the Earl of Thurlston's attentions she had managed to compose herself and repair her toilette before she had returned to the ballroom. Any unusual imperfections in her appearance had gone unnoticed by her aunt – who had imbibed several glasses of champagne – and by her cousin who was too busy flirting from behind her fan with a handsome young marquis. She had happened upon the duke twice more before they had left the party and each time he had regarded her as frostily as in the stable-yard. Her fury at him for not allowing her a chance to explain herself had certainly not abated but was somehow tempered, she realized with dismay, by the fact that each time she saw the man he appeared more devilishly handsome than the last.

CHAPTER 16

'GOOD lord, there's been another one,' declared Uncle Ernest from the depths of the newspaper the following morning.

'What's that, dear?' enquired Aunt Clementine, helping herself to a generous portion of eggs from the silver chafing dish on the sideboard.

'A second kidnapping,' clarified Uncle Ernest. 'Baroness Ormington's gone missing now. Note says if the family don't do as they're told, she'll be a good two foot shorter when they see her next.'

'Baroness Ormington?' echoed Lavinia, wrinkling her brow. 'Is she the tall, slim lady we were introduced to at Lady Pontington's musical soirée, Mama?'

'With the blonde hair dressed *à la Tite*,' confirmed Aunt Clementine. 'Why the woman is elegance itself. Indeed the regal way in which she carries herself has been compared to none other than the Queen of France.'

'Well, she won't be walking elegantly for much longer, unless her family pays up,' affirmed Uncle Ernest from behind his paper. 'Shocking business if ever I heard any.'

'My,' tutted Aunt Clementine, as she turned from the sideboard and made her way to the table, 'if I am not mistaken, Mr Crump, I do believe London is becoming one of the most dangerous cities on earth. Do you not agree, your grace?'

'Oh, wholeheartedly, Mrs Crump,' concurred the duke, glancing up at his hostess from the slice of toast he had been buttering. 'And I cannot deny that it is partly for that reason that I have decided I no longer need to impose on your generous hospitality. I have decided to take my leave of London within the next few days.'

A horrified Aunt Clementine stumbled against her chair, a look of panic spreading over her round, powdered features.

'Oh, but I can assure you there is absolutely no need, your grace,' she asserted in a wavering voice.

The duke reached for the crystal pot containing the coveted strawberry jam and began smearing a thick layer over the melting butter of his toast. 'Your hospitality has been invaluable, ma'am,' he informed genially, 'however the house in Bourdon Street has been in dire need of some serious renovation for quite some time. I therefore thought it sensible to take advantage of the situation and carry out the work at the same time as the redecoration. In the meantime, once I have put in place all the necessary arrangements, I intend to withdraw from the city and take up residence at Linthorpe Hall – my family seat in Kent.'

Aunt Clementine's face fell before she declared, with the utmost of sincerity, 'But I assure you it has not been the slightest imposition, your grace. Indeed it has been a positive pleasure having you here. We have so enjoyed your company, have we not Mr Crump? Girls?'

Whilst a strange grunting sound could be heard from the area of the newspaper, Lavinia appeared to be absorbed in the unabsorbing task of stirring a spoonful of sugar into her cup of tea. Wilhelmina, meanwhile, was experiencing a strange and worrying medley of emotions ranging from utter relief that she would not be forced to face the man every day, to something which, despite herself, she could only identify as disappointment. As his cold eyes briefly met hers, an equally strange shiver flashed down her spine. She was grateful, but even more confused, when he eventually broke the gaze and turned his attention back to his flustered hostess.

'I cannot thank you enough for your hospitality, Mrs Crump,' he said in the most courteous of tones. 'I only hope you will allow me to repay you in some way.'

At these words, Wilhelmina detected the unmistakable signs of a plan beginning to formulate in Aunt Clementine's quick mind.

'Oh, but we couldn't possibly, sir,' declared the older woman, a flush of excitement beginning to steal over her face and neck. 'Although I must admit it would be rather refreshing. As I recall you yourself saying, your grace, it can be quite stifling here in London.'

'Indeed it can, ma'am,' concurred the duke, looking somewhat baffled as to the direction in which the conversation was now being steered.

'Very well then,' declared Aunt Clementine victoriously, beaming at her fellow breakfasters. 'That is settled. We accept your kind offer, your grace, and should be most delighted to join you at Linthorpe Hall.'

At this announcement, a number of unforeseen events occurred: the duke's thickly smeared slice of toast, which had been *en route* to his mouth, tumbled to the floor; Lavinia's teacup clattered noisily onto its saucer, tipping a large quantity of brown liquid onto the lace tablecloth; and the sound being emitted from behind the newspaper was now akin to someone choking. Choosing brazenly to ignore all of this activity, Aunt Clementine ploughed on undeterred, setting down her knife and fork with great purpose.

'We shall set to packing immediately. Come now, girls,' she commanded in a brisk, businesslike tone, wiping her hands on her napkin. 'We have much to do if we are to be on the road today.'

Rather than rallying to attention however, the command was met by an array of four astounded faces, including Uncle Ernest's. He had now stopped choking and, having lowered the newspaper, was staring, open-mouthed at his wife in utter amazement.

'Mouth, Mr Crump,' instructed Aunt Clementine briskly.

Her husband snapped it shut.

The look on Lavinia's face, meanwhile, could only be described as horror.

'I cannot possibly go, Mama,' she protested with a toss of her head. 'Why, how on earth is the Comte de Roxford expected to find me if I am stuck out in the middle of nowhere?'

'It is not in the middle of nowhere, dear,' pointed out Aunt Clementine matter of factly. 'It is in Kent.'

'Well it might as well be ... be ...somewhere quite foreign, Mama. Indeed it might as well be ... *Scotland* as far as I am concerned,' she declared with more than a hint of panic. 'The point is I shall be away from London and away from absolutely anyone of any consequence.'

'Ahem,' coughed Aunt Clementine, indicating her head towards the duke. 'I think you are forgetting, my dear, that we are to be the guests of the Duke of Linthorpe.'

'My point exactly,' confirmed Lavinia with a pout.

A similar feeling of dread was also affecting Wilhelmina as she realized that if she too disappeared off to Kent, then she would most likely forego the opportunity to solve the mystery in which she had become unwittingly embroiled.

'I'm afraid I can't go either, Aunt,' she blurted out. 'I really need to stay here.'

'Whatever for, my dear?' enquired Aunt Clementine, failing to keep the lilt of irritation out of her voice. 'Why, if I do recall, you had no wish to come to London in the first place. I'm sure you shall enjoy it much more in the countryside, Wilhelmina dear.'

'But I shan't, Aunt,' countered Wilhelmina. 'I have, er, things to do here. Important things.'

'Don't be silly, child,' remonstrated Aunt Clementine, rising from the table. 'What on earth can you have to do that is so important? Now, we are going to accept his lordship's exceedingly kind invitation with the good grace it deserves. I will not hear another word on the matter, girls. We are going to Linthorpe Hall.'

At a loss as to what to do or say next, Wilhelmina looked despairingly around the table. The duke was regarding her through narrowed, suspicious eyes and had, she concluded with yet more indignation, no doubt formed his own opinion that her 'important things to do' involved romping with the Earl of Thurlston. Well, she had had just about enough of the Duke of Linthorpe jumping to the wrong conclusion. At that moment she could quite happily have slapped the accusatory sneer from the man's smug, but incredibly handsome, face.

Despite the duke informing Aunt Clementine that he was required to remain in London for several more days to attend to some urgent business matters, that woman, obviously allowing him no opportunity at all to change his mind regarding his 'invitation', wasted not a moment in organizing the packing of their belongings. It was while this process was underway that the Earl of Thurlston appeared on the doorstep, calling, he informed Wilhelmina, as he met her in the hallway, to enquire as to her welfare given the state in which he had found her the previous evening.

'What on earth is going on, Miss Crump?' he asked, squeezing against the wall to allow a footman bearing a large pile of band-boxes to pass.

'We are to remove to Linthorpe Hall, sir,' explained Wilhelmina, grateful at least that their move would mean she should be rid of the man's unwanted attentions.

A tide of disappointment washed over the earl's face. 'To Linthorpe Hall?' he repeated. 'But whatever for?'

'I have no idea, sir,' admitted Wilhelmina truthfully, 'other than that my aunt seems to think it an exceedingly good idea.'

He observed her strangely for a few seconds, obviously mulling over this unexpected news, before concluding, 'Well, I must confess I am somewhat disappointed to hear of you leaving London, ma'am. However, Linthorpe is not too far from here. If I have your permission, I should be delighted to visit you there.'

'No. Please don't,' spluttered Wilhelmina hastily. 'That is, I mean, er, there is really no need, sir.'

'Oh, but there is, Miss Wilhelmina Crump,' he contradicted gravely. 'There is a very great need indeed.'

'Oh, is this not splendid?' declared Aunt Clementine as the four Crumps, seated in their carriage, made their way out of the city and into the lush Kent countryside. 'We – the Crumps of Chipping Sodbury – are on our way to stay at Linthorpe Hall. Goodness only knows what Venetia Drinkwater will make of it when she receives my note informing her of our invitation. I believe she will be so jealous, she will most likely take to her bed for the remainder of the Season.'

'Not long enough by half,' muttered Uncle Ernest through his whiskers.

Lavinia, however, made no attempt to hide the fact that she was not at all impressed by the impromptu upheaval. 'I have told you, Mama,' she argued, 'that the duke did not invite us. He was as surprised as the rest of us when you announced your intentions.'

'Don't be ridiculous, Lavinia,' countered Aunt Clementine stoutly. 'Of course the duke invited us. He did not do so directly, I grant you, but that is simply as a result of him being far too polite to put us on the spot. Such a gentleman and forty thousand a year into the bargain, Mr Crump.'

'Hmm,' mused Uncle Ernest, stroking his bearded chin. 'A decent sum by any standards, Mrs Crump.'

'Indeed it is, Mr Crump,' agreed Aunt Clementine. 'And you will do well not to forget that fact, Lavinia dear.'

'How many times do I have to tell you, Mama,' reiterated Lavinia, 'that I have absolutely no interest in the Duke of Linthorpe. The Comte de Roxford is much more handsome and I'm sure has an income just as grand as the duke's. But how on earth the man is to find me when you have dragged me away from London, is beyond comprehension.'

Aunt Clementine regarded her levelly. 'It is not that I am dismissing the comte out of hand, Lavinia dear,' she said. 'After all, a man of such station is certainly not to be sniffed at. However, you should remember that little saying, my dear, regarding eggs and baskets. You would do as well to try and be a little more charming to the duke just in case the comte does not appear in London.'

'Well, as I am now not to be found in London myself, it signifies little whether the man turns up there or not,' pointed out Lavinia petulantly. 'Except, of course, if he falls in love with Verity Drinkwater and then I shall have no choice other than to kill myself.'

'If you say so, dear,' murmured Aunt Clementine.

Had it not been for her concerns regarding The Stag and the messages, Wilhelmina would have been exceedingly grateful to be leaving behind the incessant social whirl of London, the bickering with the Drinkwaters and the unwanted attentions of the Earl of Thurlston. Indeed she had been pondering long and hard on the earl's comments earlier that day regarding there being a very great need to see her. It had not escaped her attention that whenever she was involved in a message delivery, the Earl of Thurlston was never far away. In addition, she was acutely aware that there was something odd about the man that she could not quite put her finger on. Could he somehow be involved in this mystery? She sat chewing her nails in the carriage, wondering what on earth was to happen next.

Linthorpe Hall

The journey to Linthorpe Hall took some two hours longer than expected due to a number of unforeseen factors including, firstly, an unruly herd of cows crossing the road and secondly, an event infinitely more desperate than that of the spider incident, when a wasp took it upon itself to explore the inside of Aunt Clementine's hooped skirts. When they arrived at their destination just as daylight was beginning to wane, no one was in the best of spirits.

Although Wilhelmina had been expecting an imposing building, Linthorpe Hall surpassed all her previous expectations. Built of warm, golden sandstone, not only was the house some four times larger than she had imagined but it was quite the most magnificent example of architecture she had ever set eyes upon. Being perfectly symmetrical in shape, the centrepiece was a huge porticoed entrance supported by eight large, ornate pillars. This was flanked on either side by a three-storey wing, containing at least twenty large windows behind which were undoubtedly hidden an enormous number of rooms.

Much to Aunt Clementine's delight, the butler informed her that the duke had forwarded instructions to his staff that they were to do everything within their power to make the guests feel at home. Interpreting this as an invitation to roam freely around the building, Aunt Clementine subsequently examined seven different bed chambers before agreeing with the stern-looking housekeeper that the one the woman had originally chosen for her was perhaps the most suitable after all.

Wilhelmina could find no fault with her own room, which was spacious, comfortable and lavishly furnished. Despite the comfort of her exquisitely carved four-poster bed, however, her first night at the hall was passed in yet another fitful, anxious night's sleep, the result of which was her being able to manage only a few unenthusiastic grunts in response to Aunt Clementine's incessant chatter at breakfast the following morning.

Most of this chatter concerned the reporting in *The Times* that a third beautiful, blonde female aristocrat, had been kidnapped in London and that another gory threat had been issued. The paper reported that the whole of London Society was now living in increasing fear of the kidnapper, with several members of the *haut ton* being so terrified, they were even considering such drastic, self-sacrificing moves as giving up the Season and retiring to their country estates.

CHAPTER 17

DESPITE the indisputably comfortable surroundings of Linthorpe Hall, its tranquil setting, and the fact that its intimidating master was absent, Wilhelmina found herself decidedly on edge and unable to concentrate on anything at all over the following few days. She was only grateful that her restless, fidgety behaviour passed by unobserved by her relatives, all of whom were busily indulging in their own diverse activities: Aunt Clementine continued to snoop around the hall; Uncle Ernest calculated the amount of money required for the upkeep of the hall; and Lavinia in a deeply entrenched fit of the sullens at having had to come within a twenty-five mile radius of the hall.

After three days of such diversions, they were informed by the butler at breakfast, that his grace had sent word to say that he would be taking up residence himself that day and that he should arrive at Linthorpe in time to take dinner with his guests. This news had the effect of sending Aunt Clementine into a fit of the raptures, Lavinia into an even darker depression and Wilhelmina into a worse state of nervous agitation.

The duke arrived a little before dinner and was already in the small drawing-room where they were to take aperitifs, when the Crumps entered *en masse*. They found him standing by the fire, one booted foot resting on the brass fender, staring intently at the mantelpiece. He turned to greet them with his usual faultless manners as they entered, but not before Wilhelmina had noticed the anxious, worried expression on his face. He also looked exceedingly tired, with dark shadows under his eyes. Despite this, however, Wilhelmina was loath to admit that the duke, dressed in brown velvet, was still the most infuriatingly attractive man she had ever seen.

'So,' he began, once they had exchanged greetings and accepted a drink from the liveried footman – ratafia for the ladies and claret for the gentlemen, 'what do you all make of Linthorpe Hall?'

'Oh, it is all that is delightful, sir,' enthused an animated Aunt Clementine. 'Why Lavinia was just saying to me this morning how she thinks it most likely to be one of the grandest houses in the whole of England.'

'Was she indeed?' replied a doubtful duke, as Lavinia looked crossly at her mother. 'Can I take it then that the house meets with your approval, Miss Crump?'

Lavinia shrugged her shoulders. 'I suppose so,' she responded haughtily, 'however, are you aware, sir that the chateaux in France are much larger than the houses here in England. The Comte de Roxford owns an exceedingly large chateau.'

'Does he now?' said the duke, amusement tugging at the corners of his mouth.

Lavinia met his gaze defiantly. 'Yes, he does, sir. I do believe it is three times the size of Linthorpe.'

The duke gave a strange snort.

'Do you have something stuck in your throat, sir?' enquired Lavinia.

'I do believe I do,' he spluttered, making a show of thumping his chest.

'Of course, we should clear up the confusion, your grace,' pointed out Aunt Clementine with alacrity, 'that Lavinia is not actually *betrothed* to the Comte de Roxford.'

Lavinia shot her mother a reprimanding glare. 'Not *yet*, Mama,' she pointed out defensively.

'Yes well, "not yet" means that you are *not yet* betrothed, my dear,' insisted Aunt Clementine. 'Which is exactly the point I am making.'

'But I soon shall be betrothed, Mama,' insisted Lavinia.

'We do so hope so, my dear,' acquiesced Aunt Clementine, throwing the duke a conspiratorial smile.

Correctly interpreting the older woman's intentions, the duke then made another strange sound as he choked again – this time on his glass of claret. Wilhelmina, with whom he had exchanged only the curtest of greetings, before going on to ignore her all evening, could not help but derive some pleasure from the sight.

With her uncle and the duke enjoying their after-dinner brandies, and her aunt and Lavinia engaging in a game of piquet in one of the many drawing-rooms, Wilhelmina wandered out into the gardens to breathe some evening air. The grounds of the estate were extensive, stretching as far as the eye could see and during the three days of her sojourn so far, she had already explored a great deal on foot. By far her favourite spot was the orchard, situated at the back of the house and crammed with a plethora of fruit trees, their branches currently weighted down with heavy, lacy mounds of sweet-smelling pink and white blossom. Sitting on an old stone bench there, she looked back at the house and started slightly as she became aware of a lone face at one of the upper floor windows. She recognized the figure immediately as the red-haired woman who had been locked in the duke's cabin on the ship during their journey over from France. She appeared no happier than she had done then, as she stared forlornly out into the grounds. Wilhelmina sprang to her feet and began running towards the house waving frantically to try to catch the woman's eye. She succeeded but, rather than her attentions being welcomed, was dismayed to see a horrified expression fall over the woman's countenance before she shrank back into the shadows of the room.

'Well, I'll be blowed,' declared Uncle Ernest from behind *The Times* the next morning.

'Not *another* kidnapping, my dear?' enquired Aunt Clementine, bustling over to the table with a plate of ham.

'Only taken the ransom money from all three and now refusing to hand over the hostages,' informed Uncle Ernest, shaking his head despairingly. 'Threatening to kill them all now if they don't pay up again.'

'No!' gasped Aunt Clementine, shuddering as she lowered her plump frame into one of the Chippendale chairs. 'Why, is that not the very height of impudence, Mr Crump?'

'Oh, when may we return to London, Mama?' enquired Lavinia

innocently. 'We have been here for quite some days now and we do not, after all, wish to impose on his grace for too long,' she added, flashing the duke a sardonic smile.

'My dear, we have been here less than a week and regardless of the length of our stay, we cannot possibly return to London until all this kidnapping business is resolved,' declared Aunt Clementine. 'Why I'm sure his grace would not hear of us leaving for the city when there is quite obviously a veritable monster on the loose.'

'No, indeed,' confirmed the duke. 'You are welcome to stay as long as you like, ma'am.'

'Oh my,' fluttered Aunt Clementine, obviously – from the hint of colour which rose in her cheeks – deeply flattered at the open invitation. 'You are all that is kindness, sir. Is he not Lavinia, dear?'

'Generosity itself, Mama,' concurred Lavinia, glaring at her host.

The duke returned this comment with the most winsome of smiles, which, from the dark glower cast his way, evidently served to infuriate Lavinia even more.

Wilhelmina's agitated state had not been eased in the least by the sighting of the red-haired woman at the window. Indeed she had scarce been able to push the thought of her out of her mind since the incident. Who was she? What was she doing at Linthorpe? And why did she appear so upset? Wilhelmina had spent every spare moment trawling the extensive house and sitting for hours on the same bench, in an attempt to see her again. So far, however, there had been not a solitary sign of the woman. She had also endeavoured to make some discreet enquiries of the staff but this form of investigation had also met a dead end, with all the servants she questioned informing her that there was no one, other than the Crump party and his grace, currently in residence. She therefore had not one single, solitary clue as to the identity or whereabouts of the elusive female.

It was while the ladies enjoyed afternoon tea on the terrace at the back of the house that afternoon, that the butler appeared to inform them they had a visitor in the shape of the Earl of Thurlston.

'Oh, how simply splendid of you to come all this way to visit us, my lord,' gushed a beaming Aunt Clementine.

The earl bestowed on her a gracious bow. 'I simply could not rest, ma'am,' he informed her, 'until I had assured myself that you were all comfortably settled at Linthorpe.'

Aunt Clementine giggled girlishly. 'Oh, we could not fail to be, sir. We are having quite the most marvellous time, are we not, girls?'

'I own that you are, Mama,' concurred Lavinia with unconstrained frankness. 'I, on the other hand, am finding it the very height of tedium here and cannot wait to return to London. Are you aware, my lord, that there is absolutely nothing at all to do in the country other than go for yet another wretched walk?'

'Good lord, girl,' contradicted Aunt Clementine, 'there are a million and one things to do here. Why do you not suggest a ride around the estate with the duke, my dear? That should prove a most pleasant distraction.'

'Because, quite frankly, Mama, I should rather remove every one of my own toenails with a rusty old nail than be alone with that man. I am, as you may be aware, my lord, almost betrothed to a French comte.'

'So I believe you may have mentioned,' muttered the earl.

'Yes, well, that is all very well, my dear,' pointed out Aunt Clementine bluntly, 'but eggs and baskets, my girl. Do you not agree, my lord?'

'Oh absolutely, ma'am,' concurred the earl, looking as though he had not the first idea what she was talking about.

Aunt Clementine leaned towards him. 'Now do tell me, sir,' she enquired, feigning beatific innocence, 'if you have seen anything of our most cherished friends, the Drinkwaters, since we left London.'

Wilhelmina noticed a smile tugging at the man's lips. 'Indeed I have, Mrs Crump,' he told her. 'The lovely Verity and her mother were in attendance at Ranelagh Gardens yesterday evening.'

'And did you perchance happen to inform them of your intention to visit with us?' asked Aunt Clementine making an attempt at nonchalance.

'That I did, ma'am. Although I must confess the information did not appear to go down particularly well. In fact, if I am not mistaken, I would go so far as to say that both ladies looked a little irked.' The self-satisfied manner in which this information was relayed did not escape Wilhelmina.

It did not, however, affect Aunt Clementine's reaction to the news in the least. 'Oh, what a pity,' she pronounced looking, for all her sympathetic declaration, that it was quite the best piece of news she had heard all year. 'I have of course, written and invited them to visit with us but as yet, I fear, I have not received a reply. Of course I attribute such reluctance to timidity, my lord, for I do not suppose for one moment that poor Venetia Drinkwater has ever set foot inside a house as grand as Linthorpe. Those that are not used to dealing with the Quality can sometimes be in awe of such surroundings, do you not agree, sir?'

'Oh, wholeheartedly, ma'am,' agreed the earl earnestly.

'Of course, I have heard,' informed Aunt Clementine, with a hint of derision, 'that the Harlington-Hartsworthys own a house almost as large as Linthorpe, but I fear that is little consolation for such a dreadful affliction of the freckles.'

Wilhelmina noticed an affronted look settle momentarily over the earl's handsome features.

Obviously not sensing anything at all untoward, however, Aunt Clementine blithely carried on with a sudden change of subject. 'Now do tell us, sir, what you make of this dreadful kidnapping business. I expect it is quite the talk of London.'

'That it is, ma'am,' he confirmed, quickly regaining his composure. 'In fact it has caused such a to-do, that certain ladies are considering quite drastic measures: I have heard that both Lady Pits-Bull and Lady Bountisford are considering cutting short the Season and retiring to the country.'

Aunt Clementine shuddered as though this was quite the worst news the earl could possibly have given. 'I am only relieved,' she sighed dramatically, 'that the Duke of Linthorpe was so insistent we join him in the country, for I own I should not have had a moment's peace with such atrocities going on around me. The afflictions we upper-class people are forced to endure are quite beyond contemplation at times.'

'Quite beyond it, ma'am,' agreed the earl, with deadly earnest.

'Well, I imagine when I am a member of the French aristocracy, I shall have a great deal more of such matters to contend with,' announced Lavinia. 'The jealousy of those dreadful peasants for one thing. Why I shudder to think of the manner in which they are treating their poor queen.'

'It certainly does appear that they are kicking up quite a fuss over there, ma'am,' concurred the earl.

'What the world is coming to, I really do not know,' sighed Aunt Clementine despondently. 'Why, in my day people knew their place and everyone made sure they stayed in it.'

The earl nodded his head in solemn agreement.

'I see you have had a visitor, ma'am,' observed the Duke of Linthorpe, returning from his estate inspection as the earl's carriage rattled off down the drive.

'The Earl of Thurlston, my lord,' declared Aunt Clementine cheerfully. 'The poor man could not rest until he had seen we were properly settled. Is he not all that is consideration?'

'Is he not indeed,' remarked the duke coolly, tossing Wilhelmina a frosty glare.

Now confident in her knowledge that the Duke of Linthorpe was not the paragon of virtue he would have them all believe, she returned the look with an equal dose of animosity.

Having dwelt on what had now, in her mind, evolved into the great matter of *that look* for the following two hours, Wilhelmina had succeeded in raising herself to the point of seething with the duke by the time she returned to her room later that afternoon. Her anger soon turned to disbelief, however, when she discovered yet another note awaiting her – lying directly on top of her blue velvet jewel-box on the dressing-table. A shiver of uneasiness coursed through her entire body. How on earth did the deliverer of the messages know she was here?

The answer could only be that someone was watching her and that thought made her feel extremely anxious and more than a little terrified. Turning her attention to the note, she read the instructions:

> *Deliver to Buttercup Meadow at 3 p.m. tomorrow.*
> *Place in the bucket of the well there.*
> *Tell no one!*

At least that sounded relatively innocuous, she thought with a despondent sigh. Surely nothing could go wrong with this delivery?

CHAPTER 18

A LITTLE before three o'clock the following afternoon, having informed the butler that she was going for a ride, Wilhelmina had one of the grooms saddle up a dapple-grey mare and made her way down the long gravelled drive of the hall, after having first obtained directions from the man and assuring him that she was accustomed to riding without a groom. Although she had not the slightest inclination to carry out yet another delivery, she reluctantly acknowledged that both the weather and her surroundings could not have been more perfect for the occasion: the brilliant blue of the sky flecked with thin wisps of fleecy white cloud, while on the ground, she was surrounded by rich, glorious evidence of a typical English spring – from the abundance of wild flowers of every imaginable colour peeping from the thick green hedgerows, to the tiny lambs frolicking playfully in the bright warm sunshine. Had the purpose of her outing been of a more pleasurable nature rather than one which caused yet another bundle of nerves to well inside her, she believed she would have passed a most enjoyable afternoon.

Some fifteen minutes later, she arrived at her unmistakable destination which, from the myriad of gleaming golden buttercups bobbing merrily in the light breeze, could not have been more aptly named. The meadow was bordered on three sides by other fields, each separated from its neighbour by a low stone wall. At the bottom could be seen a small area of woodland whilst the well, complete with its wooden bucket, was located in the top right-hand corner, sitting just outside the dilapidated walls of a small abandoned cottage.

Having assured herself that there was no one else in sight,

Wilhelmina did as her instructions bade and placed the note in the bucket. Relieved that this task at least, had been completed without the least bit of fuss, she was just about to wheel her horse around and return to Linthorpe Hall when an outrageous thought occurred to her: she was tired of carrying out all these instructions without having the slightest reason why; she was tired of lying awake every night attempting to solve the mystery; and she was tired of people tracking her whereabouts when she herself had not the first clue as to who else was involved in the coil. Surely now she deserved some answers. With that thought in mind, she kicked the horse on, not in the direction of Linthorpe, but towards the area of woodland at the bottom of the meadow.

Having located a shaded spot, which afforded an excellent view of the entire meadow and the well, she dismounted and tethered the animal to the low branch of an imposing oak. She then settled herself on a tree stump, perfectly made for the occasion and, filled with trepidation and a persistent niggling concern that she could be placing herself in a great deal of danger, began her observation.

Rather than a series of heart-stopping, exciting events occurring, however, after what seemed like an eternity but in reality was little more than an hour and twenty minutes, there had been nothing of any note at all to report other than her receiving two bites on the ankle from curious ants and being pestered to the point of infuriation by one annoying, persistent fly which seemed intent on exploring the inside of her right nostril. She was on the verge of pondering whether or not to give up on her watch and return to the hall, when an agonizing scream pierced the air behind her.

Springing immediately to her feet, she picked up her skirts and headed towards the sound, which had now changed to a low, worrying moan. Having not the first idea what she was about to encounter, she gasped loudly when she came upon a young woman – not much older than herself – rolling amongst the moss and bark of the forest floor, doubled up in obvious agony. Standing watching her were two angelic little boys whose ages she would guess at as being around two and three. Clinging onto each other's hands, they were regarding the woman with wide blue eyes, looking utterly terrified.

'Oh, my goodness!' exclaimed Wilhelmina, running to the woman as fast as she could. 'What on earth has happened?'

The girl was clutching her stomach and as Wilhelmina knelt down to her, she felt her own eyes widen as she noticed the large swollen belly.

'Is it the baby?' she gasped.

The girl gazed up at her with eyes as wide and blue as those of the two little boys, only hers were swimming with tears and filled with a pleading for help which tore at Wilhelmina's heart. Obviously racked with pain, the girl could only manage a brief nod of her head.

Wilhelmina gulped. She was going to have to help the woman but, not surprisingly, she had no experience of such things. Common sense, she decided stoically, was what was needed, beginning with making the poor girl as comfortable as possible. She looked hastily about for something she could use as a pillow. It being such a warm day she had felt no need of a jacket and was wearing only a thin cotton blouse over her chemise. Well, she resolved, if she had no jacket, then the blouse would have to do. She quickly removed the garment and placed it gently under the girl's head. Observing the scene, the smallest little boy began to sob silently, large plump tears rolling down his rosy cheeks.

'Come now,' urged Wilhelmina, with what she hoped was a reassuring smile as she crouched down to both boys and gently took hold of their free hands. 'There is no need to cry. Your mama is going to have a lovely new baby. Now, won't that be fine?'

The boys both nodded their little blond heads.

'Well,' she declared, leading them a little way from their mother to where there was a large patch of daisies. 'I expect the new baby will be expecting a present when they arrive and I know for a certain fact that there is nothing they like more than daisy chains. Do you think you could make a chain for the new baby?'

Gazing up at her, they nodded their heads again.

'And I'm sure the baby will think themselves very lucky to have two such lovely older brothers,' she declared, as they both flopped down onto the grass and began, in an anxious effort to create the most favourable of impressions on their new sibling, an energetic gathering of daisies.

With the two boys thus distracted, Wilhelmina returned to the young woman who was still writhing on the ground, sweating profusely. She chided herself for not having remembered the water bottle she had brought with her sooner. Wasting not another second, she ran quickly to her horse and took the bottle from her saddle-bag. With Wilhelmina holding it to her lips, the girl took a long, grateful drink. Wilhelmina then used some of the remaining water to wet her handkerchief and gently dab at the girl's forehead. Whilst engaging in all this activity, she found herself muttering a series of soothing inanities which, she hoped desperately, completely concealed the fact that she had not the first idea what to do next.

She was attempting to quash her rising panic when she became aware of an approaching horse. Turning her head, she started with surprise as she saw that it was the Duke of Linthorpe, winding his way through the trees on his stallion.

'Miss Crump?' he called to her, as he approached. 'What on earth are you doing here?'

Before Wilhelmina had a chance to reply, he arrived at the unlikely scene and, drawing his horse to a halt alongside her, peered down open-mouthed at the writhing girl.

'Oh my!' he exclaimed, his eyes growing wide in his head.

'Oh my indeed, sir,' retorted Wilhelmina briskly. Whilst experiencing no compulsion at all even to speak to the man, let alone be pleasant to him, she was not stubborn enough, nor selfish enough, to waste the invaluable opportunity of his help. 'May I suggest that rather than standing there gawping, sir,' she instructed, 'you make yourself of some use. Go immediately to the village, seek out the midwife and bring her back here as fast as you can – I have a feeling we do not have much time.'

The woman at that point emitted a long deep moan, which seemed to throw the duke into even further turmoil. He looked aghast at Wilhelmina who was not about to give him the slightest hint that she was just as terrified as he so obviously was.

'Well, are you going to fetch help or are you just going to sit there?' she enquired truculently.

The duke gulped, nodded and in a flash had turned the horse around and was gone. Wilhelmina prayed that he had not arrived too late.

He had.

Less than half an hour later, Wilhelmina stared in awe at the tiny, bawling baby girl, the picture of robust health, wrapped in one of her white lace-trimmed petticoats. The exhausted mother, holding the babe in her arms, gazed gratefully up at Wilhelmina.

'I can't thank you enough, miss,' she said, tears streaming down her face. 'I don't know what I would have done if you hadn't been here.'

'I did nothing,' replied Wilhelmina, kneeling at the girl's side and stroking the baby's tiny velvety hand. 'It was you who did all the hard work, Cissy.'

'I'm gonna call her after you, miss,' pronounced the girl proudly.

'Oh, but I wouldn't wish you to, Cissy,' protested Wilhelmina. 'Mine is not, after all, the most fetching of names.'

The girl broke out into a diffident smile. 'I think it's the nicest name in the world, miss.'

Just at that moment, they both turned towards the approaching Duke of Linthorpe, returning with a thin middle-aged midwife seated in the saddle before him.

'Good God,' he declared in unabashed amazement as he took in the scene before him: Wilhelmina, half dressed, standing in her chemise, her long blonde hair strewn loosely around her shoulders; the glowing face of the young mother; the two little boys, each with a daisy chain around his neck; and the bawling rosy-cheeked baby girl, wrapped in a lace petticoat.

'Good God indeed, sir,' remarked Wilhelmina, before she and Cissy broke out into a nervous fit of the giggles, joined shortly by the two boys, the midwife and, eventually, the duke himself.

The news of baby Wilhelmina Woodstock and Wilhelmina's own part in the drama, caused great excitement back at Linthorpe Hall. With the new mother and baby safely ensconced back at their little farmer's cottage, Aunt Clementine had, with the duke's willing permission, delivered them a mountain of blankets, two enormous baskets of food and a promise to visit every day of her stay, much to the amazement of Mr Thomas Woodstock, a very amiable young man with hair as blond as that of his two sons, and who appeared both delighted and dumfounded by all the attention the birth of his new daughter was creating.

The Duke of Linthorpe had appeared only slightly less dazed at the results of the afternoon than Mr Woodstock himself. He had said very little for the remainder of the day and Wilhelmina had caught him looking at her strangely on at least four occasions. Each time she had done so, he had averted his eyes rather guiltily while her heart had insisted upon skipping an annoying beat.

It wasn't until she was lying in bed that night, having recited the tale of the drama innumerable times throughout the afternoon and evening, that Wilhelmina remembered the note and her intentions to spy on its collector. With all the excitement of Cissy and the baby, the whole matter had completely slipped her mind. Now that it had returned, however, it was accompanied by a niggling suspicion regarding the Duke of Linthorpe's presence in the wood and his subsequent behaviour towards her – had he been on his way to collect the note?

CHAPTER 19

'LOOK what I have, Mama,' declared a delighted Lavinia the following afternoon as she held out a tiny white and golden puppy. 'Is she not all that is adorable?'

'Well, she is very pretty I am sure, my dear,' replied Aunt Clementine, tickling the little creature under the chin. 'However, I do think you had better first ask the permission of the duke if you are to keep her here.'

'I already have, Mama,' pronounced Lavinia triumphantly. 'We saw him on our way back to the hall, did we not, Mr Dartford?'

A very good-looking young man with high chiselled cheekbones and a head of thick black curls dressed in the uniform of the clergy stepped forward and bowed to the older woman.

'Indeed we did, ma'am,' he affirmed with a disarming smile, 'and his grace was good enough to agree that Miss Crump may keep the puppy here.'

'Did he now?' simpered Aunt Clementine.

'Well, it should not have signified in the least had he said otherwise,' confessed Lavinia. 'She is so adorable that I should have kept her anyway, even if that odious man had made me sleep in the stables with her.'

'Well,' puffed Aunt Clementine, her voice lilting with relief, 'thank goodness it hasn't come to *that*. But where on earth did you find her, dear?'

'She ran directly out of the church just as I was passing by, Mama. I do believe it was fate itself bringing us together.'

'If I can explain, ma'am,' cut in the rector, 'I found the dog's mother, with pup, and quite obviously abandoned, several weeks ago. She was in an exceedingly poor state of health. I have been caring for her at the rectory ever since but when she gave birth to five puppies, I'm afraid I didn't have room for them all. I'm glad to say that I have managed to find good homes for all of them – now,' he informed, beaming gratefully at Lavinia.

Lavinia giggled as the puppy playfully nuzzled her neck. 'Oh, but you must come to visit her, Rector,' she insisted. 'You are, after all, her guardian angel.'

The rector grinned broadly. 'Nothing should please me more, Miss Crump. Meanwhile however, I shall leave you to think of a name for her.'

'I shall give it a great deal of thought, sir,' informed Lavinia earnestly.

'And I shall very much look forward to hearing the outcome of those thoughts,' replied the rector with another delighted smile.

The two stood beaming at each other for another good minute or so before he took his leave of the group.

'Oh,' sighed Aunt Clementine, pressing a hand to her chest. 'Is that not the most kindest thing you ever heard, girls: the Duke of Linthorpe allowing Lavinia to keep her puppy. Why, one cannot help but be encouraged by such selfless gestures.'

Rather than jumping immediately down the woman's throat at such an inference, much to the amazement of her mother and cousin, Lavinia, with the puppy now contentedly dozing on her shoulder, merely smiled serenely before whisking around, breezing up the steps and disappearing into the house.

Having taken yet another fruitless turn about the gardens following dinner that evening, Wilhelmina retired to her bedchamber just as night was falling. Lying wide-awake, gazing at the ceiling, she realized that she could not remember a time when she had last had a decent night's sleep. Tonight was proving to be no exception as she glanced at the clock and saw that it was a little after two. All at once, her thoughts were interrupted by the sound of a horse thundering down the drive. She bounced out of bed and sprinted to the window. It was too dark for her to make out anything other than the outline of the rider but the horse, with its distinctive white flash on its hind leg, was most definitely that of the Duke of Linthorpe.

★

There was no sign of the duke at breakfast the following morning and when Wilhelmina nonchalantly enquired as to his whereabouts, the butler informed her that he was still abed. He also failed to appear at luncheon, when Uncle Ernest announced some quite shocking news.

'Are you aware that there has been yet another incident, Mrs Crump?' he enquired over his plate of cold beef.

'There have only been *six* incidents so far, Father,' countered Lavinia defensively. 'Which I really don't think for such a new puppy is any great—'

'I'm not talking about the dog, girl,' interjected Uncle Ernest. 'I'm talking about the kidnappings. Got another one last night and still haven't released any of the others, despite all the ransom monies being paid.'

'Shocking,' pronounced Aunt Clementine, shaking her head furiously. 'Why we upper-class people are not safe in our beds, Mr Crump.'

The duke appeared for dinner later that evening, offering no explanation for his absence during the day. Although he was still impeccable in both his address and his appearance, Wilhelmina could not help but note that he was lacking his usual polish, seeming somewhat exhausted and more than a little irritable. They were halfway through their main course when the butler appeared and slipped a note to him.

Wilhelmina observed all colour drain from his face as he read the missive. He then announced, 'Please do excuse me,' and, adding no more explanation and nothing at all in the way of an apology, he rose from the table and marched out of the room, leaving Aunt Clementine in a state of agitated pondering, and Wilhelmina adding yet another mysterious incident to the ever-increasing list of the duke's strange behaviour.

Her suspicions now well and truly aroused, she wandered – with contrived casualness – down to the stables after dinner and enquired of one of the grooms if his grace had ridden out. Having been informed that he had not, she then set about trying to find her host, starting with the grounds. So extensive were they, however, that it was almost an hour later when she eventually spotted him through the window of an old summer house. Sitting alongside him was none other than the beautiful Baroness Beaumont looking as anxious as the duke himself as the two of them engaged in what was obviously another intimate exchange. From the Baroness's swollen eyes, it was obvious that she had been crying. The sight set another round of questions spinning about Wilhelmina's head – which, not least, was whether the Duke of Linthorpe made every woman of his acquaintance miserable.

'I'm afraid I shall have to leave you all to your own devices for several days,' informed an exhausted-looking duke at breakfast the next morning.

'Oh, you are not going up to London again, your grace?' enquired Aunt Clementine, her tone pregnant with consternation. 'It is not at all safe and I for one should not sleep a wink if you—'

'Not London, ma'am,' he cut in abruptly. 'I am bound for France.'

'*France?*' shrieked Aunt Clementine, 'but I fear that is even worse, sir. Why it is so dangerous I have written to my cousin, Mrs Ermintrude Fitzgibbon, and instructed her and her husband to return to England immediately.'

'I'm afraid,' said the duke, 'that however dangerous it may be, I have some unavoidable business there.'

'Oh, but surely there is someone else who could attend to it on your behalf, sir?' suggested the older woman. 'After all, a man of your position and such . . . *substantial* means could, I am sure, find someone to—'

'I am afraid, ma'am,' cut in the duke, 'that in this case there is no one else who could possibly take my place.'

With the duke away and the mystery surrounding him deepening, Wilhelmina stepped up her efforts to find the red-haired woman. Yet again, however, her searches revealed nothing and she found herself growing increasingly despondent and frustrated. She sat in the window seat of the green drawing-room watching her cousin and Mr Dartford, who had called at the hall yet again to check on the progress of the still unnamed puppy. Thanks to Lavinia's surprisingly patient attentions and assiduous care, the animal was thriving and extremely content with her new home. Today, the two of them were attempting the engaging task of teaching the pet to retrieve the stick they were throwing for her. Failing to grasp the point of the exercise, the puppy sat and watched bewilderedly as the article was thrown, gazing at her playmates with huge brown eyes. As soon as Lavinia or the rector then retrieved the stick themselves, the puppy, having evidently concluded that this was the point of the game, bounded energetically after them, darting playfully between their feet and causing the rector to fall flat on his face on at least two occasions that Wilhelmina had witnessed. All three participants were, from the sounds of laughter, squealing and yapping, drifting in through the open drawing-room window, deriving a huge amount of pleasure from their playful antics. Wilhelmina, meanwhile, having no doubt that, under normal circumstances, she too would have found the scene highly amusing, could not even muster so much as a smile.

'Mrs Drinkwater and Miss Verity Drinkwater, ma'am,' announced the butler some five days later while the three women were sitting taking tea in the garden, having just bid goodday to Mr Dartford.

A smug smile tugged at Aunt Clementine's lips. 'How charming,' she declared, setting down her tea-cup. 'Do show them in at once, Hives, and please arrange for more tea and some raisin cake.'

The butler bowed politely and took his leave.

'Venetia, dear, and Verity. How good of you to come all this way,' gushed Aunt Clementine, as the two women breezed out through the open floor-to-ceiling windows which opened on to the garden terrace.

'Well, we should have come sooner, Clementine,' pronounced Mrs Drinkwater, fiddling with the strings of her bonnet, 'but we have been so busy in London our feet have scarcely touched the ground.'

'Really,' muttered Aunt Clementine uninterestedly. 'Now do tell me, dear, what do you make of our new lodging?'

'Well,' mused Mrs Drinkwater, carrying out a pursed-lipped perusal of the exterior of the building from the wrought iron chair she had just claimed between Lavinia and her mother. 'It is certainly big enough, I give you that, Clementine, but it is hardly what one would class as "homely". Why I'm sure one would never find one's way around such an enormous building.'

'Oh, I can assure you we have managed quite well, thank you,' informed Aunt Clementine.

Mrs Drinkwater eyed her friend suspiciously. 'I own if I were staying in such a grand house, I should have been tempted to peep around all the rooms,' she confessed with a little affected titter, 'and I do not mean those which are of everyday use.'

Two spots of colour appeared on Aunt Clementine's cheekbones. 'Goodness no, Venetia,' she exclaimed with forced indignation. 'Why it would be the very height of discourtesy. The thought has never entered my head.'

'Of course not, dear,' remarked Mrs Drinkwater, as she observed the guilty flush. 'Why, I should have known that it would not. Now I do believe we have the most exciting news, Clementine. You will never in a million years guess who was in attendance at Lady Canterbury's ridotto yesterday evening.'

'I have not the slightest idea,' replied Aunt Clementine, visibly flustered, as she raised her cup of tea to her lips.

'None other than the' – began Mrs Drinkwater, pausing for dramatic effect – 'Duke of York himself.'

Aunt Clementine gasped loudly, a large splash of tea landing in her saucer. 'The Prince Frederick?' she confirmed, in wide-eyed amazement.

Mrs Drinkwater gave a single, smug nod of her turban-clad head.

'And did you . . . did you make the prince's acquaintance?' stammered an astounded Aunt Clementine, the tea-cup now rattling noisily on the saucer she was holding.

Mrs Drinkwater waved a dismissive hand. 'Well, of course, I'm sure we should have done, had the man not arrived so late but I did happen to catch his eye upon several occasions and he smiled most charmingly towards me.'

'Did he now?' murmured Aunt Clementine, looking suitably miffed.

'Quite, quite charmingly,' confirmed Mrs Drinkwater, adding salt into the rapidly gaping wound.

'Hmph!' huffed Aunt Clementine, setting down her cup and saucer and crossing her arms over her rounded bosom.

'Word has it that the king has ordered him to take a wife,' continued Mrs Drinkwater. 'And I must say, he did seem rather intent on the task yesterday evening. Do you know, he smiled directly at Verity as we were leaving? Did he not, dear?'

'Directly at me, Mama,' confirmed Verity, with a toss of her gleaming blonde ringlets. 'And I have heard word that he is to attend Mrs Harlington-Hartsworthy's ball tomorrow evening.'

'The Harlington-Hartsworthys of Herfordshire?' enquired Aunt Clementine with raised brows.

'The very same,' confirmed Mrs Drinkwater, with an affirmative nod of her head.

Wilhelmina watched Aunt Clementine's narrowed eyes darting quickly from Mrs Drinkwater's smug countenance to that of Verity.

'Well then, there is nothing else for it,' she suddenly announced briskly. 'Given that his grace is away, we shall move back to London for a few days until his return. I see nothing at all wrong in keeping all our options open, girls. Eggs and baskets. Eggs and baskets.'

Whilst, much to Uncle Ernest's stunned amazement, Aunt Clementine began immediately busying herself in arranging the packing of items for the intended short trip back to the capital, Lavinia, in a most uncharacteristic show of selflessness, appeared to be paying more attention to the needs of the puppy, than to her own, usually meticulous packing requirements.

'Now,' Aunt Clementine pronounced later that evening, 'if you are to make the acquaintance of the Duke of York tomorrow evening, Lavinia, we must ensure you are looking your very best. I suggest your pink silk – what do you think, dear?'

'Hmm?' murmured Lavinia distractedly, glancing up from the floor where she was rolling around playfully with the delighted dog.

'I am suggesting your pink silk for tomorrow evening,' repeated Aunt Clementine stiffly. 'What do you think, dear?'

'I confess I have not given it a thought, Mama.'

Aunt Clementine's brow puckered in the most puzzled of fashions as she regarded her daughter in silence for a few minutes. She then rang the bell and ordered the footman to bring her a little hartshorn and a glass of water.

London, England

'Now, Lavinia dear,' instructed Aunt Clementine as they made their way to the ball the following evening, having settled back into Number 22, Grosvenor Square, 'it is imperative that you are on your very best behaviour this evening. It would not do at all for the prince to witness that dreadful face you pull when you are the slightest bit piqued, girl.'

'I do not pull a dreadful face, Mama,' insisted Lavinia, crossing her arms over her chest and sticking out her bottom lip petulantly.

Aunt Clementine's raised eyebrow needed no vocal accompaniment.

CHAPTER 20

THE Harlington-Hartsworthys resided, much to Aunt Clementine's dismay, in a grand mansion house in Mayfair, some double the size of Number 22, Grosvenor Square. The fact that the family owned the house and were not just renting it, added greatly to the older woman's consternation.

'Well, some people consider size the only way in which to demonstrate their wealth, girls,' she muttered away as they entered the magnificent rococo hall. 'Whilst we, of course, are quite aware that there is a very fine line between large and ostentatious.'

The girls exchanged a questioning look.

As if in search of further evidence to support her views, Aunt Clementine continued her speech as they threaded their way through the throng towards the Drinkwaters, whom they had located at the far end of the room observing the proceedings. 'Why look no further than the size of that feather in Venetia Drinkwater's turban, my dears,' she murmured under her breath as she approached the woman with a disingenuous smile on her face. 'The very height of bad taste— Ah, Venetia, dear,' she exclaimed as they reached the pair. 'And looking as elegant as usual.'

'As indeed are you, my dear,' rejoined Mrs Drinkwater, carrying out a disapproving appraisal of Aunt Clementine's lilac silk creation.

'Well? Has he arrived yet?' enquired Aunt Clementine eagerly, as she cast a shrewd eye about the room.

'Who, dear?' replied Mrs Drinkwater, feigning complete innocence.

'Why the prince, of course,' tutted Aunt Clementine.

'Oh, silly me,' remarked Mrs Drinkwater, with an affected titter.

163

'No, I do believe he is not yet here.'

'Oh, well,' sighed Aunt Clementine, disappointed, 'there is time enough yet, I suppose.'

'And what a great pity there is yet another person absent from the proceedings whom we are all still anxious to meet,' remarked Verity superciliously.

'To whom are you referring, dear?' enquired Lavinia artlessly.

'Why the Comte de Roxwood, of course,' replied Verity wryly. 'I take it the man continues to be . . . *detained* in France?'

'It is the Comte de *Roxford*, Verity and yes the man is still detained,' clarified Lavinia coolly. 'But of course I am hoping he will be returned in time for your wedding to the Earl of Thurlston. Do you have a date yet for the ceremony, my dear?'

Verity glared at her. 'You know very well he has not yet offered,' she admitted petulantly.

'Goodness, I am such a silly goose,' announced Lavinia, slapping the palm of her hand to her forehead. 'That tiny fact had quite slipped my mind. Now, please do excuse me. I am going to the withdrawing-room for a little peace and quiet for I have no wish at all to endure a headache this evening.'

Some thirty minutes later, a puce and flustered Aunt Clementine approached Wilhelmina, who had just been escorted back to her seat after dancing the quadrille with the Marquis of Hetherington.

'Have you seen Lavinia, dear?' she enquired anxiously. 'The prince has just arrived and I cannot find her anywhere.'

Wilhelmina wrinkled her forehead. 'She did go to the withdraw-ing-room, Aunt, but I own that was rather a long time ago.'

'Indeed it was,' concurred Aunt Clementine, 'and I am newly returned from seeking her there myself. I could see no sign at all of the girl.'

A strange prickling sensation began crawling slowly over Wilhelmina's skin. Not wishing to cause any unnecessary concern to her aunt, however, she declared, in as blithe a tone as she could muster, 'Then she is most likely chatting, Aunt. You know how desperate she was to catch up on the London gossip.'

'Yes, of course she was,' agreed Aunt Clementine, with a large sigh of relief. Then, as an horrific thought occurred to her, she added somewhat panic-stricken, 'Oh goodness, but that will not do at all. What on earth will the prince think if he sees the girl engaging in gossip? One must exercise the utmost discretion when one is a princess. I must seek her out immediately and ensure she is acting with nothing but the greatest propriety.' And with that mission in mind, she waddled busily away.

As she observed her aunt bustling through the throng of guests, a worrying thought had taken root in Wilhelmina's mind and was growing at an alarming rate. Chiding herself for overreacting, she, too, began anxiously skirting the crowd in search of her cousin. A thorough search of the ballroom, the garden, the withdrawing-room and even the rooms set aside for cards, however, did nothing to allay her concerns. The indisputable fact of the matter was that Lavinia was nowhere to be seen.

'But she cannot have simply disappeared,' pronounced an agitated Aunt Clementine some two hours later. 'She must be here somewhere. Go and check the garden again, Wilhelmina.'

'I have already checked it ten times, Aunt,' replied Wilhelmina, trying to curb the impatience and anxiety of her tone. 'She is not here.'

'But if she is not here, then where on earth is she?' declared Aunt Clementine, tears beginning to brim in her round blue eyes.

'I wish I knew, Aunt,' muttered Wilhelmina, not daring to voice her outlandish thoughts for fear they might be true.

Several hours later, with still no sign of Lavinia, and the last guest having departed the Harlington-Hartsworthys' mansion, Mrs Harlington-Hartsworthy, her equally flummoxed husband and her sweet, freckle-faced daughter, were all at quite a loss as to what to suggest.

'Perhaps she had a romantic liaison, my dear,' suggested the hostess to Aunt Clementine, who, clutching her vinaigrette, had adopted an indelicate position on the sofa: legs akimbo and her head, upon which a cold compress had been placed, tilted directly upwards towards the ceiling. 'You know, after all, how these young people can be, Mrs Crump.'

'Impossible!' insisted Aunt Clementine. 'Lavinia would never do such a thing. Never. Why she is innocence itself.'

'Well, perhaps she had the headache and needed to go home

early,' proposed Mr Harlington-Hartsworthy, somewhat tentatively.

This suggestion evoked an even more frantic response directed to the hanging crystal chandelier. 'Never!' pronounced Aunt Clementine. 'Why the girl is all that is consideration. She would not dream of leaving without first telling me.'

'Well, then, I confess, I have no idea, Mrs Crump' admitted Mrs Harlington-Hartsworthy, pulling a rueful face.

'Perhaps we should return to Grosvenor Square, Aunt,' suggested Wilhelmina in as light a tone as she could manage. 'After all, Lavinia could well be there.'

Aunt Clementine did not look at all convinced. 'Very well then,' she agreed reluctantly. 'Although quite what Mr Crump will say when he hears of the girl's behaviour I dare not even think.'

'Haven't seen her since you left for the ball this evening,' admitted Uncle Ernest who was beginning to appear just as anxious as his wife. 'Can't think where the devil she could be.'

'There is, er, one thing, we haven't thought of, Uncle,' pointed out Wilhelmina reluctantly.

'What's that, my girl?' asked the old man, rubbing his chin.

'Well,' she pronounced, taking a deep calming inhalation. 'I do not wish to sound dramatic but I think perhaps she may have been . . . kidnapped.'

There followed a heavy thud as Aunt Clementine slid right off the sofa and landed in a heap of crushed lilac silk on the blue Aubusson carpet.

'Hmmm,' mused the large man from the Bow Street Runners who had arrived following Uncle Ernest's summons. 'So nobody has seen her for at least five hours?'

'Without wishing to appear rude, Mr Curtis,' replied Aunt Clementine, who was now reposed on the chaise-longue in the lemon drawing-room, under a thick, quilted puce coverlet, 'I have informed you of that fact some six times. Now what I wish to know is what you intend to do about finding the girl.'

'Hmmm,' drawled Mr Curtis, in his thick west-country accent. 'Well, I'm not really sure, ma'am.'

'Not sure! Not sure!' repeated Uncle Ernest, springing from his chair and beginning to pace about the room like a caged animal. 'Damn it man, if you're not sure, then what hope is there for the rest of us?'

'Hmmm,' admitted Mr Curtis. 'Well, I'm not really sure about that either, sir.'

Uncle Ernest had momentarily ceased his pacing and appeared to be on the verge of punching the ineffectual runner, when there was an almighty rap at the door, causing all four occupants of the room to start. Being already on his feet, the older man ran immediately into the hall and reappeared some two minutes later, a deathly shade of grey and holding an envelope in his hand.

'Wilhelmina was correct,' he announced in a quaking voice. 'Lavinia has been kidnapped.'

The note from the kidnappers was rather a shabby affair, constructed by crudely cut out letters from newspapers unevenly glued onto a crumpled sheet of yellowing paper. It was, so Mr Curtis informed them, exactly like all the other notes he had seen and was, just as they had been, straight to the point. It stated, quite simply:

We have your daughter.
Do as we say if you wish to keep her safe.
Further instructions will follow.

Having taken one look at the note, a disturbing gurgling sound had been emitted from the back of Aunt Clementine's throat, before she suffered yet another fit of the vapours. This time, however, Uncle Ernest insisted on leaving her in her sleeping state claiming, quite rightly, that the rest should be of much more use to her than lying awake fretting.

With the ineffectual Mr Curtis having undertaken yet another round of the same questions he had already asked at least half a dozen times, the man at last bid them goodnight, leaving Wilhelmina alone with her uncle and her sleeping aunt who was now snoring so loudly that the poor puppy, who had been dozing quite contentedly, jumped out of her basket, cast a despairing look at the woman and then dived headlong under the sofa. This amusing activity went on unnoticed by Wilhelmina and her uncle, both of whom were positively dazed by the events of the evening.

'What should we do, Uncle?' enquired Wilhelmina weakly.

Uncle Ernest ran a worried hand through his thick white hair. 'There is nothing we can do, my dear,' he muttered despairingly, 'other than wait for them to contact us again with their instructions.'

'You will let me know if there is anything I can do to help?' she enquired, with a gentle smile.

He returned her smile and reached out to squeeze her hand. 'You can assist me in looking after your aunt,' he said, looking affectionately at his snoring spouse. 'She is going to need all our help to get through this.'

'And she shall have it,' resolved Wilhelmina.

Two days had passed since the kidnapping and they had heard nothing. Wilhelmina had, as promised, been keeping a watchful eye on her aunt who had taken to her bed with enough hartshorn, lavender water and smelling salts, to last her a good many weeks. The puppy, obviously picking up on the anxious state of the household and missing her mistress dreadfully had, in an imitation of Aunt Clementine, taken to spending the majority of her time lying in her basket observing the proceedings with large brown worried eyes.

There were a number of visitors to the household over those two days, all of whom, with Aunt Clementine indisposed and Uncle Ernest in no mood for company, were left to Wilhelmina to deal with.

The Earl of Thurlston was the first on the scene. He had not been present at the Harlington-Hartsworthys' ball but had of course heard the news, which had spread like wildfire all over the city.

The information had also found its way to Kent and as a result a concerned Mr Dartford appeared at the house to enquire if he could be of any assistance. His offer to take the puppy back to the rectory with him was rejected by Wilhelmina not only because she found the animal's presence a comfort, but also because she knew Lavinia would wish to see her the moment she came back. The possibility that she might not come back was evaded by all.

The third set of significant visitors was the Drinkwaters who carried out their own interrogation of Wilhelmina in such an intense fashion that she could not help but conclude that the pair would make much more competent Bow Street Runners than the ineffectual Mr Curtis. Despite the runner failing to inspire the least bit of confidence in her, she had debated long and hard with herself about whether or not to confess her suspicions to him, suspicions which had been preying heavily on her mind for some time now and which concerned the Duke of Linthorpe. With her thoughts insisting on returning to the red-haired woman, she could not help but wonder that, if the man was capable of holding captive one woman, then was there any reason why he could not make it more? And what of his strange behaviour? Had not all of the strange incidents she had witnessed taken place the night before the other kidnappings? The only mitigating factor she could find in the man's defence was that he could not possibly be responsible for Lavinia's disappearance. He was, of course, in France.

In an effort to kill an hour or so that afternoon Wilhelmina took the puppy to the park where she absent-mindedly engaged in throwing sticks for her. The animal had now grasped the concept of the game and returned them all with a self-satisfied look upon her little face and a busily wagging tail. Throwing the stick distractedly again, it landed behind a large furze bush smothered with yellow flowers. She watched the excited pup dart behind the shrub and was amazed to see her appear a few seconds later with not a stick between her teeth but rather a rolled up piece of white paper. Suspecting immediately, with a shiver of apprehension, what it was, Wilhelmina retrieved it as quickly as she could from the animal's tiny mouth and smoothed it out. It said curtly:

Meet me by the duck pond in Hyde Park at midnight.
Tell no one!
The Stag

She ran at once to the bush to see if she could spot any sign of the deliverer. Just as she had suspected, however, she found that whoever it was had melted into the surrounding scene of other dog-walkers, promenaders and riders enjoying the pleasant afternoon. She blinked back the hot tears burning her eyes as she regarded the note again. Was it some kind of trap? Did it have anything to do with Lavinia's kidnapping? Should she really tell no one given the dangerous state of affairs? Was she really, after all this time and all that had happened, going to make the acquaintance of The Stag? She looked down at the puppy who was standing at her feet, her tail wagging as she waited for another stick to be thrown. Next time, she resolved, she too was coming back as a dog. Life as a human being was far too complicated.

CHAPTER 21

AFTER having deliberated long and hard again – this time over whether or not to inform Uncle Ernest or the ineffectual Mr Curtis of the note – Wilhelmina had opted to do exactly as the instructions bade and tell no one, despite the fact that her normally reliable instincts remained stubbornly divided on the matter.

The wait for the allotted hour seemed interminable and, as the time slowly dragged by, she had the feeling that every nerve in her body was being gnawed away by the ravages of fear and apprehension. Indeed, as midnight crawled around, every other nervous feeling she had ever experienced when delivering the notes, paled into the realms of insignificance as her heart began beating uncontrollably.

Suspecting that her usual evening attire was likely to prove rather inappropriate for the occasion, she dressed in a riding habit and a simple cotton blouse before wrapping her black cloak around her and slipping unnoticed out of the house and into the velvety darkness of the night. The walk to Hyde Park was short and, apart from the occasional sound of chatter and laughter, which wafted out from behind the closed curtains of the Mayfair mansions, she found the streets bathed in an eerie silence and the dim lights of the flambeaux.

Briskly making her way towards her destination, every one of her nerves standing to keen attention, she was aware that not only was she placing herself in grave danger by agreeing to meet a stranger alone in the middle of the night, but that a woman wandering around the capital unprotected was perfect game for the notorious footpads and cut-throats who trawled the streets, the atrocity of whose crimes she did not wish to even contemplate. So heightened were her senses to these dangers that at one point she almost convinced herself someone was following her, but swinging around to check, she was relieved to see nothing and, with her heart pounding wildly, quickened her steps.

She arrived at her destination at exactly one minute before the stipulated hour, at the same moment as the loud piercing shriek of a fighting tomcat in the near distance rudely severed the calm of the night. Her chest constricted as a bolt of fear lanced through her.

'There is no need to be so nervous, Miss Crump,' assured a voice she instantly recognized, from behind her. She spun around and saw a tall, slim figure approaching from the direction from which she had just come.

'You!' she exclaimed in amazement as the man's face came into view.

'At your service once again, *mademoiselle*,' declared the Comte de Roxford, coming to a standstill directly before her and sweeping into a deep bow.

Utterly stunned at the sight of the man, all coherent thought deserted her as she found herself gawping at him in unabashed astonishment. 'So you-you sent me the note? – you are The-the Stag?' she stammered, a million questions beginning to whirl around in her head.

The comte flashed a smile before inclining his head in affirmation, 'Of course, *mademoiselle*.'

'But I did not – that is – I had not the faintest idea you were even in England, sir,' she faltered, shaking her head in disbelief.

He nodded understandingly. 'As I'm sure you can appreciate, Miss Crump, it has been of the utmost importance that I used a great deal of discretion during my visit here.'

'Which you have done quite admirably, sir,' suddenly interjected another deep male voice.

Wilhelmina started and wheeled around to find herself gaping at yet another familiar figure: that of the Duke of Linthorpe. She gasped as he too came to stand before her, bowing his head in greeting.

'Miss Crump,' he said with cool politeness.

She continued to regard him in bewildered amazement, absorbing the fact that he was attired in entirely black riding wear – a sight which, although extremely pleasing to the eye, served only to add to the considerable confusion reigning in her mind.

'Wh-what are *you* doing here, sir?' she demanded in a distinctly unsteady voice.

He fixed her with a gaze as cool as the tone in which he had greeted her, before declaring bluntly, 'I am come to detain this man, madam.'

While a mocking scoff came from the comte, Wilhelmina's brow puckered in bafflement. 'Detain the Comte de Roxford? But . . . but . . .why?'

The duke looked with disdain at the comte before directing his reply to Wilhelmina. 'Because, Miss Crump,' he explained with some impatience, 'it is this man – the Comte de Roxford, who has been carrying out the kidnappings.'

Wilhelmina's eyes widened. 'Not the Comte de Roxford, sir,' she exclaimed.

'It certainly is,' replied the duke, as he turned to accuse the Frenchman. 'Correct, me if I am mistaken, *my lord*, but were you or were you not, intending to add a second Miss Crump to your list of victims this evening?'

'Do not believe a word this man says, Miss Crump,' snorted the comte. 'Why he is obviously here to kidnap you himself.'

Wilhelmina looked from one to the other, her head spinning at the surprise of not only having two such familiar figures before her, but also the outrageous accusations each was making of the other. For all that her acquaintance with the comte had been of a fleeting nature and though she knew nothing at all of the man other than the information he had chosen to divulge in the coach in Paris, it was her lingering suspicions regarding the Duke of Linthorpe which were clamouring for attention in her mind. She eyed him now suspiciously.

'What, may I ask, *are* you doing here, sir?' she asked guardedly. 'I was of the belief that you were in France.'

The duke glared at the comte as he replied, 'I am newly returned this afternoon, ma'am. When I learnt of your cousin's predicament I came immediately to London.'

This information, along with his strange attire, did nothing to dispel her qualms. She continued to regard him warily. 'If you were so concerned about my cousin's welfare, sir,' she questioned, 'then why did you not visit the house and enquire after her?'

A flash of irritation swept over his face as his head turned very slowly towards her. 'Because, madam,' he explained tetchily, 'I considered it more beneficial to all concerned if I engaged my energies in somewhat more constructive activities than sitting around drinking cups of tea. A fact for which, I might add, you should be extremely grateful, Miss Crump, given that my presence here has undoubtedly prevented you from a most unfortunate fate.'

At this remark, the comte gave a crack of affected laughter which caused Wilhelmina's gaze – intently focused on the duke at that moment – to jerk immediately to the Frenchman. She found him regarding his accuser contemptuously.

'Do not believe a word of it, Miss Crump,' the comte scoffed haughtily. 'It is *I* who am – once again – your knight in shining armour. *I* who have come to rescue you from *this* man.'

Wilhelmina looked uncertainly from one to the other as she observed the dark shadow of anger she had been witness to on several occasions, creeping once again over the duke's features.

'For God's sake, woman,' he declared, running a despairing hand through his thick, wavy hair, 'you know nothing at all of this man. Are you really such a dimwit as to suspect me over him?'

A sharp jolt of resentment at the insult banished all her inhibitions. Jutting out her chin, she met his cold gaze defiantly. 'It is what I know of *you*, sir,' she stated candidly, 'that is causing me most concern. Not only have you treated my cousin and me quite appallingly since we first made your acquaintance, but it has also not escaped my notice that you appear to have a woman held captive at Linthorpe Hall.'

Her misgivings voiced, she was aware of an uneasy wave of trepidation creeping over her as she observed his dark eyebrows snap furiously together.

'I have a *what*?' he demanded, his dark eyes now burning with anger.

Her momentary courage having now deserted her, she replied with a confidence she was far from feeling, 'A woman imprisoned at Linthorpe Hall, sir, and there is not the slightest use in denying it for I have seen her with my own eyes.'

She gulped as she awaited his reply. It seemed an interminable time in coming as he stared at her in such a smouldering manner that she experienced an overwhelming urge to turn on her heel and flee from him as fast as her legs would carry her.

Before either of them could say another word on the matter however, the comte broke in.

'Hah,' he sneered somewhat unpleasantly. 'What more evidence do you need, Miss Crump that it is *this* man who is responsible for the kidnappings? If he has imprisoned one woman then he is capable of taking hostage four more. You must let me deal with him at once, *mademoiselle*, and put a stop to his crimes before he abducts you too.' And on that heroic note, with a theatrical flourish, he produced a small silver dagger with a glittering jewelled handle from under his jacket.

Wilhelmina's eyes almost popped out of her head. She gasped and took a step back before casting a despairing look at the duke who, to her surprise, was now gazing bewildered at the Frenchman.

'That,' said the duke, nodding his head at the shining blade of the weapon, 'is supposed to frighten me, I assume?'

The comte's mouth broke into a sneer. 'That is entirely your privilege, sir,' he replied with mock courtesy. 'However, as interesting as I am finding this little exchange, I am afraid I do not have time to stand around conversing all evening. As Miss Crump cannot accompany both of us, I suggest we narrow down the lady's choices. Do you not agree, sir?'

Wilhelmina, who had no desire at all to accompany either man but to go instead straight back to Number 22, Grosvenor Square and take refuge under her coverlet, found herself rooted to the spot.

'But I—' she began in a wavering voice.

'Be quiet, Miss Crump,' snapped the duke, in such a wrathful tone that she felt her already quaking knees beginning to shake uncontrollably. She watched in mortified silence as the two men then began circling one other in the unsettling manner of two feuding predators.

After less than a minute of this circling activity, the comte suddenly lunged forward, aiming the blade of the knife directly at the area of the duke's heart. Wilhelmina was aware of a small warbling cry, which, although it had been emitted from her own mouth, had the strange sensation of appearing not to belong to her at all.

In the flurry of activity that followed, which was over so quickly she scarcely had time to absorb what had happened, the duke skil-

175

fully sidestepped the comte's lunge before expertly kicking the dagger out of the man's hand. Then, before the comte had even had time to take stock of the fact that the weapon was flying through the air and landing in a group of bullrushes, the duke planted a hard, bone-cracking blow directly in the centre of his face.

Wilhelmina watched in stunned silence as the Frenchman wobbled unsteadily on the spot for a few seconds before tumbling to the ground like a sack of oats.

She stared open-mouthed, first at the collapsed heap of the comte and then at the duke who was standing alongside her, rubbing his knuckles.

'Come along now, Miss Crump,' he instructed brusquely, producing two lengths of thin rope from his breeches' pockets. 'We have no time to lose.'

Wilhelmina balked at the suggestion as he bound together the unconscious Frenchman's wrists and ankles. Surely he could not expect her to go with him after what she had just witnessed. Granted the Comte de Roxford had displayed quite another side to his character from that which she had witnessed in the coach in Paris, but her doubts regarding the Duke of Linthorpe had not been alleviated at all.

She remonstrated silently with herself for being stupid enough to come out alone, without informing a single soul of her whereabouts. As useless as Mr Curtis, the Bow Street Runner, had proved himself to be, she wished vehemently that she had turned the entire matter over to his hands. However, being led by her foolish, overpowering curiosity, she had not and she now realized that she had either to suffer the consequences of her irresponsible actions or remove herself from the situation as swiftly as she could. She surveyed the park. There was not a soul to be seen. Her eyes landed on the duke who was concentrating on the trussing up of his adversary. This could be, she recognized with some anxiety, the only opportunity for her to escape. Without wasting another second, she turned on her heel and began to run as fast as she could towards the park gate, a potent mixture of fear and determination driving her onwards. She was not even halfway towards the park entrance, however, when she felt a man's strong restraining arms around her.

'What on earth are you doing, young woman?' spat the duke, spinning her around to face him.

176

Wilhelmina wriggled, trying desperately to free herself from his firm, unyielding grip.

'If you do not release me this instant, sir,' she commanded, 'I shall scream so loudly I will wake the whole of London.'

'And what would be the point of that, madam?' he demanded irascibly, 'when I have just gone out of my way and quite likely broken a few bones in my hand to boot, to rescue you from abduction?'

'I have only your word for that, sir,' she replied, writhing madly, 'and quite frankly, I am not sure I believe you.'

The look upon his face told her his levels of patience were rapidly depleting. 'But why on earth not?' he persisted brusquely. 'Although our acquaintance is but short, Miss Crump, surely it has allowed you *some* insight into my character.'

Wilhelmina narrowed her eyes as she made a futile attempt to remove his arms from her. 'That is my point, sir,' she declared stoutly. 'As well as seeing that poor woman locked in your cabin on the ship and at Linthorpe, you ride out at all hours of the night dressed as some kind of . . . of . . . highwayman; and then, if all that were not extraordinary enough, you-you turn up this evening, completely unexpected, whilst everyone was under the impression you were in France. You must confess, sir, that such behaviour is not that of a normal gentleman.'

His grip on her tightened as he regarded her coolly. 'One thing that I have never professed to being, Miss Crump,' he remarked in icy tones, 'is a *normal gentleman.*'

His frosty manner had the effect of reigniting the spark of anger which had burned in her, albeit briefly, a few minutes earlier. 'That sir,' she retorted with some indignation, 'is perfectly clear, for *normal gentlemen* do not go around kidnapping innocent women.'

'Lud, woman,' he snarled, holding her so tightly that she flinched. 'You are enough to drive a man to distraction. What do I have to do to convince you that I am not the kidnapper? I suppose if I were a charming dandy like the Earl of Thurlston, you would believe every word I said.'

'Well, unlike yourself, sir,' she rejoined tartly, 'at least the Earl of Thurlston *knows* how to be charming.'

He gave a disparaging snort. 'I can assure you I can be perfectly charming when I need to be, madam.'

'Well, quite obviously you have never felt that need in my presence, sir,' she pointed out, seething.

'It is not in my nature to pander to gold-digging chits, who wish only to shackle themselves to men for money and titles,' the duke stormed.

'Are you implying, sir, that I am a gold-digging chit?' Wilhelmina demanded.

'There is no use in denying it, ma'am,' disdained the duke. 'You forget that I have witnessed, on several occasions, your . . . *relationship* with the Earl of Thurlston.'

At that Wilhelmina's spark of anger burst into a red-hot, roaring inferno. 'I can assure you, sir,' she hissed furiously, 'that there is no *relationship* with the Earl of Thurlston.'

He raised a doubtful eyebrow. 'But I have only your word for that, Miss Crump. And, I confess, I'm not sure I believe you.'

'Why you-you—' spluttered Wilhelmina who, at a complete loss for words, could think of nothing else to do other than to stamp as hard as she possibly could on the duke's booted foot.

'Ouch!' he cried, immediately releasing his hold of her. 'Why on earth did you do that, woman?'

'Because, sir, you have jumped to the most outrageous of conclusions without giving me the first chance to explain myself.'

'And I could well say the same about you, madam,' rejoined the duke, anger colouring his tone. 'I can assure you I am not in the habit of kidnapping women, Miss Crump.'

She shot him a derisive look. 'I think we should leave that to the Bow Street Runners to decide, don't you?' she asked. 'Now if you do not allow me to go, sir, I shall scream this very instant.'

'Like hell you will,' countered the duke and, before she could work out what was happening, he pulled her to him and kissed her so hard that all coherent thought was at once banished from her mind.

'Now,' he remarked, as he drew his lips from hers after what seemed like several long minutes, 'are you still feeling the urge to scream, madam?'

Experiencing a strange – but not unpleasant – sensation, Wilhelmina found she could only manage a feeble shake of her head.

'Good,' concluded the duke, obviously satisfied that his drastic action had produced the desired result. 'Now we must—'

At that moment, their attention was drawn to the comte who, propped up against a tree with his arms bound behind his back, his legs in front of him, was groaning strangely.

'Ah, good,' announced the duke, with some relief. 'I was beginning to think we might have to wait quite some time for him to awake. I must confess I acted a little in haste, Miss Crump for I should have obtained the information I required before I rendered the man unconscious.'

She blinked at him, puzzled.

'Now, if you will excuse me a moment, Miss Crump,' he said, inclining his head.

She watched perplexed as he sauntered over to where the knife had fallen, retrieved it from the patch of bullrushes and returned to the Frenchman whose moans were growing increasingly louder. The comte was trussed up like a pig, with two rivulets of bright red blood trickling from his nostrils, and Wilhelmina could not help but make a comparison with the charming, refined image the man had presented in Paris a few short weeks before.

The duke, on the other hand, appeared to be giving very little thought to the comte's appearance as he knelt down on one knee beside him and with his left hand roughly grasped a clump of the man's hair. This he used to jerk up the Frenchman's head to regard his own. With his right hand, he positioned the sharp, pointed tip of the knife-blade directly in the centre of the comte's throat. The Frenchman's eyes bulged in their sockets as he struggled for breath.

'Now, sir,' began the duke with affected civility, 'I should be much obliged if you would do me the courtesy of telling me where you have hidden the hostages.'

The comte coughed before spitting out an emphatic, 'Never!'

Undeterred, the duke pushed the tip of the knife a little harder into the Frenchman's skin. Wilhelmina grimaced.

'Are you quite sure, sir?' the duke enquired with yet more contrived politeness as he pulled up the comte's head a shade further.

'Quite sure,' wheezed the comte.

'Very well then,' concluded the duke matter-of-factly. 'If you insist on not telling me, I shall have no choice but to cut your throat, *my lord*.'

179

'You wouldn't dare,' spluttered the Frenchman.

'Oh believe me, I would, sir,' replied the duke, with a dangerous smile. 'I *never* make idle threats.'

Wilhelmina's grimace deepened as she observed the duke deliberately move the tip of the blade to the right side of the man's neck where he jabbed it so hard that he broke the surface of the skin, causing a tiny trickle of blood. At this, the comte's breathing became noticeably more agitated.

'No, please,' he implored.

'Then the location, sir,' commanded the duke.

There was a brief pause while the comte's eyes darted frantically about like those of a terrified animal caught by its slaughterer. 'The old woodcutter's cottage at Biggin Hill,' he murmured in all but a whisper.

'How very kind,' remarked the duke with a smile. 'And if I find out you have deceived me, sir, I can assure you I shall have not the slightest hesitation in finishing what I have started.' He then tossed the knife aside and landed another punch in the Frenchman's face before pulling a kerchief from his pocket and stuffing it into the once again unconscious comte's mouth.

'Now,' he claimed, fixing her with an earnest expression as he sprang to his feet, 'surely that must prove that I am not the kidnapper, Miss Crump?'

Dumfounded, Wilhelmina merely stared at him.

Taking her blank expression as one of affirmation, the duke continued speaking as he once again retrieved the knife and this time tucked it into his waistband. 'Well, now that we have cleared up that little misunderstanding and I have the vital piece of information regarding the hostages' whereabouts, I shall take you home, Miss Crump, before I go on and rescue these poor women.'

Her eyes widened at this statement and she was relieved to find that her power of speech had returned. 'Surely you cannot expect me to go home *now*, sir,' she argued. 'After everything I have just witnessed. I want to come with you.'

'Out of the question, madam,' he informed, rubbing his right hand. 'It will be far too dangerous.'

'But surely then, it would be best if we went and told the whole story to the Runners, sir,' she suggested.

The duke shook his head dismissively. 'I do not wish to waste the entire night explaining everything to the Runners a dozen times or more,' he said curtly.

Given what Wilhelmina had witnessed of Mr Curtis, she could find no argument with this point and her mind began searching for another suggestion. Before she could think of a single one however, the duke, intent on his plans, began issuing a set of instructions.

'Now come, Miss Crump,' he commanded briskly. 'I shall take you home and then collect my horse from Bourdon Street.'

All reasoning failing her, she replied with the only word she could think of. 'No,' she contradicted.

His dark brows shot to his hairline. 'What?' he demanded.

'I will not go home, sir,' she said. 'I think you forget that it is *my* cousin you are intending to rescue.'

His eyes clouded over once again with anger. 'You will go home if I have to carry you myself,' he told her.

'Then carry me you shall, sir and I shall scream every inch of the way,' she stated defiantly.

He looked at her through narrowed eyes and she began to think she had pushed him a little too far.

'Damn you woman,' he suddenly declared. 'You may come, but one word from you and I shall tie you up just like I have done with the comte. Do you understand me?'

Not daring to disagree, Wilhelmina meekly nodded her head.

CHAPTER 22

A Journey to Kent

WITH a million questions swirling around in her head, but not daring to voice a single one of them, Wilhelmina made her way to Bourdon Street in complete silence, the duke striding ahead of her in such a purposeful manner that she was forced into a jog in order to keep pace. Arriving at his house and not wishing to arouse any suspicion, he quickly saddled up his stallion and a second horse, a chestnut bay, for Wilhelmina. Having mounted their steeds, the two of them then began their journey.

The duke took the lead, in no doubt as to the exact location of their destination. They rode quickly through the mainly empty streets and were out of the city in some fifteen minutes, heading south towards Kent. Eventually, having ridden along a number of country lanes and traversed several fields, he slowed his horse to a trot and indicated to Wilhelmina to do likewise.

'We will dismount here,' he instructed, pulling the stallion to a halt. 'They may hear us if we ride any nearer.'

Not daring to speak in case he lost his temper with her again, Wilhelmina nodded her acquiescence and the two of them dismounted and led the horses to a small wood where they tethered them to a tree.

'The woodcutter's house is on the other side of these trees,' informed the duke, tying off his mount's reins.

Wilhelmina bit her lip, while he regarded her stonily for a few minutes. To her great relief, he then conceded, 'You may come with me, Miss Crump, while I assess the situation but I warn you—'

As he repeated his threats, Wilhelmina experienced a strong

urge to tell him exactly what she thought of them and him. With his treatment of the comte fresh in her mind however, she decided it wiser to bite her tongue.

They made their way silently through the group of trees, and then as the house came into view, bent down low. The building was outlined in the dim light of the moon, and Wilhelmina noted that it was not only small but also in a state of some dilapidation. It consisted of one floor only, with a door in the centre and one window to either side of it, indicating that the structure was likely to consist of no more than two rooms.

They headed first towards the right-hand window, which was poorly covered by a pair of ragged curtains. The room was in darkness but, squinting through one of the fraying holes, Wilhelmina could just about discern the dark outlines of four slim bodies slouched against the walls – their ankles and wrists obviously bound. Her hand shot to her mouth as she spotted a figure she instantly recognized as Lavinia, huddled in the right-hand corner. Hot tears immediately flooded her eyes and resentment and anger coursed through her at the appalling treatment of her cousin – and indeed all the poor women. She should have liked nothing more at that moment than to rush into the building and drag them all out herself.

The duke, sensing her desire for action, placed a restraining hand on her arm and raised a finger to his lips, reaffirming the need for her to remain silent. He then inclined his head to the left, indicating that they should move onto the other window. Bright candlelight was filtering its way from this room, the curtains here being as ineffective as the previous pair, and so allowed the observers an excellent view inside. There were two scruffy men in the room, seated on upturned beer barrels and engaged in a game of whist. Two more barrels were lying on their side on the floor and, from the men's raucous laughter, there remained little doubt as to the fate of the contents. Having observed the drunken scene for a few seconds, the duke then inclined his head again – this time back towards the wooded area.

Back at that destination, Wilhelmina collapsed in a stunned and furious state onto the ground and looked imploringly at the duke. 'We must do something immediately, sir,' she urged with a catch to her voice. 'We cannot allow those poor women to languish in such appalling conditions for a moment longer.'

'I fully intend not to allow them to languish, Miss Crump,' he replied brusquely as he marched over to his horse. To her amazement, he then reached up to the saddle-bag and drew out a pistol. 'This time you *will* stay here,' he commanded.

Wilhelmina's eyes widened in dismay. 'But you cannot go in there alone,' she gasped, raw panic pulsing through her. 'There are at least two of them. Possibly more. Surely we should go to seek help.'

'I do not wish to waste more time, madam,' he stated firmly. 'I can assure you I have dealt with much more dangerous enemies than two drunken louts. Now stay here,' he instructed calmly, 'and if I do not return within twenty minutes, then you may go to the Runners.'

Not wishing even to contemplate that possibility, Wilhelmina merely nodded.

Rather than turn directly on his heel and march away, however, the duke continued to look down upon her in such a disconcerting manner that it brought an embarrassed flush to her cheeks. Then, without uttering another word, he turned around and strode away.

With that look adding to the confusion of the kiss and the other improbable events of the evening, a perplexed Wilhelmina watched the outline of his retreating broad back slowly disappear into the darkness. A thousand questions still remained unanswered about the duke's behaviour but there was now no doubt in her mind that the heroic, handsome Duke of Linthorpe was the perfect man to be The Stag.

She was still absorbed in her reverie when a rough, blistered hand clamped itself tightly around her mouth and a voice laced with alcohol slurred into her ear, 'Now then, what's a pretty little thing like you doing out here?'

Instinctively she bit into the hand as hard as she could causing the culprit to yelp and at once release his hold of her. Without wasting a moment, she was on her feet and about to run away. She found however, for the second time that evening, that as his arm reached out and pulled her back, she had completely misjudged her opponent's reflexes.

'My, feisty little thing, ain't yer?' he said, leering at her. 'Makes it a bit more exciting though, I always find.'

Taking her by surprise, he then spun her around, roughly forcing her back against a tree. She noted that he was a short, stout fellow, dressed in a grubby white shirt, with a spotted kerchief knotted around his thick neck and a pair of tight-fitting fawn breeches.

'Now then,' he continued, sneering, 'let's be 'aving ourselves a bit o' sport.' His thin lips then formed an evil grin revealing two rows of cracked, yellow teeth. As he lowered them to her face, Wilhelmina did the only thing she could think of and spat at him.

His head jerked back immediately. 'Hmm,' he slurred drunkenly, wiping his face with the back of his hand. 'Looks like I might 'ave to use a bit more force that I'd reckoned.' He raised the same hand as if to slap her across the face.

She closed her eyes, bracing herself for the impact of the blow, but immediately opened them again as a male voice boomed with nerve-shattering authority, 'Take your hands off her this instant, man!'

Wilhelmina's gaze darted from the duke to the drunk. With the latter's eyes still fixed upon hers, he lifted one thick bushy eyebrow as his mouth formed yet another evil sneer. He then, very slowly, released his hold of Wilhelmina and turned around to face the duke who was standing some ten feet away from him.

Wilhelmina shrank back against the tree, her body flooding with a mixture of relief at being free of the man and dread at what was to follow.

'Well, what 'ave we here?' sniggered the drunk. 'Little rescue party, is it?'

'Something like that,' replied the duke, eyeing the man contemptuously.

'Well now, ain't that nice?' remarked the drunk. 'Don't normally get many visitors, we don't.'

'You do surprise me, sir,' informed the duke, his tone dripping with sarcasm. 'Particularly as your hospitality appears to be second to none.'

The man's eyes narrowed as he regarded the duke with menace. The younger man however, appeared not in the least intimidated.

'Now, I should inform you that I have already apprehended your two colleagues – who submitted themselves quite willingly. May I suggest you do the same, sir.'

185

'Think yer clever, do yer?' snarled the man.

The duke flashed a satirical smile. 'Clever enough to deal with you.'

'Are yer now?' scoffed the adversary. 'Well, let's see how clever yer are when yer lying on the ground ... dead.'

In a flash he whipped a pistol from his pocket and fired it directly at the duke. Two reports sounded within split seconds of each other. Indeed, the whole incident happened so quickly that Wilhelmina was too astounded to make a sound as she waited, with a sickeningly numb feeling, for the duke to fall. It was, however, to her utmost amazement and relief, not the duke but the drunk who landed face down on the ground with a deadening thud. She looked askance from him to the duke from the barrel of whose own gun rose a little puff of smoke. She then watched in stunned silence as the duke dropped his pistol and clamped his right hand to the top of his left arm, all colour draining from his face.

She rushed over to him, observing the dark patch of spreading blood – evident even against the black fabric of his jacket.

'Come and sit down,' she instructed, leading him to a sawn-off tree trunk.

'It is only a scratch,' he muttered weakly.

'We'll decide what it is once we've had a look at it,' insisted Wilhelmina.

He made no protest as he sat down and she carefully removed his jacket. Then, crouching down to him, she rested his left hand in her lap and gently rolled up the sleeve of his shirt. As her hands came into contact with his bare skin, she was shocked to find some rather disturbing thoughts intruding her mind. Not without some difficulty, she reined these in and meticulously peeled away the thin cotton from the area of the wound. She could see no sign of the bullet being lodged within. Indeed, it appeared that it had flown directly past him, grazing his arm badly on its journey.

She pulled out her handkerchief from her skirt pocket and wrapped it tightly around the wound. She would make him comfortable and then go in to do what she could for the hostages before riding off for more help, she decided.

She was in the throes of tying off the knot in the handkerchief when they heard the sound of a snapping twig. The duke's head jerked upwards and they gazed at each other in silence, but before they had a chance to do or say anything, a figure came into view which they were astonished to recognize.

Wilhelmina leapt to her feet. 'Tipping!' she exclaimed, her voice crammed with relief. 'Thank God you are come. But how on earth did you know we were here?'

As astounded as they were, Tipping wrinkled his forehead in bewilderment. 'Miss Crump,' he remarked puzzled. 'And his grace. But I had not the slightest idea you were here. What are you—'

'But if you didn't know *we* were here, then why on earth are *you* here?' she enquired with equal bewilderment.

'I'm here with The Stag, ma'am,' informed Tipping. 'To apprehend the perpetrators and rescue the hostages.'

Wilhelmina scratched her head. 'But the Duke of Linthorpe has already apprehended the perpetrators.'

'Ah,' nodded Tipping, with a knowing smile. 'So his grace was responsible for the capturing of the Comte de Roxford? We did wonder who had been there before us when we arrived at the park this evening – a little later than we had planned, Miss Crump – due to a problem with my horse's shoe.'

'So it was *you* I was to meet in the park?'

'Yes, ma'am,' clarified Tipping. 'Who did you think you were to meet?'

'Why The-The Stag of course – the Duke of Linthorpe,' she blustered somewhat nonplussed.

'Oh no, ma'am,' rejoined Tipping shaking his head gravely. 'The Duke of Linthorpe is not The Stag.'

No sooner had the words left the man's mouth, than they became aware of another approaching figure. Wilhelmina felt her head beginning to spin when she saw who it was.

'This, ma'am, is The Stag,' informed Tipping with a knowing smile.

Staring wide-eyed at the man, she stammered, 'But I never . . . that is I would never have . . . I mean I didn't for one moment think—'

'And nor were you supposed to ma'am,' replied the rector, Mr Dartford with a disarming grin.

'But I-I don't understand,' stammered Wilhelmina, shaking her head in bafflement. 'What on earth is going on?'

'You have been working for the rector and me, Miss Crump,'

informed Tipping, rushing over to the duke.

Wilhelmina gasped. 'So *you* have been delivering the notes to me all this time?'

'Indeed, I have, ma'am,' replied the valet, with an apologetic smile.

Wilhelmina stared at him blankly, attempting to assimilate yet another astonishing revelation.

'Would you like us to explain, ma'am?' enquired the rector, sensing her obvious confusion.

'I should be much obliged, sir,' she muttered softly.

He took a deep breath. 'Well,' he began, 'Mr Tipping and I work very closely with our colleagues in France. As you are aware, that country is experiencing a great many problems at the moment – not least of which is a political battle between various members of the aristocracy, who are hoping to exploit the situation to further their own positions.'

None of this made anything any clearer to Wilhelmina, who merely continued staring. The rector meanwhile, calmly continued.

'Two of these prominent power-seekers are the Comte de Roxford and his rival the Duc d'Orléans. The duc, as you may be aware, Miss Crump, is a very rich and powerful man. He plays on – and indeed exacerbates – the mob's hatred of the French monarchy. He wishes to be rid of the king and queen and take over power himself, as indeed does the Comte de Roxford.'

'But how could they possibly even hope to do so?' she asked, still completely bewildered.

'The Duc d'Orléans is exceedingly clever and a master of propaganda,' continued the cleric evenly. 'He has set up various scurrilous leaflet campaigns to discredit the royal family and has been highly visible in giving out thousands of *livres* to the peasants. In other words, he is using every trick in the book to buy his popularity with the French people. The Comte de Roxford, on the other hand, having very limited resources, could not hope to compete with the duc on such a scale. He therefore needed to raise funds for his own campaign via other methods – such as kidnapping.'

'But I thought he was rich,' said Wilhelmina, wrinkling her brow as she attempted to assimilate all the information. 'He told us that he owned a chateau.'

'Oh, and I believe he does, ma'am,' piped up Tipping as he carefully untied Wilhelmina's hastily bound handkerchief from his master's arm. 'In fact I think he owns the entire ruin.'

'Oh,' replied Wilhelmina, taken aback. Then, as another question occurred to her, 'But why has he come to England to carry out the kidnappings?'

'Because,' explained the rector, 'he suspected his plans of being discovered in Paris and no longer dared proceed with them there. He has too many enemies in France to risk being exposed as the rogue that he is. His image to the people must be of an honest citizen doing his utmost to ease the suffering of the lower classes.'

'So he thought that if he came to England he could avoid suspicion and still carry on raising his monies?'

The rector nodded his head. 'Exactly, Miss Crump. He has, of course, been keeping his presence in the country as secret as possible. Indeed, in my extensive efforts to track down the man, he has proved as slippery as a barrel of eels.'

'But how did you find out about these plans of his?' asked Wilhelmina.

'The very first letter you brought with you from Paris,' confirmed Mr Dartford. 'That informed us that the comte had been planning an extensive kidnapping campaign in Paris but, suspecting his plans had been thwarted, might attempt to try his luck in England instead. We have been trying to track him down ever since although, as I have already said, he has proved a highly elusive character.'

There was a brief silence while Wilhelmina attempted to digest all this astonishing information. As she did so, however, yet another question came to mind.

'But, if the Duke of Linthorpe was not involved in your investigation, then what on earth is *he* doing here?'

She turned to the slumped figure of the Duke of Linthorpe sitting on the sawn-off tree trunk. He lifted his pale face to her.

'Why, is it not perfectly obvious, Miss Crump? When I found out what had happened to your cousin, I was worried that you would be next.'

'But why ever should you have thought such a thing, sir?' she asked, flummoxed.

'Because,' he replied with more than a hint of impatience, 'the

189

kidnapper appeared to be targeting beautiful blonde women and by my reckoning there cannot now be too many of those remaining in the city.'

Wilhelmina's brow furrowed still further. 'So you-you followed me this evening with the sole purpose of protecting me?'

'Indeed, madam,' he confirmed. 'Or, to be more precise, I followed the Comte de Roxford, following you. I had an idea that the kidnapper might well resort to alternative measures to lure his prey and therefore considered it prudent to keep watch on your house. I spotted the man lurking in the shadows and then, when you did appear, I knew that I had been correct in my assumption although, I must confess, until this evening I did have another suspect in mind – one whom I have been observing very closely.'

'May I ask who that was, sir?' enquired Tipping.

'Indeed you may, man. It was that damned Earl of Thurlston, of course,' admitted the duke scornfully. 'The man seems to thrive on surrounding himself with beautiful blondes. Been following him for a couple of weeks now trying to catch him in the act – and at the most unsociable hours, I might add.'

Wilhelmina said nothing but stared at the duke in utter amazement. Not only had he risked his own life to protect her, but he had implied that he thought she was beautiful. Despite the rather incongruous circumstances in which they currently found themselves, a little bubble of happiness expanded deep inside her.

Unaware of the reaction his confession had evoked in Wilhelmina, the duke, as flummoxed as she was, began his own round of questioning.

'But what is your part in this, Tipping?' he asked, wincing with pain as his valet inadvertently touched the wound.

'Oh, I have many talents other than shining boots, sir,' informed Tipping, grimacing slightly as he peeled away the makeshift bandage. 'In fact I have been a secret agent now for some twelve years.'

'Secret agent? For twelve years. But I never suspected a thing.'

'That is why it is "secret", your grace,' pointed out Tipping, applying a pad to the wound which he had made from his own handkerchief.

'And we must of course congratulate *you*, Miss Crump,' interpolated Mr Dartford, 'not only on the successful accomplishment of all the tasks we required of you, but also of your complete discretion at all times.'

Wilhelmina flushed slightly at the praise. 'Well, I confess, it was not always easy, sir,' she muttered diffidently as she recalled some of the more awkward moments of her experiences.

The duke flinched again as Tipping secured the pad with Wilhelmina's handkerchief. 'What on earth are you talking about now?' he enquired with a hint of irritation.

'Miss Crump has been an invaluable help to us throughout the entire operation sir,' informed the Reverend. 'We suspected that our usual contacts were being observed and therefore needed some fresh blood to help us with our lines of communication. Miss Crump was chosen by our contact in France for her quick thinking and her level head and has proved a first-class choice. She has risked her own safety on numerous occasions in the successful accomplishment of all that we asked of her.'

The duke regarded her strangely before declaring, 'Good God. And she delivers babies as well.'

Tipping nodded his head in admiration. 'Now that, sir, is a skill which even I do not claim to possess.'

Having done as much as he could for the duke's wound, given their limited resources, Tipping then announced, 'Well, I am sure you must both have a hundred and one other questions but our first priority must now be to release the hostages. His grace's disposal of the perpetrators has made our task much simpler. Now that you have done all the hard work this evening, sir, you may leave it to the rector and me to remove the hostages. I suggest you stay here, Miss Crump, and keep an eye on his lordship.'

Wilhelmina nodded obediently.

The rector and Tipping then produced black kerchiefs from their pockets and tied them around the lower part of their faces.

'As I'm sure you can appreciate, Miss Crump,' explained the clergyman gravely, 'we have no desire to reveal our identities. This is particularly important to me in this mission, given that I do not wish your cousin to recognize me.'

Wilhelmina nodded understandingly. The duke, meanwhile, said nothing, but gazed in astonishment at all three of his accomplices.

CHAPTER 23

AS IT happened, there was no need at all for the rector and Tipping to disguise themselves for it was discovered, upon entering the house, that every one of the hostages had been drugged, so that they were all unconscious.

Mr Dartford, having considered the finer details of the mission, had not only forwarded word to the Bow Street Runners informing them of the Comte de Roxford's whereabouts and his involvement in the kidnappings but had also arranged for a farmer's cart to convey the women back to London.

'Not quite the mode of transport they are used to,' he confessed, grimacing as the unconscious bodies were carefully placed inside and covered with blankets, 'but given the circumstances, I do not think they will judge me too cruelly for the lack of velvet squabs.'

As Lavinia was carried out, Wilhelmina briefly left the side of the duke and went to assist. Her cousin looked so very pale and vulnerable that a tear escaped her as she watched the cleric deposit the girl gently in the cart.

'She is very beautiful, Miss Crump,' he uttered softly, gazing affectionately upon the girl's sleeping angelic face.

'Yes, sir. She is,' agreed Wilhelmina, wiping away the tear.

With the two unconscious drunken guards trussed up in a similar fashion to that of their leader and left behind in the cottage for the Runners to deal with, the little cavalcade wound its way to London with its sleeping cargo, including the injured Duke of Linthorpe, in the back of the cart.

Mr Dartford had, much to Wilhelmina's amazement, secured a house in an unassuming street on the edge of the city where the hostages were to be taken, before being returned to their homes at a more reasonable hour of the day once they had received the necessary medical attention and awoken from their drugged state.

With all of the women placed under the care of the two doctors awaiting them, the rescue party retired to a small saloon. The Duke of Linthorpe, whose wound had been cleaned and dressed by one of the medics, was now reposing on a red velvet sofa looking decidedly wan but, Wilhelmina considered, still incredibly handsome. One of the servants brought in a welcoming tray of tea, a plate of ham sandwiches and a large raisin cake. They all tucked in heartily, regardless of the fact that it was a little before five o'clock in the morning.

'One thing I can't understand, Tipping,' admitted Wilhelmina, breaking up a piece of cake on her plate, 'is what on earth you would have done if I had stayed in Chipping Sodbury and not come to London at all?'

'Well, then things would most definitely not have proved so easy, ma'am,' confessed the man, cutting a slice of cake. 'It did make our job a whole lot simpler when you came to London and then I could scarce believe my luck when we ended up residing under the same roof.'

'But how did you know I *had* come to London?' she continued, puzzled.

'Believe me, ma'am,' informed Tipping solemnly. 'There have been very few moments when you have not been observed by a member of our group since you came back from Paris.'

Wilhelmina raised a questioning eyebrow. 'You mean I have been *followed* ever since my return?'

Tipping nodded his head a little sheepishly. 'For most of it, ma'am. For your own safety, of course.'

'I see,' she murmured, with an involuntary shiver. Then, persisting with her questioning, 'But tell me about the notes, Tipping. I assume it was easy for you to deposit the envelopes in my bedchamber and my reticule when we were residing under the same roof but how did you manage to slip the first one into my reticule at Lady Carlton's ball?'

'Ah, my brother, Howard, helped me out there, ma'am. He is one of Lady Carlton's footmen and was waiting on at the ball. In fact, I believe the two of you almost collided as he walked by you carrying a tray full of champagne glasses.'

Wilhelmina recalled the incident and nodded. 'But I was sure someone was watching me that evening when I delivered the note, Tipping. I distinctly saw someone lurking around the fruit barrow.'

'Oh, that was just the fruit boy, ma'am,' clarified Tipping. 'Apparently he had had one barrow stolen the week before and had no intention of losing another.'

'I see,' muttered Wilhelmina, feeling a little deflated that it had not been something more exciting – particularly as the revelation of her part in the drama appeared to be making quite an impression on the Duke of Linthorpe, who was regarding her with a look she desperately hoped was of admiration. 'And the last note? The one I received via the puppy – in the park?'

'I paid a flower girl to deliver that one, ma'am. Although I've seen the day I would have gone crawling around myself, my knees just aren't up to it any more.'

'Well,' exclaimed Wilhelmina, with a sigh of relief. 'Thank goodness it has all turned out for the best. Can I now be assured that I shall receive no further notes, Tipping?'

'Oh, I'm afraid I can't promise you that, ma'am,' replied Tipping gravely. 'We never know when we need to call upon our special agents.'

'Special agent?' repeated the duke astounded. 'Miss Crump? A special agent?'

'Yes, sir,' confirmed Tipping with some alacrity. 'She has proved herself to be most reliable. Now if you don't mind me saying so, your grace, I think we should be getting you back to Bourdon Street so that you may rest properly.'

'Good idea, Tipping,' agreed Mr Dartford. 'I will have one of the carriages take Miss Crump home at the same time.'

Wilhelmina experienced a pang of disappointment as the group began to disband. Before they took their leave of the little house, however, the cleric assured them that he would arrange to deliver all the hostages safely home later that day. He also stressed once again the importance of confidentiality: no one, he insisted, should reveal under any circumstances, anything of their part – or indeed of anyone else's – in the mission. With those words resounding in their ears, Tipping and the duke headed off in a carriage to Bourdon Street and Wilhelmina was deposited by another conveyance to Number 22, Grosvenor Square, just as the first fingers of dawn began streaking across the sky.

Number 22, Grosvenor Square

Having slipped quietly into the house and up to her room just minutes before the first servants arose to begin their daily duties, Wilhelmina lay in bed, her head spinning with the events of the previous evening. She could, of course, scarcely contain her excitement at the thought of Lavinia coming home later that day – thank the Lord, unharmed. In order to savour the moment properly, she knew she should at least make some attempt to sleep a little. Every time she closed her eyes, however, the same handsome face flashed before her and the memory of his lips on hers. If she did not know better, she would think that she had quite lost her heart to the man with whom she had experienced so much in just a few hours that evening. But, she reminded herself quickly, he had only kissed her to shut her up. Why, she pondered dolefully, would the man pay her the slightest bit of attention when he was already involved with God knows how many beautiful women? She had best rid herself of all ridiculous notions regarding the Duke of Linthorpe. The man belonged to one – or two – others. For now, however, she was content to imagine that none of those others existed.

At nine o'clock, having slept for no more than a few minutes, Wilhelmina was seated at the breakfast table with a silent, morose Uncle Ernest, when there sounded a loud rap on the door. As had been the case every time there had been a knock at the door since Lavinia's disappearance, the man was on his feet and out into the hall at a speed which completely belied his two-and-sixty years. Desperate to go with him but not wishing to arouse the slightest suspicion, Wilhelmina held her breath for several seconds before she heard her uncle cry joyously, 'Oh thank God! Mrs Crump! Mrs Crump! Our daughter is returned. And unharmed!'

Contrary to the drugged, unconscious state in which Wilhelmina had witnessed her cousin only a few short hours before, Lavinia, having undergone an emotional and tearful reunion with her parents, her cousin, the puppy and even Hodge, the butler, now appeared in the brightest of spirits, lapping up all the attention which was justly awarded her. Having been fed, bathed, attired in clean clothes and brought up-to-date with proceedings by an uncharacteristically animated Mr Curtis, Aunt Clementine deposited her daughter on the chaise-longue in the lemon drawing-room and piled a mountain of blankets and pillows around her.

'And it is the strangest thing, Papa,' declared Lavinia, as she peeped out from under the mound of coverlets, 'but when we all came to this morning, there was no one at all in the house – only a row of hackneys with our names and directions awaiting us outside. We have not the slightest idea who was responsible for our rescue.'

'Well, we shall not worry too much about that, my girl,' remarked Aunt Clementine briskly as she busied herself with the plumping up of one of Lavinia's many pillows. 'The fact of the matter is that someone *did* rescue you and whoever it was, we shall be eternally grateful to them.'

'Hear, hear,' concurred Uncle Ernest.

'What I can't believe, my love,' continued Aunt Clementine, now attempting to tuck the covers under Lavinia's chin, 'is that the monster who carried out these atrocities was none other than the man you had your heart set upon marrying.'

Lavinia grimaced. 'Well, not any more, Mama,' she stated firmly. 'In fact I had quite gone off the idea of marrying the wretched man even before this escapade.'

Aunt Clementine's brows shot to her hairline. 'Oh really?' she enquired hopefully. 'And do you perhaps have your heart set upon another, dear?'

'Perhaps,' mused Lavinia with a coy smile.

'Oh, how perfectly splendid,' declared Aunt Clementine, clapping her hands together in delight.

The following day, the mysterious rescue of all the hostages and the involvement of the Comte de Roxford claimed the headlines of every one of the newspapers and brought with it a stream of curious visitors including, of course, the ubiquitous Drinkwaters.

'We came as soon as we heard, my dear,' gushed Mrs Drinkwater, flouncing into the drawing-room where Lavinia could just about be spotted under the mound of blankets, the sleeping puppy balancing precariously on top. 'Oh, thank the Lord that you have returned –

and unharmed, my love,' she went on, bustling over to the chair next to Lavinia. 'We have scarce slept a wink since you went missing, dear girl. Indeed Verity has been quite out of sorts – despite the fact that the prince himself brushed passed her on Tuesday evening. And not only that, but he also apologized for doing so. "Your pardon, ma'am," he said. Just like that. Why, with all these goings on, is it any wonder I am so exhausted?' she puffed.

'Well, please do not concern yourself any longer on my behalf, Mrs Drinkwater,' said Lavinia. 'As you can see, I am quite well.'

'Which is more than can be said for that odious man, the Comte de Roxford,' remarked Verity, elegantly lowering her slender form into one of the striped armchairs. 'Who would have believed that your "almost-betrothed" could be capable of carrying out such horrific deeds?'

'Who indeed?' replied Lavinia, as she began stroking the silky fur of the pup.

There then followed a brief pause as all occupants of the room awaited a cutting retort from Lavinia, but to their amazement, the girl appeared not the least perturbed by Verity's gloating, and carried on stroking her sleeping pet.

A number of astounded looks having been exchanged around the room, Mrs Drinkwater then broke the silence by enquiring, 'But what of your mysterious rescuers, my dear? Do you really have not the least idea who they were?'

'Not the least, ma'am,' confessed Lavinia with a beatific smile.

The second person of note to visit Grosvenor Square, immediately following the none-too-soon departure of the quizzing Drinkwaters, was the Earl of Thurlston who had been present in the lemon drawing-room for fewer than five minutes when the Duke of Linthorpe arrived. Wilhelmina's heart leapt when the butler announced him.

Looking as handsome as ever, despite the dark smudges beneath each of his eyes, no one would ever have guessed that he had been involved in a bloody skirmish just hours before. His wounded left arm, hanging rather limply by his side, was concealed under his jacket.

Wilhelmina noted that his charming smile faltered very briefly as he set eyes upon the Earl of Thurlston. His greeting to her, much to her chagrin, was the usual curt exchange of words, which revealed to no one the fact that the two of them had shared a passionate kiss only hours before. Or at least, she reflected, that with her limited experience of kissing, she had thought it passionate. To the duke, of course, it might have been an everyday run-of-the-mill kiss which, for all she was aware, he could carry out ten times a day with any number of his admirers.

The duke's timely arrival, coinciding with that of the earl, meant that he was not forced to expend too much energy in feigning a lack of knowledge of Lavinia's adventure. It also benefited Lavinia, who had only to repeat her story once more for the ears of her two handsome male visitors.

With every detail of the escapade fully recited and examined, the duke then politely enquired of Aunt Clementine, 'I was wondering, Mrs Crump, if you should all like to return to Linthorpe. I believe the fresh air there will greatly aid Miss Crump's recovery.'

Aunt Clementine's mouth spread into a large pearly grin. 'How very thoughtful of you, your grace,' she enthused. 'We should be delighted to return to Linthorpe, should we not, Lavinia dear?'

'Yes, we should, Mama,' beamed Lavinia, her eyes shining brightly. 'Indeed I can think of nothing I should like more.'

CHAPTER 24

Linthorpe Hall

ALTHOUGH it seemed a positive age since they had left Linthorpe, it was in fact only a matter of days and Wilhelmina was therefore not surprised to see that nothing had changed – at least on the surface. The fact that the Duke of Linthorpe was invading her thoughts on rather too frequent a basis and disturbing her sleep with worrying regularity, was a matter which she was not about to divulge to anyone – particularly not the man himself, who had resumed his usual cool, off-hand manner towards her. She hoped that this coolness, was perhaps because he did not wish to arouse any suspicion – that being, after all, the manner in which he usually treated her. More likely, however, she realized that it was probably because he had not given her a moment's thought since the rescue evening.

'I am delighted to inform you that we shall be joined by another party of guests tomorrow,' announced the duke over dinner that evening. 'My sister and her family are to visit.'

Aunt Clementine dropped her fork as a flush of excitement spread over her countenance. 'Your sister, your grace? How positively thrilling. Is that not thrilling that we should get to meet his grace's family, Lavinia dear?' she trilled excitedly.

'It is, Mama,' concurred Lavinia, without the slightest hint of her usual belligerent tone. 'Quite thrilling indeed.'

'And may I enquire as to the young lady's name, sir?' probed Aunt Clementine, her eyes shining with exhilaration.

'You may, Mrs Crump,' replied the duke, calmly. 'She is Lady

Grace, Duchesse de Fontainebleu.'

Aunt Clementine almost choked on her capon. 'A *duchesse*? Oh, this is simply too marvellous for words, sir. What do you think of that, Mr Crump? Not only will we have the presence of the duke himself at dinner tomorrow but we will also be joined by French aristocracy.'

Uncle Ernest nodded in the manner of one suitably impressed. 'Splendid, splendid,' he muttered through his whiskers. 'Any idea what we'll be having for dinner tomorrow, your grace? Could do with some more of this buttered crab. Best I've ever tasted.'

Aunt Clementine glared at her spouse. 'Manners, Mr Crump,' she scolded.

Uncle Ernest looked contrite. 'Sorry, dear,' he muttered remorsefully.

If Wilhelmina had thought that, given the events of the previous week, nothing else could surprise her in the least, she was soon to discover that she was mistaken. Having been dragged to an upstairs window by Aunt Clementine, who was attempting to hide her own plump form together with that of Lavinia and her niece, behind a single blue velvet curtain, she found herself unwillingly sharing a surreptitious observation of the new aristocratic arrivals. As the elegant green carriage pulled up at the front door and the duchesse stepped out, Wilhelmina's eyes grew as wide as saucers for, dressed in a beautiful gown of green velvet, was none other than the red-haired woman she had seen on the ship and at Linthorpe previously. This time, however, rather than the tearful, miserable expression she had sported on both those occasions, the happiness emanating from her beautiful face was visible for all to see. And the surprise did not stop there. Not only was the woman accompanied by a tall, handsome gentleman with a head of thick blond hair, but there also appeared two little boys of some four years who bore not only a striking similarity to their father but an identical resemblance to each other. The woman, catching sight of her trio of eager observers, waved to them with a broad smile on her face.

'Oh my,' muttered Aunt Clementine through gritted teeth, as she schooled her features into an expression of surprise and attempted to wave blithely back. 'We must simply say that we were admiring the gardens, girls, for it will not do at all if Lady Grace thinks we were spying on her. Indeed I do believe I can think of nothing more embarrassing. Pass me a chair, Lavinia dear – I feel one of my turns coming on.'

As it turned out, Lady Grace, much to Aunt Clementine's relief, was far too charming to mention anything at all about the 'spying' incident. Indeed the duchesse and her family proved to be charming company – particularly the twins, Henri and Edouard, who formed an immediate bond with the delighted puppy.

With all the happenings of the last few days, Wilhelmina was grateful for a little time alone as she strolled around the gardens after dinner that evening. She was sitting on her favourite bench in the orchard marvelling at the deep flashes of orange, pink and purple cast by the setting sun, when she spotted the duchesse walking towards her, a genuine, concerned look hovering over her beautiful features.

'My dear Miss Crump,' she opened anxiously, upon reaching the bench and seating herself alongside her. 'I have been desperate to speak to you alone all day. You must be wondering what on earth has been going on, child.'

Taken aback at this candid statement, Wilhelmina hesitated, 'Well – I, um – I own I was, er, rather worried about you, ma'am.'

'So my brother informs me,' said Lady Grace, her knowing smile causing two spots of colour to appear in Wilhelmina's cheeks. 'And I can assure you there is not the slightest need for you to be embarrassed, my dear,' she continued softly. 'Your concern has been extremely touching and our actions were, after all, not conventional behaviour. I would, if I may, like to explain.'

Wilhelmina nodded her consent and was surprised to see a sudden wave of sadness wash over the duchesse's countenance as she turned her eyes away from her and focused them on the folds of her ivory gown. 'I believe you were in Paris on the evening of the riots, Miss Crump,' she began, with a tremor to her voice.

Wilhelmina nodded again.

'Well, that evening my husband, Olivier, was in Italy on a business matter and little Edouard and I were returning to Paris in our carriage, having spent the day visiting friends near Versailles. When we reached the city we could scarce believe what was happening. I had never seen such chaos in my entire life.'

'Nor I, ma'am,' concurred Wilhelmina, recalling the hatred of the mob, the fires, the looting and the terrorizing.

'Our carriage was attacked,' continued Lady Grace, producing a lace handkerchief from her sleeve and twisting it anxiously between her fingers. 'It was terrifying. They killed our poor driver, Jules. Just left him on the ground. Then they ... they dragged Edouard and me from the carriage and began taunting us; pushing us around as if we were—'

She broke off as a lone tear streaked its way down her velvety smooth cheek.

'I tried to be strong, of course, for Edouard's sake. He was terrified, poor little mite, but my attempts to stand up to them only served to anger them even more. Then one of the men ... he ... he tried to carry me off, but not before telling me exactly what he was going to do to me. Edouard was screaming. The women were laughing—'

She trailed off again, taking a moment to compose herself.

'We were very fortunate,' she sniffed. 'Had it not been for the soldiers arriving at that moment I dread to think what would have happened. But one of the soldiers ... he was very young, very ... eager. He ... he shot dead the man who was threatening me.'

Wilhelmina gulped.

'It was all over in a second. He fell to the ground like a—'

Tears began tumbling freely on to the ivory silk of the duchesse's skirts.

'The man's brother was part of the crowd who were taunting us. He watched his brother die right in front of him. He blamed me. He said that it was all my fault his brother had been killed. He said I should not have made such a fuss. He called me all sorts of terrible names and then he threatened to ... to kill us: Edourd and me. Slaughter us like pigs was what he said. If it was the last thing he did.'

Wilhelmina grimaced.

'My first thought of course, was to flee the city immediately but there was Henri. He had stayed at home with his governess. He had a cold.'

She took a deep breath before proceeding. 'We ran to the house as quickly as we could but when we arrived it was on fire – flames pouring from all the windows. There was nothing I could do, Miss

Crump, other than pray that Henri and the governess had escaped. I didn't even know where to begin looking for them. There were people everywhere – shouting and screaming and . . . and all the while there was that man. That dreadful, wicked man following us—'

Wilhelmina felt a tear of her own escape.

'I . . . I just stood there, in the middle of street, with all this chaos going on around me. I had not the first idea what to do. Had it not been for William, then I dare not even think of what our fate would have been.'

'William?' repeated Wilhelmina slightly baffled.

The duchesse nodded her head of glistening red curls. 'His ship had docked in Calais the day before and he had ridden to Paris to visit us. He appeared just at that very moment. When I had lost all hope.'

'Thank God,' murmured Wilhelmina, who could only imagine the terror the woman must have experienced.

'He took us both back to Calais immediately,' continued the duchesse. 'I, of course, was in a dreadful state: worrying about what had happened to Henri and what could happen to Edouard and me if that man found us and . . . and—'

Wilhelmina nodded her understanding.

'Then, having made sure we were safe – or as safe as we could be given the circumstances – William returned immediately to Paris and began searching for Henri. He searched all day. For hours and hours. But he could find no trace of him or the governess. He returned to the ship that evening: the evening you were aboard. He had responsibilities to his crew too, of course. He promised that once Edouard and I were in England, he would return to Paris and renew his search, which he did. As soon as we were safely settled at Linthorpe, he headed back to that dreadful place, but yet again he could find no sign of the child. I, of course, was frantic with worry and still living in dread of that man discovering my whereabouts. To make matters worse, we had no way of contacting my husband. He had no idea what was going on.

'Upon his return, William decided to spend some time in London to see if he could find out anything from his sources there. A great many French had come over to London, you see, in order to escape the trouble. It took a while, but last week, thank the Lord, we received news of Henri's whereabouts. He was being held captive by that . . . that evil man. He thought he was Edouard, you see, and was waiting for me to try to rescue him so that he could have his revenge.

'Upon receipt of the news, William returned immediately to France. I dared not even ask what he did whilst he was there, but he returned with Henri and the promise that that wicked man would no longer be able to harm us.'

Tears were now streaming down both women's faces.

'William is a good man, Miss Crump,' concluded the duchesse, turning to Wilhelmina and clasping both of her hands in hers.

'I know,' whispered Wilhelmina, releasing a new wave of tears for quite a different reason.

CHAPTER 25

'WOULD you care to come for a walk with Lady Grace and me today, Lavinia dear?' enquired Aunt Clementine over breakfast the following morning.

'I'm afraid I can't, Mama,' informed Lavinia brightly. 'I met Mr Dartford by chance yesterday and we arranged for him to visit today. We are going to teach the puppy to sit – although, I must confess, the man is of such a sweet nature that I'm not at all sure he has the ability to be firm enough with her.'

Despite her low spirits, Wilhelmina found herself biting back a smile. The duke, meanwhile, obviously lacking her restraint, released a strange strangled sound, which he quickly adapted to a cough.

His mirth however, did not go unnoticed by Lavinia, who regarded him coolly. 'Just because Mr Dartford is of a gentle disposition and does not go around blowing people's heads off in battle like yourself, sir,' she pointed out, 'it does not mean he is any lesser a mortal.'

'Oh, believe me, Miss Crump,' replied the duke with the utmost sincerity, 'I could not agree with you more.'

'Now, Lavinia, dear,' cut in Aunt Clementine, quickly steering the conversation around to a less controversial topic, 'you really must decide on a name for that dog. We simply cannot go around calling the poor little thing "the puppy" for there will soon come a time when she outgrows that description.'

Lavinia pulled a rueful face. 'But it is so difficult, Mama,' she groaned. 'Yesterday I considered calling her Mimi but I fear the rector did not like it – although, of course, he was too much of a gentleman to say so directly.'

'Hmmm,' mused Aunt Clementine. 'Well, I must say I agree with him. It is far too . . . too. . . .'

'Repetitive, ma'am,' pronounced the duke.

'Exactly, sir,' concurred Aunt Clementine, throwing him a grateful smile.

In an attempt to lighten her mood, Wilhelmina decided to make the most of the pleasant afternoon and indulge in a ride around the estate. She had been thus engaged some three hours and was feeling slightly better, when she turned into the long drive to the hall to find the duke riding towards her on his black stallion. Her heart skipped its customary beat. She had had no chance to speak to him alone since the night of the rescue mission but that fact had not deterred her in the least from thinking about him every spare minute of the day – and night. Indeed, following her conversation with Lady Grace and the revelation of yet another admirable facet of the man's character, he had scarcely been out of her thoughts at all.

He drew his horse to a halt directly before her. 'Good afternoon, Miss Crump,' he said, with his usual coolness.

A swarm of butterflies began drumming inside Wilhelmina. 'Your grace,' she murmured, with a slight inclination of her head.

'A very pleasant day,' he remarked politely.

'Yes, sir,' she replied, feeling gauche.

There then followed a brief, uncomfortable pause where the duke regarded her in a disconcerting manner, forcing her to lower her eyes and focus them on a spot on her horse's left ear. Then, before she could stop herself, she suddenly blurted out, 'I should like to apologize, your grace.'

He raised his brows to her. 'Really?' he enquired. 'Do go on, Miss Crump.'

She felt colour burning her cheeks as she now gazed directly into his dark eyes. 'I should like to apologize for saying that your behaviour towards my cousin and me was appalling, sir, when all the while you had gone out of your way to protect me and to rescue Lavinia.'

'I see,' he replied, in an infuriatingly neutral tone. 'Is that all, Miss Crump?'

She stared at him blankly. Was that not enough? What else did he expect her to say?

'Er – I believe so, sir,' she found herself muttering.

'Then I shall bid you goodday,' he declared frostily, before steering the stallion around her mount and kicking his horse to a brisk trot.

Wilhelmina remained staring at the space he had newly vacated for several long, confusing minutes while she pondered what on earth she was supposed to have done wrong now.

Neither Wilhelmina nor the duke had seen anything of the rector since the night of the rescue mission. Visiting later that afternoon, dressed in the uniform of the clergy, he appeared as unassuming as ever and one would never have guessed that he was the mastermind behind the hostage rescue operation and goodness only knows what else, from a number of things Tipping – obviously having the utmost respect for the man – had proudly let slip.

Lavinia, despite not having the first idea of the important role the clergyman had played in her rescue, was delighted to see him, as indeed was the puppy. The two of them and the twins spent the entire afternoon in the garden frolicking with the pet who, much to their combined hilarity, seemed to think that the word 'sit' was a command to roll onto her back and waggle her legs in the air.

Wilhelmina, meanwhile, had been wallowing in her thoughts of the duke. His cool treatment of her at their brief encounter in the drive had had the effect of plunging her into even deeper despair. She was beginning to feel, not without some panic, that her feelings for the man were spiralling dangerously out of control. A fact which, when she had found herself alone in the library with Lavinia and the puppy later that evening, had evidently not escaped the older girl's attention.

'Is there something you are not telling me, Cousin?' enquired Lavinia as she feigned interest in a book of poetry.

Wilhelmina's heart stopped for a solitary moment. Had her cousin remembered something of the rescue evening after all? 'I, um, haven't the slightest idea what you are referring to, Lavinia,' she stammered, aware of a culpable flush stealing over her cheeks.

'There is!' exclaimed Lavinia, slamming shut the book and jerking to an upright position. 'Why else would you look so guilty, Cousin?'

'Well, I, er, that is I – shouldn't really—' she stuttered, having not the first idea where to begin with her explanation.

'Well, I must say, I am a little surprised,' launched forth Lavinia as she relaxed back into her seat. 'Quite what anyone could see in the man is positively beyond me. I suppose that he is quite pleasing to the eye – although not half as handsome as the rector – but I am afraid I shall never be able to forgive him for the treatment of my lace-trimmed petticoats,' she concluded stoutly, with a resigned shake of her head.

'Wh-what are you talking about, Lavinia?'

'Why your Duke of Linthorpe of course,' replied the older girl in a tone which, much to Wilhelmina's relief, indicated there could be no other possible subject.

'*My* Duke of Linthorpe? What on earth do you mean?'

'Well, it is perfectly obvious to all but Mama, Cousin, that you are head over heels in love with the man.'

Wilhelmina gasped. 'Indeed I am not,' she protested, aware that her cheeks were now burning red.

'Oh really, Wilhelmina,' chided Lavinia. 'There is not the slightest use in denying it. Why even Lady Grace has noticed.'

Wilhelmina felt mortification seeping from every pore. She had better take more care for she certainly had no wish at all for the duke to discover the intensity of her feelings for him. Particularly not when there was still one vital piece of the jigsaw which remained missing: the matter of the beautiful Baroness Beaumont, which was hanging over her like a dark, oppressive cloud.

May was turning out to be a most glorious month for the weather at least, contemplated Wilhelmina, as she did her best over the next few days to attempt to conceal her feelings for the duke. Although her brooding mood was not eased in the least when he suddenly announced that he was to spend the next two days in London, forcing her thoughts once again to the baroness.

Despite her own low spirits, she was pleased to see that the rest of the household all appeared to be enjoying their sojourn: Lavinia and Mr Dartford were becoming a regular sight together and she could not recall ever seeing her cousin look prettier as she glowed with happiness, blooming under the man's avid attentions.

Lady Grace and her family – obviously revelling in their reunion

– presented the perfect family picture as they strolled around the garden: Henri, perched on his father's shoulders and Edouard being carried piggy-back style by his mother, while the puppy skipped about their ankles.

Even Aunt Clementine and Uncle Ernest seemed to have been bitten by the romantic bug as Wilhelmina had spotted her uncle the previous day giving his wife a playful peck on the cheek as she lightly scolded him for his poorly arranged cravat.

Her relief at having the duke return to Linthorpe Hall, unaccompanied – some two days later was shortlived, lasting only until dinner when he made an unexpected – and unsettling – announcement.

'We are to hold a garden party,' he declared, over his dessert of chocolate mousse.

'How thrilling. I do so love garden parties,' Aunt Clementine said.

'And I am sure this one will not disappoint you in the least, ma'am,' replied the duke, smiling broadly. 'Mrs Crump, you shall be in charge of invitations; Grace, you shall command the housekeeper and cook and the two Misses Crump shall direct the decoration of the gardens in whatever way they please.'

'Oh, did you hear that, Mr Crump?' beamed Aunt Clementine proudly. 'I am to be in charge of invitations. What do you think Venetia Drinkwater will make of that, sir?'

'One cannot even begin to imagine, my dear,' muttered Uncle Ernest, reaching for his glass of burgundy.

Leaving the men to their brandies and cigars after dinner, the four ladies retired to Wilhelmina's favourite drawing-room overlooking the garden, where they were served with tea and sweetmeats.

'Do you know, I am so excited, Lady Grace, I do believe I shall not eat another thing between now and the garden party,' pronounced Aunt Clementine, shaking her head as the footman offered her the plate of delicacies.

'But one must keep up one's strength, Mrs Crump. Particularly when one is to be so busy over the next few days,' observed Lady Grace, with just a hint of humour to her tone.

Aunt Clementine considered this statement for all of two seconds before replying, 'Of course you are quite right, my lady.

Perhaps I shall just take one . . . for my strength of course.'

'Of course,' agreed Lady Grace, winking at Wilhelmina as her aunt selected a sugared plum.

'Now, ladies, what on earth do we think of this garden party?' asked Aunt Clementine. 'I rather suspect that his grace is about to make an offer to a young lady and that the betrothal shall be announced at the party.' She shot an optimistic look at her daughter who was gazing aghast at Wilhelmina.

Wilhelmina's heart seemed to stop beating as she returned her cousin's look with ten times more intensity.

'Oh, I shouldn't think it's anything of the sort, Mrs Crump,' countered Lady Grace dismissively. 'In fact I am sure there will be no announcement at all.'

'But do you know that for certain, ma'am,' enquired Aunt Clementine intently. 'Some men can be terribly romantic.'

'Well, I'm afraid my brother is most definitely not one of them, Mrs Crump,' informed the duchesse evenly. 'William has been accused of being many things, but never a romantic. He is far too much of a . . . a man's man. Not one to show his true feelings,' she added, directing this comment to Wilhelmina.

Wilhelmina, who had not the faintest idea what the duke's true feelings were, merely stared back at her blankly. Lady Grace and her cousin could attempt to cheer her up as much as they liked, but she had a strong feeling that this time it was Aunt Clementine who was correct and her unhappy thoughts turned, yet again, to the beautiful Baroness Beaumont.

The party was due to take place the following Saturday, a mere ten days away, a fact which Aunt Clementine insisted on repeating every waking hour of the hectic period before the event. Due to the lack of time for preparation, a simple 'May Day' theme had been agreed and Lavinia had even had the idea of constructing a maypole which, with the help of several of the grooms, was positioned in the middle of the lawn at the back of the house, complete with streams of ribbons of every imaginable colour.

As predicted, Aunt Clementine had thrown herself into her allocated task of organizing the invitations, although Wilhelmina did wonder if the duke had any idea at all of the number of people who had been asked, her aunt wasting not one opportunity to send out the beautiful white cards printed with the tasteful Linthorpe Hall insignia. She had also, she had advised, included a 'little note' with each of those cards forwarded to her personal acquaintances which, so far as Wilhelmina could discern, involved just about everybody her aunt had ever stumbled across in all her five-and-fifty years.

CHAPTER 26

PREPARATIONS began early on the much-awaited day with Wilhelmina, Lavinia, the twins and the puppy spending the entire morning in the gardens, supervising the erection of the refreshment tables and the hanging of the colourful streamers the twins had helped prepare. As the heat was increasing with each new day, the refreshments were to be kept inside, in the pink drawing-room, which opened directly out onto the raised terrace of the gardens. Music was to be provided by a nervous-looking quartet who were to be seated under a small canopy, especially constructed for the purpose, at the bottom of the lawned area.

With the grounds looking their very best, all the organizers then retired upstairs, hoping to effect similar results on their own, somewhat dishevelled appearances. When they convened in the drawing-room some ninety minutes later, they had all done another admirable job: Lavinia looked delightful in a gown of lilac organza, while Wilhelmina had been informed by Lady Grace that she looked 'positively charming' in her dress of white chenille decorated with tiny white pearls. Even the puppy looked more adorable than usual, Henri having put a chain of daisies around her little neck, which she trotted around proudly displaying. The only blot on the day so far – albeit a very large, dark blot – was that Wilhelmina had not yet set eyes upon the Duke of Linthorpe and, not wishing to arouse even more suspicion about her feelings for him, had not dared enquire of even the diplomatic Tipping, as to his master's whereabouts.

Amongst the first guests to arrive was the Earl of Thurlston who, in time-honoured fashion, placed a charming kiss on Wilhelmina's hand at exactly the same moment as the Duke of Linthorpe chose to enter the garden. Upon absorbing the scene, the faint smile which she was sure she had detected hovering over his lips as their eyes met, was wiped from his face as he chose instead to stride directly by her. Wilhelmina's spirits plummeted and in a dazed and deflated state she allowed herself to be steered, unheeding, by the earl towards the orchard, failing to notice the way the duke's dark gaze followed the pair of them.

Upon reaching their destination, the earl sank down onto the old stone bench. 'Miss Crump,' he announced, with deadly earnest. 'I have an embarrassing confession to make.'

Sighing, Wilhelmina sat beside him. 'A confession?' she echoed. 'Regarding what, sir?'

'My ... my feelings,' he stammered, with more than a hint of embarrassment.

Wilhelmina sighed again. She was in no mood at all to hear more of the earl's nonsense. 'Look, sir,' she began, unable to conceal the impatience in her tone, 'I am deeply flattered but—'

'Oh, no, please do not reject me, Miss Crump. You are the only one who can help me. No one else understands me like you.'

Wilhelmina narrowed her eyes. 'Help you? What on earth are you talking about?'

'Why, the love of my life, of course. The girl who has quite stolen my heart from the moment I first set eyes upon her.'

'Verity Drinkwater?' asked Wilhelmina, screwing up her nose.

The earl shook his head. 'No,' he replied stoutly. 'Octavia Harlington-Hartsworthy, of course.'

She furrowed her brow. 'Octavia Harlington-Hartsworthy?'

'The very same, ma'am. And pray do not mention her freckles for I find them positively enchanting.'

'But ... but I have never seen you so much as dance with the girl,' observed Wilhelmina. 'Indeed rumour has it that she is desperate for you to make her an offer and you refuse to do so.'

The earl emitted a mournful sigh. 'That is a rumour put about by that cad, James Fraserburgh. Oh, it is all such a coil, Miss Crump,' he concluded, leaning forward and resting his chin in his hand.

She regarded him somewhat baffled. 'I'm afraid you have lost me, sir,' she confessed, shaking her head.

213

'I cannot blame you for not understanding, Miss Crump. Why some days I cannot even make sense of the predicament myself despite the fact that it has largely been of my own making. Well, mine and that cad, Fraserburgh's. If I can explain—'

'Please do,' murmured Wilhelmina, wondering what on earth was to follow.

'Well,' he began, 'last year, the year in which Miss Harlington-Hartsworthy made her come-out, and before I had even set eyes on the girl, that cad Fraserburgh wagered me that I would not dare be seen dancing with the girl with the largest fortune in the room. Never one to refuse a wager, Miss Crump, I of course agreed but when the man pointed out that his target was Octavia, I was in despair. And not only that, Miss Crump, but when I did dance with the girl I found her to be quite the most delightful little thing imaginable.'

'But if you feel as strongly about her as you claim,' remarked Wilhelmina regarding him puzzledly, 'then why have you not offered for her?'

'But I have,' he continued miserably. 'On several occasions. The problem is, you see, that Miss Harlington-Hartsworthy found out about the wager and now she and her family think I am the most despicable man on earth and only wish to marry her for her fortune.'

'And her fortune has nothing at all to do with it?'

'Good lord, no,' he exclaimed with some asperity as he turned to face her. 'I have more than enough money of my own. Indeed I have even offered to have a legal document drawn up forsaking any claim at all to their blasted fortune.'

'I see,' replied Wilhelmina, not knowing quite what to make of the shocking revelation. 'But one thing is puzzling me, my lord. If you have quite lost your heart to Miss Harlington-Hartsworthy, then what on earth were you about flirting with myself and Verity Drinkwater and goodness knows who else, right in front of the poor girl?'

He sighed again. 'Because, Miss Crump, that cad, Fraserburgh told me the best way to jolt a girl's interest is to make her jealous. I therefore thought that if I could create a stir amongst some of the most beautiful girls in Society – and perhaps even have them bickering over me – then perhaps Miss Harlington-Hartsworthy would realize that she really did want me after all.'

Wilhelmina shook her head despairingly. 'And you have told Octavia all this?'

He shook his head gloomily. 'I have tried but she will not speak to me. I even went down on my knee outside Lady Carlton's ball a few weeks ago, pleading with her, but her Mama just whisked her away, declaring that her daughter was not an object for a wager and would not marry a man who was only interested in her money. That was why I no doubt looked so dejected, Miss Crump, when I came across you in the hall immediately following my rebuke.'

Wilhelmina nodded, recalling his doleful expression at that encounter.

'I then had the most marvellous idea of buying her an engagement ring,' continued the man. 'I had just purchased the most exquisite one in the shop when I happened to meet you that morning in Oxford Street. But when I tried to give it to her that afternoon, which I hoped would leave little doubt as to the seriousness of my intentions, I was turned away yet again, accused of being a fortune-seeking rake.' He fixed Wilhelmina with an imploring gaze. 'You must believe me, Miss Crump,' he professed with a hint of desperation, 'that I would love the girl if she had not a penny to her name.'

'I do believe you, sir,' replied Wilhelmina, reading the sincerity in his eyes. 'If you wish, I will speak to the girl myself and pass on all that you have told me.'

He grabbed her hand. 'I should be eternally grateful to you, ma'am.'

'But tell me,' enquired Wilhelmina, as she rose to her feet, 'is this what you meant when you said you had a very great need to see me, the day we were moving to Linthorpe?'

'But of course. Could there possibly be anything of more import, Miss Crump?'

'No, my lord,' she replied, biting back a smile. 'Nothing at all.'

The news of the earl's devotion and his assiduous, albeit unsuccessful, efforts in securing her affection, was met with several happy tears and a spontaneous hug by the delightful, freckle-faced Octavia. Having gone on to compose herself a little, she had subsequently deigned to speak to the earl who, when informed of this progress, had also thrown his arms around Wilhelmina in a further impulsive gesture of gratitude. As the pair, under the watchful eye of Octavia's mother, began their stroll around the gardens, deep in conversation, Wilhelmina could not help but feel a stab of envy as yet another couple seemed to have found one another. She stood at the side of the garden, observing how the earl and Octavia were so engrossed in their exchange that they almost collided with Mr Dartford and Uncle Ernest – similarly absorbed in their own discussion as they ambled about the grounds. Her attention switched to the two men as they suddenly came to a standstill and, each with broad grins, began hand-shaking and back-slapping. Uncle Ernest then took his leave of the younger man and marched purposefully over to his wife, who was busy dragging around a radiant Cissy Woodstock – looking as pretty as any of the grand ladies in attendance – and the little sleeping baby, Wilhelmina.

'All alone, Miss Crump?' suddenly enquired the Duke of Linthorpe in a familiar supercilious tone.

Startled, she turned to face him. 'Are you implying that I ought not to be, sir?' she replied wryly.

'Not at all,' he retorted with icy matter-of-factness. 'But I confess it is rare to see you unaccompanied by the Earl of Thurlston.'

'The Earl of Thurlston, sir,' she remarked tetchily, 'is currently putting forward an offer of marriage to one Miss Octavia Harlington-Hartsworthy – the love of his life.'

The duke raised his brows. 'He loves Octavia?' he enquired with an element of surprise.

'Indeed he does, sir.'

'But I thought that you and he ... that is, I mean, you were always—'

'His presence whenever you observed us together was nothing but coincidence, sir. The man was playing a little game: attempting to make Miss Harlington-Hartsworthy jealous. It did in fact serve the opposite purpose and the young lady would have nothing at all to do with him.'

'But how are they now—?'

'Because I have informed the young lady of the earl's true feelings, sir. Some men do know how to express their true feelings.'

The duke stood as though contemplating that notion for a

moment before turning his back to her and, to her great dismay, striding away.

The tears which began stabbing at her eyes did not abate in the least when, a few minutes later, the Baroness Beaumont, as late and as stunning as ever, whirled into the garden – a vision in shimmering lemon silk. As she observed the duke, and Lady Grace and her husband, bestow an enthusiastic greeting upon the beauty, she was aware of a choking sob rising in her throat.

The four of them engaged in a quick and animated conversation for several minutes before the duke bounded up the stone stairs to the upper terrace and called the attention of his guests. After a speech which all but Wilhelmina appeared to find humorous, and a profuse expression of gratitude to all the organizers, much to Aunt Clementine's delight, he then uttered the words Wilhelmina had been dreading:

'I am both proud and delighted to announce that we are soon to be joined by a new family member.'

A murmur of anticipation floated over the crowd. Wilhelmina's knees weakened.

'My sister, the Duchesse de Fontainebleau is expecting another baby in five months' time and I have no doubt that this one shall bring as much happiness to our lives as have the twins.'

Relief flooded through her as a huge cheer burst forth, followed by an enthusiastic round of applause.

'And I, if I may, your grace, have an announcement of my own to make,' asserted Uncle Ernest, mounting the steps.

Silence fell again upon the curious crowd.

'I am delighted to announce that my daughter, Lavinia, who was returned safely to us recently, is to marry the Reverend Daniel Dartford, as soon as possible.'

Another cheer and more rapturous applause resounded as all eyes turned towards the happy couple who were, at that moment, engulfed in one of Aunt Clementine's eager embraces.

'What do titles and money matter when one's daughter is so obviously happy,' Wilhelmina heard her pronounce to Mrs Drinkwater as she stepped aside to allow the stream of other congratulators to reach the couple. 'Why, we could not ask for more for the girl.'

'Hmph,' huffed Mrs Drinkwater reluctantly. 'I suppose I cannot argue with that, Clementine. There is certainly no denying that the girl is the very picture of happiness which is more than can be said for Verity.'

Wilhelmina glanced over to where Mrs Drinkwater was indicating and found Verity poised with her arms crossed over her chest and her bottom lip pouting. The target of her annoyance was one Penelope Prestwick, of musical soirée notoriety, whose mother, despite being a 'ghastly ambitious woman', had done an extremely impressive job on grooming Penelope. In fact, Wilhelmina would have said that she was one of the prettiest girls at the party, a fact which had obviously not gone unnoticed by Prince Frederick, who had slipped into the gathering without drawing the slightest attention to himself and was now chatting away to the girl who undoubtedly had not the first idea as to his true identity.

With the party well underway and everyone appearing to be having the most marvellous of times, Wilhelmina, finding herself at a loss, wandered aimlessly about the grounds. For all her relief that the duke's announcement had not been his betrothal to the Baroness Beaumont, she was only too aware that this did not prove that the pair were not lovers, nor did it mean that he felt anything at all for Wilhelmina. She was deep in melancholy when Lavinia joined her, slipping her arm through hers.

'Can you believe it, Cousin,' she pronounced dreamily, 'me – betrothed? And to a rector?'

'I am truly happy for you Lavinia,' said Wilhelmina, squeezing her cousin's hand affectionately. 'He is a wonderful man.'

'He is the most wonderful of men, Cousin,' sighed Lavinia contentedly. 'And I know he shall make me the happiest of women. Of course, I own he is not as daring or as dashing as your duke but he is kind and gentle and quite the most perfect man on earth.'

Wilhelmina smiled at her cousin's adoration. 'Indeed he is,' she agreed sincerely, 'and I know you shall be very happy together.'

'And he is not at all rich,' pointed out Lavinia unnecessarily, 'but that is of absolutely no import, Cousin, for I should still choose to marry him above all men even if he had not a penny to his name.'

'I know,' replied Wilhelmina, chuckling at the change in the girl since she had made the acquaintance of the rector.

'Of course, you must be my chief maid of honour, Cousin,' she continued solemnly. 'Although I confess I have not yet given a thought to the colour of the dresses. Do not tell Daniel for it is not a very Christian thing to do,' she continued, lowering her voice to a whisper, 'but we simply cannot have yellow for that is the colour in which Verity Drinkwater looks best and I simply refuse to be outshone by that girl on my wedding day.'

'I doubt there will be any chance of that, Lavinia,' pointed out Wilhelmina.

'Oh, I can scarcely wait to go back to Chipping Sodbury to begin the preparations, Cousin,' enthused Lavinia. 'It is going to be quite the most wonderful day.'

Wilhelmina had the distinct impression that whatever preparations she had witnessed her aunt and cousin engaging in so far, were nothing compared to those there would be for the wedding.

As the light began to wane and the guests slowly to depart, Wilhelmina's hopes of slipping away to her bedchamber to break her heart in private were thwarted by the appearance of two late, and completely unexpected, arrivals.

'Ermintrude Fitzgibbon, my dear girl – what on earth took you so long? You should have left that dreadful place weeks ago,' chided Aunt Clementine, bustling over to her cousin with a welcoming smile. She embraced her tightly.

'I am so sorry, Clementine dearest,' apologized an evidently flustered Mrs Fitzgibbon, 'but we have been rather – um, busy, in Paris.'

Aunt Clementine shook her head despairingly. 'Now I know insurance is important, Percy dear,' she reproached, 'but it is not nearly so important as ones' lives. You should have left that ghastly city the moment all that disturbance broke out. Now come inside and I shall find a room for you. There are so many here to choose from you know – although I haven't, of course, seen even half of them myself.'

Mr and Mrs Fitzgibbon each raised a questioning eyebrow.

As the last of the guests trickled away, Mr and Mrs Fitzgibbon, having made the acquaintance of the duke and his family, were seated with the rest of the residing party in the pink drawing-room, finishing off the refreshments.

'So, Mr Fitzgibbon, can we take it that things are improving in

Paris at last?' enquired the duke.

Mr Fitzgibbon shook his head in sorrow. 'I'm afraid not, your grace. We were speaking to the king about the matter yesterday and he is deeply concerned.'

Lavinia dropped her macaroon. '*You* were speaking to the *king*?' she repeated.

Mr Fitzgibbon nodded his head. 'Well, to be more precise, my wife was receiving an honour from him.'

'An honour?' repeated Aunt Clementine. 'Ermintrude? Receiving an honour? From the King of France? But what on earth for?'

Mrs Fitzgibbon flushed guiltily. 'We have a confession to make, Clementine dearest. We have not been involved in insurance in Paris. We have been working as spies. For the government.'

Uncle Ernest choked on his glass of claret.

'Spies?' echoed Lavinia, wrinkling her forehead. 'You two were spies?'

Mrs Fitzgibbon nodded. 'We may tell you now because we have decided to retire and find a little cottage in the Cotswolds. We have, however, been working for the king for some twelve years.'

A dumbfounded Aunt Clementine whipped out her vinaigrette, whilst staring at her cousin in utter disbelief.

'Indeed,' continued Mr Fitzgibbon, 'the day of the rioting in Paris – the day in fact you made the acquaintance of the Comte de Roxford, Lavinia – Mrs Fitzgibbon had just uncovered the man's plans for the kidnappings in Paris. That was the reason we could not allow you to have the carriage.'

Lavinia's mouth dropped open.

'When you announced that evening that you had made the man's acquaintance and were to meet him at *Le Bal de Printemps* later that week, we knew we had to remove you from Paris as soon as we could. The rioting provided an excellent excuse.'

'Good lord,' muttered Lavinia. 'When I think of the fuss I created. Was I really quite dreadful?'

Mr and Mrs Fitzgibbon nodded their heads in unison.

CHAPTER 27

THE following day, with Lavinia and Aunt Clementine desper-ate to begin preparations for Lavinia's wedding, it had been arranged that the Crumps and the Fitzgibbons would take their leave of Linthorpe Hall that afternoon and remove to London where they were to spend several days shopping before winding their way back to Chipping Sodbury.

Wilhelmina had spent yet another restless, sleepless night, this one exacerbated by the knowledge that, with the exception of Lavinia's wedding, she would most likely never see the Duke of Linthorpe again once they had left Linthorpe. He had not even been present at breakfast that morning where, weighted down with a heavy feeling of despondency, she had barely uttered two words and swallowed only half a cup of coffee.

Returning to her room after breakfast to finish her packing, her spirits sank even lower when she spotted a white envelope lying in the middle of the damson damask bed cover. Surely Tipping and the rector were not involving her in another mystery already. She had neither the inclination nor the energy. Picking up the item she noticed that it was addressed to *Special Agent Crump*. She broke the seal and unfolded the paper, dreading what she was about to read. To her surprise, the note contained not an abrupt list of instruc-tions, but a single question:

Will you marry me?

She gazed at it in amazement, a strange buzzing sound begin-ning in her head. Was this someone's idea of a joke? If so, it was not an amusing one. Her thoughts were interrupted by the sound of a familiar voice behind her.

'Well?' enquired the Duke of Linthorpe.

Spinning around Wilhelmina looked from him to the note and then back to him again.

'Will you marry me, Wilhelmina?' he asked, walking over to her and taking both her hands in his.

She said nothing, but merely stared at him.

'I promise to curb my temper,' he said, regarding her imploringly.

She continued staring.

'I will do anything, anything you wish,' he continued, a look of deep concern spreading over his handsome face. 'I will try to be more romantic. I will even give up my career in the navy. I will—'

'The Baroness Beaumont, sir,' she suddenly blurted out.

'What?'

'The Baroness Beaumont.'

'What of her?' he asked, visibly taken aback.

'You and she – I have seen you—'

'Doing what?'

'Talking . . . and . . . and . . . meeting in secret . . . and . . . and—'

He regarded her, not for the first time, as though she were a dimwitted child. 'Isabella Beaumont is my sister's best friend, Miss Crump. She is godmother to the twins. She was deeply upset about what was happening. She has contacts in France and was doing all she could to help me find Henri.'

'She helped you find Henri?'

'Yes— Why? What did you think?— Oh, you didn't think that Bella and I were. . . ?' He broke out into a wide smile.

'Well, what was I supposed to think,' remarked Wilhelmina suddenly feeling foolish and more than a little defensive. 'Particularly when it is rumoured that you have a beautiful secret lover. And then I see you and she together – in secret – and—'

'You think I have a beautiful secret lover?' he asked, the smile continuing to hover about his lips.

She nodded miserably and averted her eyes to the floor. 'Verity Drinkwater said so.'

'Ah, then it must of course be true. Miss Drinkwater being so up-to-date with such matters.'

'I see,' muttered Wilhelmina, tears prickling her eyelids.

'But I'm afraid you don't, Miss Crump,' he countered teasingly. 'You don't see at all. That old chestnut – not very original, I own – was a rumour set about by myself some three years ago to keep the tabbies and their daughters at bay. I must say, however, I am amazed it is still circulating. I can assure you, Miss Wilhelmina Crump, that there is only one woman for me and she is standing before me right now. So, for the umpteenth time, woman – will you marry me?'

'But you cannot marry him, Cousin,' protested Lavinia, looking horrified at the news. 'I grant you he is not perhaps as odious as I first thought but surely you have not forgotten what he did to my lace-trimmed petticoats?'

'Ah, yes,' cut in the Duke, appearing around the doorway to the library where the two girls were to be found. 'Your lace-trimmed petticoats, Miss Crump. If you care to look in the hall, you will find your trunk and valises all ready for your trip back to Chipping Sodbury. All in order I think. Forgive me, but I have had quite a lot on my mind of late and I simply did not get around to having them delivered to you before now.'

Lavinia gazed at him through narrowed eyes. 'Are you saying, sir that you have returned all my luggage from the ship?'

'Every last bit that was not left behind in France, ma'am.'

'Oh,' mused Lavinia. Then, having given the matter a little thought, 'Well, then that is perfectly splendid. You may marry the man after all, Cousin.' And with that she danced out of the room.

'Oh dear,' muttered Aunt Clementine, observing Lavinia and the rector taking a final stroll, hand-in-hand, around the gardens with the puppy, before the party took their leave of Linthorpe. 'Lavinia is such a handful, I do hope Mr Dartford will be able to deal with her.'

'I'm sure the rector has dealt with far more difficult occurrences than my cousin's demands, Aunt,' remarked Wilhelmina, casting a knowing glance at the duke who was reclining in a wing chair with the newspaper.

'Do you really think so, my dear?' fluttered Aunt Clementine. 'One can't help wondering if the most drama the man has ever had to deal with has been someone dropping the collection plate during Sunday service.'

Wilhelmina had just run upstairs to fetch her reticule ready for their journey back to London when she heard Lavinia's voice floating up the stairs.

'Cousin, I have a very great announcement to make. I have decided to christen the puppy "Wilhelmina".'

'But it is so *pas de Française*, Lavinia,' shouted back Wilhelmina, recalling with a smile, their conversation in Paris.

'Nonsense,' replied Lavinia. 'It is quite in vogue. Why Lady Grace has just informed me that that is what she intends to call her baby if it is a girl, so obviously if it is good enough for her then it is good enough for me.'

'Good lord, the place is going to be full of Wilhelminas,' muttered the duke, striding into the room at that moment.

'Are you complaining, sir?' enquired Wilhelmina teasingly.

'Certainly not,' he replied, wrapping his arms around her waist from behind, 'as long as I have mine.'

'Oh, you do, sir. For as long as you like.'

'I fear that may be for quite some time, madam,' he replied, nuzzling into her neck.

'Oh, well,' sighed Wilhelmina resignedly, 'as long as you don't interfere with my lace-trimmed petticoats, I suppose I shall just have to put up with you.'

He fixed her with an earnest look. 'Oh, but I'm afraid I couldn't possibly promise not to do that, Miss Crump.'